Pastor,

Thank you for
your guidance...
for sharing your
God-given wisdom.

Steve

MURDER BY CHANCE

BLOOD MOON LUNACY OF LEW CAREW

STEVE STRANGHOENER

WESTBOW
PRESS
A DIVISION OF THOMAS NELSON

This book is a work of fiction. People, places, events, and situations are the
product of the author's imagination. Any resemblance to actual persons,
living or dead, or historical events, is purely coincidental.

WestBow Press
A Division of Thomas Nelson
1663 Liberty Drive
Bloomington, IN 47403
www.westbowpress.com
1-(866) 928-1240

ISBN: 978-1-4497-3932-4 (sc)
ISBN: 978-1-4497-3933-1 (hc)
ISBN: 978-1-4497-3931-7 (e)

Library of Congress Control Number: 2012901990

Printed in the United States of America

WestBow Press rev. date: 02/10/2012

For John Mackay, Ken Ham, David Menton, Brian Young and all those who labor in propagating the truth at considerable risk and personal sacrifice against enormous odds and formidable obstacles.

"Who changed the truth of God into a lie, and worshipped and served the creature more than the Creator, who is blessed forever. Amen." (Romans 1:25)

CONTENTS

PROLOGUE

W HAT IS THE MORE UNSETTLING proposition, that we are the product of random chance or an omnipotent designer with uncompromising, impossible standards? The world has made its ruling very clear in favor of the former. But what peace does this offer? And what does this mean for us in the scheme of things; life and death? What grounds do we have for the legal and moral concept of murder if we are no different than the animals other than perhaps a higher level of intelligence achieved across countless ages only by the whim of natural processes that have left us meandering through a mere point in time in an oblivious struggle to survive? If murder is simply a game of chance, an infinitesimally small particle of dust floating across eons of blind evolutionary toil and strife, what right do we have to adjudicate against it? Should we not applaud it as a necessary consequence of nature's governing forces which guide us down the path to becoming higher beings for the greater good?

Winter Solstice ...
Death on the Prowl

CHAPTER 1

☾

WOLF MOON

I WAS NO MORE THAN A casual observer when the first death occurred. It was later that I gained access to the inner circle and the details I can share with you now. Death can be such a harmless word when its effects are far removed from our personal lives, producing no emotions beyond those associated with this unfortunate but natural part of life. How was I to know that this was no random event and would be succeeded by a string of shocking incidents that would evoke much stronger feelings such as those associated with harsher words like killing or even murder? For now, someone just *passes on* as we say, as if taking a secluded, peaceful stroll down a one-way path to the sun's setting. Normally, I'd be too wrapped up in school and work to catch a local news teaser but it's not every day that you hear about a possible animal attack in your own neck of the woods. No, that's the stuff of cable reality shows which aren't my cup of tea. Nevertheless, it turns out that this death was anything but a peaceful passing on.

In the real world, an animal attack usually means a pit bull got loose and bit someone. That's strictly the grist of local news, unless there's a small child involved. To gain national attention, it has to be something much more unusual like a rogue bear mauling a hiker but this only happens in some far off place like Yellowstone. Here, in my new, temporary home of St. Louis you're more likely to hear about a confused deer crashing through someone's sliding glass window; pretty mundane Midwestern fare. Animal attacks that result in people dying are extremely rare. Once every ten or fifteen years you might hear of someone being killed by a grizzly or mountain lion. Even shark attacks are typically not fatal. The death or mistreatment of one of our furry friends is much more apt to make the headlines than vice versa. So yes, it caught my attention when the ten o'clock news trumpeted an animal attack resulting in the death of a local man.

In spite of all my complaining about the rubes on the local newscasts and the trivial nonsense littering their up-to-the-minute reporting, I was sucked in by the seemingly over-sensationalized lead-in, "Local man found dead … the apparent victim of an animal attack … you may be at risk … details at ten". Coming from the Left Coast and a college student to boot, I considered myself too cosmopolitan for any local Ron Burgundy wannabe. But there I was, glued to the set at ten as the story unfolded. Unfortunately, as was often the case, the report didn't contain much in the way of details beyond what I'd heard in the teaser. The location was at least a good forty minute drive away from my apartment which seemed like a world apart from my tiny, self-centered college existence. Were it not for me taking on a part-time job, I would have been clueless but instead there was a tiny connection that drew me in further.

My internship afforded me the opportunity to become very familiar with the St. Louis County Parks system. As part of my training, I had to visit all the parks which broadened my horizons beyond our campus and some of the nearby urban centers I frequented. I was about to delete the animal attack from my consciousness as inconsequential and move on when a sliver of information pierced my ear and clung stubbornly like the sharp barb of a fishing lure. The site of the attack was completely foreign to me but the body had been discovered, by chance, by a couple hiking an alternate route since the walking path at Bridgeton Riverwoods Trail was closed. Ah ha, now I had a frame of reference pulling me in.

Although they were within the county limits, the parks in the suburb of Bridgeton, like other local municipalities, were not officially part of the St. Louis County Parks' system. Still we were familiar with all the parks in the county whether under our jurisdiction or not. I had visited there once to learn about erosion firsthand. Riverwoods Trail offered a bird's-eye view of neighboring St. Charles from across the wide Missouri which had a habit of escaping its fickle banks. I remembered my earlier visit there vividly because several sections of the asphalt path along the trail's two mile length were in the process of being moved twenty to thirty yards east to escape the swirling, muddy waters that swept away tons of soil like so much dust in the wind. This had etched a picture in my mind because it was so different from the Columbia River in my hometown of Portland. In any case, I guessed the trail had been closed due to some flooding, which was unusual in January, or perhaps some of the old trees along the trail had collapsed, not an uncommon occurrence at any time during the year.

Rather than turning back and packing it in or opting for another park, our dauntless hikers elected to log their miles just due north along an abandoned stretch of Missouri Bottom Road. It was quite an unfortunate coincidence for Marsha and Jim, a couple in their late-sixties who were determined to maintain their health and vitality through a daily regimen of brisk walks; rain or shine, hot or cold. They had no way of knowing that their misfortune would be such a boon to the local media.

Marsha and Jim had set their sights on the majestic old railroad trestle that loomed on the horizon about two miles ahead. It offered a halfway marker and visually appealing vantage point to whet one's curiosity and sense of adventure. I can imagine how it must have made them feel like kids again, off on an exploration. They were not too old to enjoy the tingling sensation that might be evoked by the uncharted territory that lay before them. Although it was daytime, with the heavy cloud cover, the setting likely stirred up a bit of a creepy, mysterious feeling. This stretch of Missouri Bottom Road was never that busy but it had the feel of a ghost town ever since the old bridge across the river into St. Charles had been demolished more than twenty years before. Now, St. Charles Rock Road abruptly ended at the river and Missouri Bottom Road veered off to another lonelier dead end just beneath the rail road tracks. Nearby there was occasional traffic generated by a sand dredging business, the paint-ball park and an auto salvage yard on its last leg but further along there was nothing. It was so desolate one might expect tumbleweeds to roll by in the bone chilling breeze.

Past the point of whatever sleepy commerce remained, there was a haunting sense of isolation for any passersby. The county had long since ceased maintaining this stretch of road and the trees, bushes and vines were gradually claiming dominion. What had been two lanes was effectively squeezed to just over one. They might as well have been hacking through the underbrush on a search for a lost Mayan temple. The center line on the road was now just a faint, faded yellow. The closer they approached to the railroad, the more it must have seemed they were cut off from civilization. The trestle, still in use periodically, was a magnificent structure. A marvel of intricate, woven woodwork, it towered above them more than fifty feet. Its age was etched indelibly on its massive framework but it had stood the test of time, a testimony to the ingenuity, skill and hard work of a generation gone by. The disrespect of young contemporaries was splashed indiscriminately in unintelligible graffiti and litter.

For anyone in this situation, the titillating thrill of adventure was surely replaced by a foreboding sense of dread. This deserted place was apparently home to occasional visitors who were obviously unsavory types; troublesome teens, homeless vagabonds … perhaps even criminals on the lam. You couldn't blame them if they worried about what might happen if they encountered someone hostile out there in the middle of nowhere. What would they do? How could they defend themselves? They later reported they decided it was time for them to cut the adventure short and hurry back to the safety of their car. But just as they were preparing to beat a hasty retreat, something caught Jim's eye several hundred yards down the path along the trestle's footing. It was an old pickup truck partially hidden by bushes and weeds that jutted out from the edge.

As they recounted afterward, Marsha urged Jim to forget about it and leave but he argued that someone might be in trouble and need their help. He could see that the driver side door was wide open but the truck was not running. Jim forged ahead with Marsha reluctantly in tow. Along the way, they encountered an assortment of refuse in the midst of several "No Dumping Allowed" warnings; old tires, broken down furniture, discarded appliances and soggy rolls of moldy carpeting. As they approached the truck, there was no one in sight. Jim peered inside to see if someone might be sleeping but the cab was empty. He touched the hood and it was stone cold. Over Marsha's objections, Jim slipped into the cab and turned the key which was still in the ignition and the engine grinded groggily then roared to life. Jim honked the horn several times startling Marsha before shutting it down. Jim wondered aloud why someone would walk off and abandon a perfectly good vehicle. Marsha suspected foul play and insisted that they get while the getting was good. The old man reluctantly agreed but turned back to shut the door so the dome light would not run down the battery. It was then that his trained, deer hunter's eye caught a glimpse of something out of place. Someone's leg was peeking out from under the brush just up ahead of the truck. Jim froze in his tracks then motioned to Marsha to stay back while he crept forward to investigate.

There was a small clearing on the other side of the bushes where the body lay. Jim did his best to muffle the gasp which escaped from his lungs in order to spare Marsha the shock. He stumbled as he hurried away and caught Marsha before she could witness the carnage. Now it was Jim who urged departure over Marsha's objections. Thankfully, Jim's judgment won out over her curiosity. Pale and shaken, Jim would not share the gory details as they made their way back to their car, retrieved his cell phone and contacted the authorities. Jim led them back to the scene but did not approach the body again. Marsha overheard enough of Jim's conversation with the police officers to understand why he didn't want to see the victim's remains again. It was the last time the two of them would venture off the beaten path for a long, long time.

It was unusual for the media to be granted such quick access by the police but, in this case, they felt a little publicity might be valuable if it helped to discourage people from venturing out to this dangerous, barren stretch along the county's outer reaches. The Eye in the Sky crew wasted little time in seizing upon this rare opportunity. While the camera men were not allowed to take any footage of the victim's body, they filmed numerous shots of the surrounding area including an aerial photo as they left the scene. The lead reporter, Flip Flanagan, was granted permission to take a peek at the body before it was loaded onto the gurney. Though he was a news veteran with numerous bloody crime scenes among his many credits, this one was unique. He recoiled from the repulsive sight and swallowed hard to keep the bile down.

In spite of his natural revulsion, Flip was savvy enough to keep his wits about him and took mental notes about the unusual nature of the crime scene. Or was it better deemed an accident scene? The police seemed a little baffled by the whole thing too. Their homicide training did little to prepare them for what clearly appeared to be an animal attack. They overlooked numerous pieces of evidence that might have proved useful later on. However, under the circumstances, it would be difficult to criticize them for jumping to what appeared as obvious conclusions and being absorbed with one question, "Just what kind of beast could do this to a full grown man?"

Something seemed odd and out of place. The victim, identified as Merle Polk, was not tossed about as one might expect from the melee. He was found flat on his back, as if in a peaceful repose, with no signs of a defensive struggle. The only thing, besides the horrific wound, that belied a peaceful death was the expression on Merle's face; sheer terror etched in his craggy features and now cloudy, glazed-over eyes that seemed to pop out of his head like huge grapes squeezed right out of their skins.

Flip's natural inclination to seize upon any hint of malfeasance was subdued by his sympathy for the police officers' plight. Was failing to fully process the scene shoddy work on their part or just an honest acknowledgment of the obvious? There was no need to look for a murder weapon or collect DNA from a human perpetrator. One look at the wound, that massive, gaping, devastating wound, eliminated all of those questions. The only real question that naturally jumped into everyone's minds was, "What are we dealing with here; dogs, wolves or coyotes?" Unfortunately, there were no real woodsmen at the scene that day but even a novice could see that something strange had occurred. Merle's throat had been completely ripped out to the point of near decapitation. No one on the scene would have discounted the possibility that something very large like a bear or mountain lion had ranged into eastern Missouri. Shoot, from the looks of it, you couldn't rule out that someone's exotic pet, perhaps a tiger, had broken loose and was on the prowl. The blood drenched gash torn through Merle's neck was that ponderous.

The assumption of an animal attack was so prevalent that all the other anomalies were subordinated. Why were there no markings on the ground showing a body being shaken and strewn to and fro? How come there were no defensive wounds on Merle's hands? Why were there no other wounds on the body? What kind of animal in what state of mind kills for the sake of killing and not nourishment? Did Merle somehow present a threat to the beast or its offspring? And what was he doing out in the middle of nowhere all alone in the dark of night? Most importantly, where was this dangerous animal now and why were there no clear tracks to follow its escape route?

Due to the inexperience of the officers in such matters and the lack of attention to detail at the crime scene, the answers for many of these questions were lost. The only good evidence retained for future study by me and the others was the ravaged body of poor Merle Polk who was in the wrong place at the wrong time. The police were consumed mainly with ensuring the safety of the living. There was a concerted effort to identify, track down and capture or kill the animal or animals responsible but with no trail to follow and no sightings of any such menace, it was destined for failure. Time has a way of smothering resolve and determination when any sign of an immediate threat has evaporated into thin air. There seemed no point in wasting precious resources on a meaningless endeavor. They didn't even bother to use forensics to try to pinpoint a species. They knew enough … that whatever killed Merle was very large with a huge set of deadly choppers. Some effort went into idle speculation, mainly to comfort everyone with the notion that whatever caused Merle's death was long gone. Perhaps it was an exotic animal that had returned to its owner and proper confinement. Maybe it was a bear, wolf or mountain lion that was on the way back to its natural habitat north or west of Missouri.

Flip Flanagan was not one to let this story die a premature death. In spite of his cartoonish name, he was quite skilled and fairly well accomplished. He had gone about as far in journalism as one could expect with the name Flip. He would have changed it by now, having achieved maturity some time ago, but he was caught in a nasty bugaboo of his own making. In his youth, Francis or Frank, was a gifted athlete who excelled in gymnastics and diving. The Flanagans had a trampoline in their back yard that Frank practiced on frequently. He was so good in fact that his friends gave him the nickname Flip. In high school, he used his athletic prowess to try to cleverly impress the ladies. When a young gal asked him how he got the nickname, Frank would answer by performing his special feat right there on the spur of the moment.

The name just kind of stuck as he moved on to college and didn't seem out of place for a young reporter fresh out of school. It was too bad he didn't choose to be a sportscaster. A funny thing happened on the way to becoming a newsman. Flip was so good that he gained too much notoriety too fast. Flip became a household name in local circles before he could shed the albatross and then it was too late to change … damned if you do, damned if you don't. So flipping Francis had good skills but ethics was not his strong suit. Disappointment and frustration will do that to a man. Sensationalism and expediency in catching the public's eye often won the day over hard core, nuts and bolts journalism.

As you would expect then, Flip tried to get as much mileage out of the saga as possible. But as the immediate danger wore off, it was harder to create enough panic to keep this in the headlines. When in doubt, how about a good conspiracy theory? Flip dug up a story from the archives where eight months prior an amateur videographer had captured a mountain lion on a surveillance camera out in the deep woods near his residence in far west St. Louis County. It caused a stir to have actual footage of such a dangerous beast of prey nearby whose normal range did not extend into mid-Missouri. With a little investigation, Flip was able to capitalize on a nasty rumor that the Missouri Department of Conservation had released some mountain lions into the wild to help control the burgeoning deer population. This quickly lost steam but Flip was nothing if not persistent.

With nothing else of substance, Flip decided to focus in on Merle and the human interest element to milk the last few drops of newsworthiness out of the story. This back fired and put the final nail in the coffin for anything resembling hard news. It turned out that our poor, helpless victim had a reason for being under the railroad trestle in the middle of the night. He was a habitual illegal dumper. Not only were they able to trace some of the nearby rubbish to Merle but, apparently, numerous other deposits had his finger prints all over them. It seems Merle was an industrious booger who figured if he could get away with dumping his personal refuse, he could make a healthy dose of extra cash, tax free, by offering his services to other willing customers. Missouri Bottom Road was just one of the locations used by Merle for his illegal dumping venture. When the media brought this to light, a lot of people, especially the *green* types, wrote Merle off. Public sentiment waned and the enviromaniacs actually felt he got his just desserts. I mean, the guy was not only wantonly trashing the environment but was a tax cheat on top of it. They chalked it up to bad Karma.

Flip was not a slave to substance either. He was very creative and given to a healthy imagination. Whatever it takes, right? In surfing the web to do some research on possible culprits, Flip got off on an interesting tangent when studying wolves. In a flight of fancy, he ventured into the realm of the werewolf just to amuse himself and kill a little time and picked up a juicy tidbit on lunar cycles. By back tracking, he was able to establish that there was a full moon the night of Merle's terrible death. Putting two and two together, Flip stumbled upon the ancient Native American names for the full moon cycles and discovered, to his delight, that January was known by some as the wolf moon. It denoted the hungry wolf packs that would howl outside their villages in the dead cold of night. That's too good to be true, right? Flip had no shame so he ran with it. As silly as it seemed, he actually lured in a fair number of new viewers with his crass sensationalism. Beware the full moon when the hungry wolves are on the prowl! Don't end up like poor old Merle!

Flip's desperate attempt to keep his baby alive eventually fell flat. I lost interest sooner than most because my thin connection to Riverwoods Trail was not enough to keep me from spitting the hook. For Flip, whether reporting or sometimes creating the news, it was time to move on to more fertile ground. The whole wolf moon saga faded into obscurity. Flip didn't realize how close he had come to igniting what would become a powder keg in the months ahead. Fact and fantasy were on a collision course that would make Flip's flight of fancy seem not only erudite but prophetic.

CHAPTER 2

☾

DEATH MOON

I NEVER CONSIDERED MYSELF, SETH LOMAX, to be *green*, left wing or anything of the sort. Perhaps that's because, coming from Portland, I hadn't really been exposed to anything different. You'd say I was normal if you lived there or perhaps even a little right of center because of my parents. Walt and Gretchen were born and raised in Portland and attended the University of Oregon in Eugene. But theirs was a different time before the Northwest tilted so far left. Plus, my dad was a business guy who traveled extensively around the country and was continually exposed to other ways of thinking; like, as he called it, good, old fashioned capitalism. He worked for a large packaging corporation and liked to joke that he had made his *fortune* selling brown boxes to Midwestern bumpkins.

That's how I wound up in St. Louis at Washington University instead of becoming a Duck or attending the more familiar University of Washington nearer to home. Dad had some really big customers in Missouri in the beer, beverage and meat packing businesses to where it was almost a home away from home. He had developed a lot of friends and contacts in and around St. Louis through the years and felt like it would be good experience for me to get a taste of life in Mid-America. At first, I wasn't too thrilled with the idea, that is, until I started researching Wash U. To my surprise, its academic standards and reputation were among the tops in the nation. If there was any doubt, all you had to do was check out the tuition. It was not the Harvard of the Midwest ... I think Harvard might have been a little cheaper.

Once I warmed up to the notion, the big question was what to study. Maybe I was a greenie after all because, in spite of some strong arm twisting from Walt, I decided to pursue a B. S. in Environmental Earth Sciences. Then, left to my own will and determination, I made another choice which delighted Walt to no end. I wanted to stay in contact with the *real world* and had a good head for figures so I decided to minor in business. In spite of my *indoctrination* in the Portland Public School System, Walt and Gretchen had taught me well enough to know that good business principals and environmentally friendly behavior are not mutually exclusive. Walt laughed at how zealous corporations jumping on the green bandwagon would pay more for a lousy box made of flimsy recycled materials rather than an *evil* container constructed from strong, virgin wood fiber. A biz minor made sense to me for another reason ... while Wash U had a well-respected environmental science program, its business school was really well established and considered top notch.

During my first three years at Wash U, I found it to be much like my educational experience in Portland. After all, like most college campuses, Wash U is primarily a liberal think tank, notwithstanding a few oddball exceptions on the staff. The big difference is the surrounding region. Portland is a lime floating in a sea of green whereas Wash U is an olive bobbing in a purple lake. If you're following this metaphor you already know that purple is a mixture of red and blue which describes Missouri well; a swing state with plenty of liberal and conservative influences. The longer I was exposed to this *fair and balanced* environment, the more it grew on me.

I wasn't ready to give up on my Left Coast leanings but, during my first two years, I developed an affinity for St. Louis' provincial nature and Midwestern charm. It was a simpler, less hectic way of life and I kind of liked the laid back style. My arrogance gave way to a bit more humility and curiosity. Perhaps it was something in the air or maybe I was just maturing but my mind opened up and I was able to at least consider other points of view even if many of the more prevalent local notions still struck me as foreign. The one thing that still made me recoil in fear was the open way in which many Midwesterners embraced what I referred to as religiosity. The place was filthy with evangelicals who apparently felt no sense of guilt or embarrassment in wearing their religious beliefs on their sleeves. It would have disappointed Walt and Gretchen so I avoided bringing up the fact that I hadn't darkened the doorway of a church since coming to Wash U.

Two years into it, my feet were drenched and I had a firm grip on my studies. With no steady girlfriend or formal extracurricular activities to speak of I had enough time on my hands that I decided to apply for a paid internship the summer after my sophomore year. I preferred to stay in St. Louis rather than spending two months living under my parents' roof and their watchful eyes. Frankly, although they missed me, they were pretty happy to have me out of the house. So I applied for a job with the St. Louis County Parks Department as an assistant to the Supervisor of the Park Ranger Staff. It fit well with my environmental studies program, offered a chance for some hands on experience and, hey, I certainly didn't mind having a little extra pocket change. When I got the nod, I was thrilled at the prospect of spending time outdoors rather than in a stuffy lecture hall, lab or classroom. These internships usually run for six months but I got such a kick out of it that I put in for a permanent part-time position in January at the beginning of the second semester of my junior year.

I really liked working for my boss, Wes Woodson, and was glad he had the budget to keep me on as his man Friday. He was what I'd call a hands-on environmentalist. Wes was not big on getting into anyone's face over pet causes. Action was his thing, not rhetoric. He set a good example by doing; getting his hands dirty up to his elbows. I respected him because he practiced what he preached and based his view of the environment not solely on books or hot air swirling around in classrooms but practical experience in the great outdoors. He didn't pontificate but rather lived what he believed and vice versa. Nature is a great teacher, up close and personal, and Wes was summa cum laude in that classroom.

Wes had a very cool air about him. First, he looked the part … tall, angular, wiry … a no-nonsense guy with a hint of Eastwood in him. He didn't say much and was usually soft spoken but when he talked, people listened. He commanded attention and instilled confidence. If you were lost in the woods, trapped and hanging off some rocky ledge, dangerously exposed to the elements or ... facing a wild animal ... Wes was the guy you'd look to first for help and guidance. That's because he knew his stuff. The man was a walking almanac of everything outdoors. St. Louis was home for him but he had lived and learned throughout the country from the Rockies to the Smoky Mountains; from Glacier National to the Everglades. Wes was usually all business but he had his moments and could be as down to earth as the next guy. He really didn't like to talk about himself but sometimes you could fetch a few precious pearls, if the setting was just right, just casual enough, by getting him to share a few war stories from his colorful past.

When Merle Polk's death made the news, I asked Wes if he had ever been involved in an animal attack.

I must have caught him at a good moment because he gave me a wry smile and said in his deep, down-home, Sam Elliot voice, "Which time?" We had just wrapped things up for the day and he said, "Wanna grab a beer at Duggan's?"

How could I resist? A cold beer to cap off the day was always good but it was even better at Duggan's, a rustic hole in the wall where loud music and incessant sports TV was not allowed to get in the way of good conversation. We settled around one of the stout wooden tables with sturdy bench seats with a vantage point where we could admire all manner of stuffed wildlife trophies mounted here and there.

When I ordered a Red Hook, Wes frowned good naturedly and chided me, "Don't you know where you're at boy? Are you confused again? This here is St. Louis MISSOURI." He really drew out the last word as he put an exclamation point on his declaration of local loyalty by ordering a "frosty, crisp, cold, clean BUDWEISER".

I countered, "Sorry Wes but, you know, you can take the boy out of Portland but ..."

"I understand ... just don't let it happen again."

Not knowing where to start since Wes apparently had so many tales to tell, I tried to prime the pump another way, "So, what kind of animal do you think did in poor old Mr. Polk?"

"Well, it's hard to say without being at the scene but from what I could gather from the news, it didn't sound like any critter you'd normally find around here. Whatever it was, it had to be big and powerful."

"What's your best guess?" I coaxed.

Wes had to rub his chin to draw an answer, "It takes a lot for an animal to attack a man. They'd have to be damn hungry, trying to protect their young ... or just plain mean and ornery. Since it didn't make dinner out of Merle, I'd rule out number one. It would be very strange for a bear or mountain lion to wander so far out of its natural range with babies, so I guess I'll have to go with door number three."

I was really curious, "Do you know of any animal we might find around here that would fit the bill?"

More chin scratching commenced, "It would be very unusual but not unheard of but the meanest SOB I've ever encountered is the gray wolf."

I almost salivated, "Tell me about it, please!"

"Before I get started, there's a little business I need to take care of, son. Darl'n, can you set us up with two more cold Buds? Now, where was I? Oh yeah, the gray wolf. You know, in this whole great, big world, the only thing that a gray wolf will fear is tigers or humans. They can back down a mountain lion or even a bear. This one was a rare specimen even as gray wolves go. Anyway, one spring, I went with a small group of buddies on a fishing trip up past Minnesota into Ontario, west of Thunder Bay, north past Kenora, beyond a tiny place called Ear Falls into the middle of nowhere. We were tough young bucks who wanted to rough it. Spring in that part of the world can still get pretty cold so at night our little tents were circled closely around a campfire and only a fool would venture out of the cozy confines of a warm sleeping bag. It was not just the cold but you didn't want to stray too far from the fire since it's what kept the critters at bay." This was more talking than Wes was used to so he took a long draw on his Budweiser as if to catch his second wind and lubricate his tongue.

"I thought I was the toughest thing on two legs back then but I was probably just the biggest fool. In any case, I decided to show everyone who was the boss by going out alone before daybreak to beat everyone else to the punch. I had just cast my line in the first time when I felt a presence and noticed something moving out of the corner of my eye. It was the biggest damn wolf I had ever seen with a huge, arched back nearly as high as my chest. It had snuck up on me and was creeping into the open clearing ready to breach the remaining gap of about thirty yards with deadly intent on its brain. I was lucky it was alone. It's pretty rare for one of these things to leave the pack and go rogue but this one was a breed apart in more ways than one. What saved me is that I didn't think but instinctively dropped everything and high tailed it to the nearest pine tree which was only a few feet away. Good thing because it leaped up and took a piece of my pant leg before I got up high enough to be safe. I had taken quite a hike to my *lucky spot* so my pals were well out of ear shot. Long story short, it was a good while before they noticed me missing and were able to track me down, so I got to learn about Mr. Gray Wolf in a most intimate way."

I was so awestruck it took me a while to find the words to prod further, "What did you do, Wes?"

"What could I do? I kept my butt up in that tree and nearly froze to death. It's something I'll never forget. Looking down into those eyes that held the yellow glint of the moon was the most frightening thing I've ever encountered. They almost glowed with evil and it seemed like that ravenous, salivating tongue might stretch all the way up to swipe me down from my perch. There's no doubt in my mind that that wolf would have waited until doomsday for me to pass out from hunger and fall from that tree. The connection between us was unmistakable and haunting. I could feel his longing to devour me; his jaws had an almost spiritual grip on me. I was the happiest man on earth when I first heard my friends call out in search of me. When I hollered at the top of my lungs, their voices grew louder and then you could hear the crunch of their footsteps, I expected the wolf to flee immediately. But the scariest part of the whole ordeal was the way he stood his ground against all five of them. Losing the cover of darkness with the daybreak didn't deter him. He snarled viciously baring his gleaming fangs and lowered his head behind those piercing, menacing eyes and seemed to dare the whole group to bring it on. It wasn't until one of them took out a pistol and fired a warning shot into the air that he reluctantly, grudgingly gave ground. But he never ran. He sauntered away not even looking back as if to pay his last disrespects to us. He left with no fear, only disdain." There was a long pause and Wes took another swig from his mug before concluding, "That's the kind of animal that could kill a man just for the pleasure of it."

"So Wes, do you think it was a wolf?"

"Kid, there's just no way of knowing without seeing the body and checking out the scene of the attack firsthand. If I had to venture a guess, I'd say a gray wolf would be as good as any. We'll probably never know."

I was perplexed, "Why do you say that, Wes?"

Wes was about talked out so he said in a matter-of-fact way, "Look, we're into March and it's been almost two months without incident so whatever it was must be long gone. If we had a distant cousin of that killer I met in Canada anywhere near here, we'd know it. An alpha male gone rogue can't help it ... he has to kill." I couldn't deny the logic and wouldn't question Wes' experience so I let the junior detective's instincts in me recede back into some dusty corner of my brain. We raised our glasses together one last time, killed the remains of our beer and I headed back to my apartment, books and unfinished school assignments.

I had two classes in the morning ... one my favorite and the other not so much. Homework assignments needed to be completed for both. I had met Professor Noah Mosely my freshman year when I took one of his course's to satisfy my geology requirement. What a trip. The dude was unlike anything I had ever encountered. As a new kid on campus, I hadn't heard about his reputation so he was quite a shock to my system. First off, I had to learn a new language, Australian. Doctor Mosely was a visiting professor from the University of Queensland in Brisbane. I think he spoke English but it was hard to tell. He spit the words out in such rapid fire fashion that it forced me to really pay attention. I guess it was a blessing in disguise since it compelled me to adopt disciplined study habits in the classroom. After a few weeks of hanging on his every word, I was able to keep up with the frenetic tempo and decipher his strange accent but still found myself going online after most classes to look up some bizarre Aussie colloquialism that left me scratching my head. Speaking of rare species, this cat was definitely a different breed. Without knowing me from Adam, one day he casually invited me to partake of the Vegemite snack he regularly sampled during class when he saw me gazing at it with rapt curiosity. I had to turn him down when he gave me the chance to inspect it up close. I couldn't believe the way he gobbled up the disgusting stuff … it was like a jar of thick black jam made out of fermented bat guano.

He dressed like he was ready for a trip into the outback rather than another day in the ivy covered halls of academia. I don't think he'd ever heard of Calvin Klein. He must have bought his jeans second hand from some farmer. I would have loved to have known the actual mileage on his well-worn, waffle-soled, hiking boots. His canvas vest had more pockets and compartments than Batman's utility belt and he seemed to keep an impossible inventory of trinkets, fossils and other curiosities on his person at all times. The topper was the floppy leather hat he wore to and from class and occasionally maintained during his lectures as he paced to and fro like a caged animal. There was also the thin, scraggly beard he apparently kept for the sole purpose of occupying his fidgety fingers which constantly scratched, stroked and poked his face involuntarily when he spoke as if he needed to manually activate certain muscles to form the proper words. The hiking stick he carried when walking across campus conjured thoughts of Charlton Heston preparing to part the Red Sea. But I found out quickly that I couldn't dismiss him as some kind of offbeat loon retained by Wash U solely as an affable diversion for our merriment. Underneath the odd exterior lay an incredible mind full of an amazing array of facts and experiences.

As time passed, I was able to get the low down on Dr. Mosely. Most people saw the curmudgeon from Canberra as the odd duck that he was but dismissed him as a harmless, amusing, old fart in spite of his oft-times offensive views. When I say offensive,

I mean that his views on philosophy and theology were way outside the mainstream and highly controversial, especially on a college campus. However, he didn't seem to care much about what people thought of him personally. That's one of the things I liked most about him. Aussies have a tendency to be wonderfully direct, blunt, outspoken and possessed of a common sense that escapes most Americans. They just say what's on their mind and don't hesitate to question the conventional wisdom if it doesn't make sense to them. Listening to him I wondered if Australian politicians were equally as forthright as the regular folk. Wouldn't that be a pleasant change of pace, mate?

It was funny though because he wasn't vilified or ostracized because of his insensitive views like most people would have been. He seemed to get a pass because of his jaunty approach to teaching and jocular, Aussie charm. When it came to his archaic views on God, creation and origins, people didn't take him to task. He was so far out of bounds that people chalked it up to being a crazy foreigner … as if he had some kind of inbred sickness unique to the land down under that required pity over revulsion. Professor Mosely did not go out of his way to raise the ire of potential detractors. He never ranted, blew his stack or attacked people personally. His approach seemed peaceful and innocent; one loaded with seemingly innocuous questions and a general desire to understand opposing positions. Everything was sprinkled with an Aussie's wit and quirky humor to keep opponents off guard. Beneath it all though, his academics were impeccable.

The live-and-let-live attitude he seemed to enjoy from others was not completely charitable. Many of the hard core, committed liberals among the staff and faculty would like to have torched the nemesis they considered an unwelcome, reactionary interloper. However, some soon found out the hard way that Dr. Mosely was not a man to be taken lightly in spite of his delightful manner and seeming vulnerability. One particular firebrand, Professor Stillwell, made this same mistake just a few weeks prior when he agreed to a debate in which he figured to toy with the old man to the delight of a home crowd of his sympathetic colleagues and adoring young charges. He must not have witnessed past debates personally or suffered from poor memory or foolish arrogance. To put it bluntly, Professor Mosely ripped him a new one in a most gentlemanly way. A public colonoscopy would have been more pleasant.

Stillwell was lulled into a false sense of security and didn't prepare well. Most of his arguments rested on the premise that evolution is *settled science* and he assumed that, once this insurmountable paradigm was foisted clearly into focus, Mosely would shrink from the fight, shrivel up and blow away. The problem was that Mosely didn't accept this at face value. He had the unmitigated nerve to actually question the basis for the settled scientific conclusions that didn't seem obvious to him at all. That started a downhill slide that exposed the gaps in what appeared to be a weak, ill-conceived argument and, from there, dissolved into mean-spirited, personal attacks from Stillwell. I agreed to spend my evening in the auditorium for the quid pro quo of extra credit in Mosely's archaeology class. As part of the audience, I was an eye witness to the *carnage* that ensued.

It wasn't that Professor Mosely ever departed from his calm and friendly demeanor. He did no such thing. Every personal attack on his credibility and sanity was met with composure, dispassionate logic and a cheerful smile. There was no vitriol or returned salvos of a personal nature. The professor buried Stillwell with an amazing grasp of facts and history that confounded, befuddled and frustrated his angry colleague and all the environmentalists, atheists and secularists in the audience who had come to witness the slaughter of an academic Benedict Arnold. When Stillwell, sounding like a broken record, kept repeating his mantra about settled science, Mosely brushed it aside with questions like, "By settled science do you mean the missing link established with the discovery of Piltdown Man?" It was a low blow to resurrect the long forgotten hoax involving the combination of a human skull and orangutan jawbone that had been a source of embarrassment to evolutionists since 1953. But raising that specter served the purpose of creating some doubt and derailing the settled science express.

Many of the college students in the audience, like me, were not familiar with Piltdown man but got a real eye opener as Mosely reopened this old wound. He pressed the issue with a wink to the audience and a friendly grin for Stillwell, "How many people in the scientific community do you think were misled by this *settled science* during the forty years it was perpetuated as fact? And why would anyone need to create such a hoax in the midst of so much *settled science*? Yes, I know it was a long, long time ago and things are so much different today. But have they really changed that much? Just look at the *settled science* of global warming ... I mean ... um ... climate change or whatever they're calling it now. With so much incontrovertible data supposedly at our disposal, why would the folks in East Anglia need to tamper with their temperature readings to support their theory?" He paused to allow Stillwell to respond to his string of rhetorical questions but more so to demonstrate to the audience that his colleague had no reasonable comeback. Then he resumed, "I don't mean to cut off debate. I just want us to hold open the possibility that the theory of evolution is not so cut and dried. Why don't we look at the scientific evidence with an open mind and consider various alternatives before closing the book on it as settled science?"

Mosely then took aim at another windmill of *settled science*, "Can anyone in the audience tell me the age of the earth? C'mon now, raise your hands if you know."

Unless there was some trick involved, this was easy so hands started popping up and Dr. Mosely pointed out one fellow, "It's roughly 4.5 billion years old."

"Very good my friend; that's right according to settled science. Now, if it's permissible to my esteemed colleague, I'd like to ask for a volunteer from the audience; one of your choosing." Clearly perturbed, Stillwell grudgingly agreed and selected me from the dozen or so hands that had been raised. I'm guessing he felt comfortable with me since he knew me from one of his classes to be a well-informed, progressive young man. In any case, I stepped up onto the stage feeling like a magician's assistant who was about to be sawed in half.

"Welcome aboard mate, I guess I should reveal that I know your name, Seth, since you currently attend one of my archeology courses. Isn't that right?"

"Yes Dr. Mosely, that's correct."

"Tell the audience what your major is, Seth."

I smiled sheepishly, "I'm working toward a B. S. in environmental earth sciences."

Mosely was very accommodating, "That's excellent my lad. So you should know something about the subject at hand. If I recall correctly, you're also a business minor with a pretty good head for math." Feeling more like a sacrificial lamb, I simply nodded. "That's perfect because I need your help with a bit of simple arithmetic. If you don't mind, please take this calculator and marker and make your way to the board." Oh boy, what had I gotten myself into?

"Don't look so *happy*, Seth. I promise you I won't put you on the spot. This will be easy. We just heard that the earth is about 4.5 billion years old. How long have modern men, homo sapiens, been around, anyone?"

The same smart fellow raised his hand and Mosely pointed him out, "Most experts agree man, in some form, has been around for more than a million years but Homo sapiens first appeared somewhere between 160,000 and 200,000 years ago."

Mosely smiled politely again, "Very good and thank you for deferring to the experts on this subject. There you have it, let's be conservative and use 160,000 years to peg when the first modern humans occupied the earth. For the sake of our example, let's say we started with male and female Homo sapiens, one each, 160,000 years ago. Help me figure out what we would expect the world's population to be given expected normal birth and death rates."

From there, Mosely pulled some figures out of an almanac in his head to establish that the earth's human population, in modern, industrialized times, doubles about every fifty years or roughly 1.4% per year. Then, again taking the conservative approach, he adjusted this figure downward to .475% after walking us brusquely through a series of simple yet mind numbing assumptions and calculations to account for a higher, pre-modern death rate due to wars, plagues, disasters, the lack of technology, etc. Then to be ultra-conservative, he suggested we start by using only 20,000 years for the origin of modern man to make the math easier. As promised, he helped me with the calculation which was $1.00475^{20,000}$ x the 2 original parents in our assumption. Of course, my calculator read error because there weren't nearly enough decimal places. For emphasis, Mosely added, "Think about this for a moment, one trillion is 1,000 billion or put another way 10 to the 12th power. Our calculation of $1.00475^{20,000}$ is the same as 1.5×10^{41} The land surface of the earth is 57,506,000 square miles. That's 1.6 square feet x 10^{15}. Bear with me now, 1.5×10^{41} divided by 1.6×10^{15} would yield 9.4×10^{25} people per square foot in just 20,000 years. The densest population on earth is Bangladesh with 2,255 people per square mile. If every square inch of the earth's land mass was covered with unimaginable high rises, we couldn't find a place to put so many people," he chuckled.

Mosely let this sink in for a minute then offered an alternative, "Let's look at another scenario, shall we? Suppose that man was created a little over 6,000 years ago but then there was a worldwide catastrophe like a flood that leaves only eight people alive of which only three couples are of child bearing age about 1,656 years after the first couple was created. What does that leave us? Using the same basic formula would give us 6×1.00475^{4362} or roughly 5.7 billion people. Fancy that, simply amazing, eh folks?" The audience was hushed. Of course, no one clapped but there were no objections raised either. What he was really proposing, if you got past all the calculations and theatrics was absurd. He was basically asking us to accept Christian mythology regarding Adam and Eve and Noah's Ark as fact. It would never fly in such a well-educated crowd but no one could immediately expose the slight-of-hand he had employed to propose something so preposterous using a little mathematical wizardry. Ever the gentleman, Mosely courteously bid me adieu, "I want to thank my trusty assistant, Seth, who did the mathematical heavy lifting for us." I hadn't done anything other than serving as a convenient prop but nodded obligingly; just happy to be released from duty.

There were several other such episodes during the debate which, in the end, had the desired effect. I don't think anyone came away with a new belief in the creation story of Genesis but some questions were raised in many people's minds. The audience doesn't leave thinking a magician actually sawed a young lady in half when the performance is over but a master prestidigitator will leave them thoroughly perplexed wondering over and over about how he did it. I was no different from the rest in that I couldn't find any holes in his logic even though the conclusion seemed ludicrous to me. There was something else that stood out. I hadn't given a thought to Dr. Stillwell. Maybe Mosely was indeed a magician because he had made Stillwell disappear right before our very eyes.

Mosely's classes were very much the same ... they didn't make any sense but made all the sense in the world if you just followed the trail of facts he laid out in plain sight. I hadn't become a convert but he had expanded my mind about tenfold. As crazy as it seemed, when you really studied the archaeological artifacts and endless fossil evidence he presented firsthand, it shot so many holes in conventional wisdom that the theory of evolution resembled a Swiss cheese more than a block of granite. Being a natural skeptic and so steeped in *settled science*, I always assumed I was the victim of Mosely's slight-of-hand ... his undetected hypnotic powers were somehow preventing me from picking up on the obvious. I didn't mind though because he was so much fun ... weird but fascinating ... and just a nice fellow, completely down to earth and seeking no vain glory in his incessant probing for the truth. Every day in his class was like a trip to Ripley's Believe It or Not museum.

Associate Professor Greene could not have been more different from Professor Mosely. They were polar opposites in every way imaginable. Greene was one of the youngest members of the staff at not quite thirty years old. He was only a few years out of graduate school and was in only his third year of teaching at Wash U. If

Mosely was an academic and philosophical anachronism, Greene was cutting edge. He earned his environmentalist chops while pursuing his undergraduate degree at the University of Colorado. He was born and raised there and grew up under the watchful eye of his more accomplished mother, Gloria Greene, who was an iconic CU professor with deep roots in Colorado's environmental and feminist movements back in the 70s and 80s.

Gloria Greene's influence on her only child was unmistakable. She had put her stamp on him from day one when she named him Zebulon Pike Greene. It's not that she was a great admirer of one of Colorado's favorite sons. It was more of a lark to distinguish Zeb with the initials ZPG which referred to Zero Population Growth, one of her pet movements back then. She was still a fervent believer in Malthusian theory and a devotee of Paul Ehrlich who espoused the notion that the earth could not sustain its burgeoning population and had to limit couples to no more than two offspring to avoid the pending catastrophes of famine and environmental suicide. Somewhere along the line, modern technology had defused Ehrlich's *Population Bomb*, but that didn't matter to true believers like Gloria Greene. They had just swapped out one scenario for another to keep the bomb ticking, most recently in the form of the global warming crisis. No matter how you sliced it, humankind was the enemy. We must save the earth! It mattered little if the solutions might make our lives on earth miserable.

Professor Greene's influence on Zeb was magnified by the fact that he never knew his father. He was the product of a youthful dalliance, more harshly known as an accident, and his mother had no interest back then in getting trapped in a traditional family, especially while in the midst of her graduate studies. So Zeb grew up in the shadows of academia with the beautiful state of Colorado as the backdrop. Its natural beauty was a powerful draw that made it a hotbed for enviromaniacs. Thus, as a boy Zeb received an education through the ample opportunities for incredible hands-on experiences in the great outdoors in some of the most magnificent settings our country has to offer. He was also exposed to a lot of people outside the home that tended to reinforce his mother's philosophies. By the time he entered CU; he had quite a jump on the competition and naturally excelled in the field of environmental science. For Zeb, it was more than a course of study … it was a way of life.

Right about the time Zeb was graduating from CU, his mother received an offer to become the chair of the philosophy department at Wash U. So Zeb moved with his prominent mother to complete his graduate work at Wash U; still under her watchful eye. There's no doubt that his mother's influence helped pave the way for him being hired as an Associate Professor to teach environmental science but it would be unfair to characterize him as the beneficiary of nepotism. He possessed a sharp mind and a zeal for his field of study. Zeb worked incredibly hard and paid his dues. In spite of his relative youth, he had an impressive resume that went well beyond academia. Zeb was an active member of countless environmental societies, had published numerous articles in some of the more prestigious scholarly journals and still found time to devote to practical field work. He frequently contributed his time and talent to various endeavors sponsored by the St. Louis Zoo and was an active board member for several wildlife preservation groups such as the Mississippi River Eagle Observatory and local Wolf Sanctuary.

If Noah Mosely was on the fringe of the right wing of the spectrum, Zeb Greene was definitely at the other end. However, on a college campus, Zeb was considered more mainstream if not centrist. He was certainly more my cup of tea as far as being in my major area of study as well as, frankly, more of my comfort zone given my northwestern upbringing and education. If there was one area you might say Zeb had something in common with Dr. Mosely it would be his ability to rely on practical experience from beyond the confines of the classroom. I admired the wealth of working knowledge he had accumulated despite his relative youth and lack of longevity in the teaching ranks. But for sheer entertainment value, he couldn't hold a candle to Professor Mosely. Zeb was Mr. Serious in the classroom … to him, adding levity to the subject matter would have been a betrayal of the cause. Excuse me for being so shallow but, in spite of the questionable content, I'd pick Mosely's class over Greene's any day of the week on showmanship alone.

It really didn't matter what classes I had that day because it was Friday. I was looking ahead anxiously to cutting loose a bit that night and then being free from the classroom over the weekend. Sure, I still had my duties with the Parks Department but that was a labor of love. It was March and the weather forecast was calling for some warm, sunny, early spring weather so I was looking forward to spending Saturday outside. Little did I know that my life was about to change dramatically.

My peaceful slumber was interrupted by Wes well before daybreak, hours before the Parks were open to the public. After I fumbled around and finally put the phone to my ear, he gave me a few seconds to clear the cobwebs before saying apologetically, "Hey Seth, I'm really sorry to bother you at this hour but I need a favor."

I was thinking holy crap but cleared the gunk from my throat and managed to croak, "No problem, what can I do for you?"

Wes explained, "I just received a call from the County cops. A couple of high school kids are missing. Apparently, they were last seen at some kind of illicit party near Creve Coeur Lake and their parents are frantic. It hasn't been long enough to file an official missing person report but the cops are trying to be proactive and need our help. I'm about to head back from Jeff City and don't want to let this wait until then. Can you head over there now and check it out?"

My adrenaline kicked in and I alertly responded, "You bet, I'll throw on a pair of jeans and be there in twenty five minutes."

Wes went into coaching mode, "Okay Seth, grab a flashlight because it will still be kind of dark. According to some of the kids who were there, you should start out past the Page Extension overpass, along the gravel hiking trail toward the thickest patch of woods on the near side of the Lake. It's probably nothing. The kids are likely passed out drunk in someone's basement or still snuggled up in the back seat of a car. Their names are Mike Mohr and Carol Sue Arthur. They're seniors at Pattonville High School. Just check the whole area thoroughly to establish that they're hopefully not in our Park and then call my cell phone. I'll relay the information on to the police."

There had been no hint of panic in Wes' voice, ever the steady hand, but I was still kind of jacked up by the unexpected call to duty so I made it to Creve Coeur Park in record time. With the big lake, high cliffs and signature water fall, it was one of the more scenic locations in St. Louis County but right then it was a little creepy. After passing through and relocking the gate to one of the back entrances, I drove as far as I could and parked in the last empty lot nearest to the bridge. It was still dark in spite of the full moon which was shrouded in hazy clouds, the first sunlight was not yet starting to peak over the horizon and the Park was completely deserted. During normal hours, there'd be a gaggle of hikers, bikers, picnickers, dog walkers and sail boaters. But right then it was just me and my lonesome self. With the moon fading and dawn fast approaching, I could see well enough to keep from tripping over my own two feet but I turned on the flashlight anyway. The last thing I needed was to step on a snake. Yeah, environmentalist or not, those things still gave me the willies … even in broad daylight and certainly when shrouded in darkness.

The asphalt path ended just beneath the overpass which hovered above like a massive canopy. From there, I was accompanied by the familiar crunch of gravel as I took the path heading into the deep woods. I almost jumped out of my skin when an owl hooted from the branches no more than ten feet above my head. I shined the flashlight and caught a reflection from his iridescent eyes. My heart, still racing from his rude warning, pounded harder when he launched himself skyward with the loud flapping of expansive wings that brought visions of pterodactyls to my vivid imagination. After several minutes, just as my heart began to settle down into a normal rhythm, I was sent into another circulatory frenzy by a large animal bounding across the path five feet in front of me. Never mind that it was a fawn, probably a distant cousin of Bambi. It darn near made me soil my drawers. I was on high alert thereafter but the rest of my hike was uneventful, that is, until I came upon the trail left by our uninvited teenage guests.

You didn't have to be an eagle scout or have any Native American blood running through your veins to pick up the scent of this prey. The beer cans and fast food wrappers led me off the path and through the woods to a makeshift clearing, the *scene of the crime*. Judging from the mess, it must have been one heck of a PHS Pirate party. They had been very drunk, really bold or perhaps both because they went so far as to make a nice fire. Maybe they figured the folks in the houses up beyond the cliff's edge would be sleeping, too far away to see the flickering flames or too disinterested to call the cops. Judging from the number of footprints, I'd say there were at least thirty kids at the impromptu bash. Apparently, there was at least one fastidious adolescent in attendance who tried to gather most of the seventy-five or so beer cans into a large trash bag before apparently giving up on a lost cause.

I nosed around a bit more but it wasn't hard to see that the party had long since petered out. It didn't take Daniel Boone to spot where the troops had beaten their retreat out of the woods back toward the exit and, I assumed, cars parked somewhere outside the locked and closed gates; a fairly good trek especially for a bunch of wasted kids in the wee hours of the morning. As I was taking one last stroll around the perimeter before making my way back, I noticed a single pair of tracks headed off deeper into the woods. It was probably just an alternate route to a different rendezvous point. Everyone had probably parked in scattered locations in the neighborhoods around the park in order to avoid drawing attention. Nevertheless, I decided to follow the tracks a bit to be sure.

Thirty yards into my quest, I had second thoughts when I walked right through a fresh, giant spider web. I spasmodically swiped at my face and shoulders hoping to rid myself of the cloying silk strands before I might encounter the hairy, little design engineer with its dripping fangs. Forgive me for being such a wuss but with the dense foliage and high cliffs blocking the sunrise, it was still pretty dark and my nerves were already on edge from too many surprises. At least I had the fortitude to forge ahead instead of turning back prematurely. I almost wish I had given up because the worst surprise still lay just ahead.

Once free from the architectural arachnid's masterful snare, I pressed on with my antennae up and eyes focused firmly down the flashlight's beam. Then, about twenty-five yards ahead I caught a glimpse of something that caused my heart to skip a beat. No, it wasn't an animal but rather looked like human forms. Yes, there were two people on the ground in front of me. Unbelievable I thought; I had found the two missing teens and they were still snoozing away ... like I should have been. I crept up quietly so as not to startle them and bent down to carefully jostle them out of their slumber when I recoiled in horror. I had been fooled by their posture which made it look like they were casually reclining on their backs resting peacefully. No, they were sleeping alright but it was the sleep of the dead. Their skin, drained of blood, shone even paler in the artificial light and provided a ghastly contrast to the devastating, blood red wounds which brought about their demise. I was staggered as though thunderstruck by the surreal scene that was unlike anything I had ever encountered in my life. Their throats had been completely torn out leaving gaping, jagged remains as if they had been attacked by a huge land shark.

I suddenly felt more alone than ever and it took every ounce of resolve I could muster to keep myself from screaming at the top of my lungs and bolting from the scene. With my eyes shut tight, I stood frozen for a good minute before I could think rationally. My first instinct was to call Wes, "I need your help! What should I do? It's bad, real bad!"

Wes didn't sound like a man caught off guard, "Seth, settle down. Take it easy. Just stay calm and tell me what's wrong."

He remained silent while I tried to corral the wheezing torrents escaping from my heaving chest, "Wes, I found the missing kids in the Park. They're dead, Wes, both dead!"

Even that shocker produced no panic, "Seth, are you sure, absolutely sure?"

I tried not to sound exasperated by the question, "There is absolutely no doubt, they're dead. Their heads were nearly ripped off!"

After a long silent pause, "Seth, hang up the phone, call 911 and then call me back." When I rang him again, Wes stayed on the phone with me until the police arrived. There really wasn't a lot of meaningful information exchanged. I think he just wanted to make sure I didn't flip out.

When the police arrived, everything kind of went into slow motion for me. My adrenaline rush wore off and left me drained, in somewhat of a stupor. I felt much safer with the police around but quickly tired of them asking me the same questions over and over. The process lasted so long that Wes arrived on the scene before the officers wrapped things up. They didn't ask for his advice but Wes was able to talk them into giving him access to the scene of the attack. I could almost see the wheels turning in his head as he took mental notes. Even from a distance, I still wanted to retch when I looked at the bodies so I looked away or tried to train my focus on Wes. It was a welcome distraction and very interesting to watch him work the scene. He was cool, calm and completely detached like a laboratory researcher or grizzled medical examiner performing an autopsy. Only later would I get a glimpse into the level of emotion he was able to keep bottled up.

The similarities between the deaths of Mike and Carol Sue and the demise of Merle Polk were so obvious that even the neophytes who arrived first on the scene couldn't miss the apparent connection. The wounds and positions of the bodies were identical down to the expressions of terror frozen on their faces. It didn't take long for them to reach the conclusion that St. Louis County had not been so lucky after all. There was apparently a very large, vicious animal on the prowl that had a taste for human flesh. Beyond that, the analysis was pretty shallow. So it was a relief when an experienced veteran, Detective Stan Sloan, appeared on the scene. He was a no nonsense guy who immediately took charge. The only drawback was that I had to sit through another round of questioning. This time, Wes stayed with me for moral support and tried to interject a few observations of his own.

Sloan was adept at multi-tasking as evidenced by his ability to carry on a conversation with us while barking occasional orders to his team to keep things flowing along some scheduled path in his brain. It was nearly time for the Park to open so he instructed two officers to close off the entrances to the gravel path. Wes winced because he could already hear the grumbling complaints from bikers and walkers in being restricted from using such a large section of the Park on a busy Saturday but he understood the need to isolate the scene and control the flow of information. Sloan instilled confidence with the way he quickly connected the dots, "This is obviously the work of the same thing that killed that man in Bridgeton. But what has it been doing for the past two months? And how did it manage to kill these two kids, laying side-by-side, without one of them making a run for it? Something doesn't add up here." Then our confidence waned as he offered a rather disturbing confession, "Mr. Woodson, I'm a homicide detective and pretty good at it. When it comes to violent crimes, crimes of passion, even gangland violence, I'm your man. But I'm a city boy, a child of the suburbs. To me, exploring the great outdoors means mowing my backyard. I understand this is some kind of animal attack but when it comes to something like this that is well off the beaten path, far from the asphalt, concrete pavement, high rises, strip malls and subdivisions that make up normal civilization, I'm a fish out of water."

Wes, cool as a cucumber, offered, "Well, welcome to my world, detective. If I can help in any way, just let me know. This is personal to me now. This thing, as you call it, has invaded one of my Parks, my home. And please call me Wes."

Sloan was not one to cede an ounce of control but he welcomed any useful resources at his disposal, "Okay Wes, I appreciate that. So, what's your take on this?"

Wes had to massage his chin to elicit the right response, "Unlike you, I'm an outdoorsman through and through ... but there are still a lot of things that don't add up. These poor kids and Mr. Polk had their throats ripped out but there are no other signs of violence and they weren't killed for food. There are no defensive wounds which I could reconcile when it came to Mr. Polk alone but not with these two. I see no natural reason for one animal to be able to kill two people like this in such close proximity with no signs of flight or struggle."

Sloan wanted to get past the obvious, "I hear you Wes. So can you tell me anything affirmative based on your experience?"

Wes trained his steely eyes on Sloan, "I can tell you this for sure. We've got one big, mean bastard on our hands and it will do this again if we don't catch it or kill it. I can't say for sure but I'd be willing to bet that there's a large gray wolf on the prowl in St. Louis County and it has a mean disposition ... it kills people for pleasure."

Sloan's pragmatic mind was already racing ahead thinking of pulling together the right kind of task force to hunt down the beast. At the same time, the wheels were spinning on how to manage the media and avoid setting off a panic. He was envisioning a rush on gun shops and people setting dangerous traps that would only wind up mangling the leg of some poor, unsuspecting child or family pet. Other than asking for some general guidance on where to find knowledgeable trackers and professional varmint control types to launch a search and destroy mission, Sloan apparently saw no other use for me and Wes and dismissed us to our own duties. Wes wasted no time in putting together his own plan to try to secure the safety of our park guests. As for the media, Sloan was fighting an uphill battle. The cat would soon be out of the bag when the police informed the Mohrs and Arthurs about poor Mike and Carol Sue.

What a shame it was. They were just a couple of teenagers doing what kids do. Sure they were stretching the rules a bit with the party but there was no harm or malice intended. They were just out to have some fun and camaraderie with their pals. And, unlike some of the wilder ones in the bunch, they weren't looking to get ripped on beer and wine. They had a few but it had nothing to do with their demise. There biggest mistake was breaking from the pack to get some time alone to fan the flames of teen romance. It was pretty innocent stuff ... Carol Sue was not the type to let things go too far and Mike was too much of a gentleman to force the issue. And yet, none of it mattered because they had paid for their error in judgment and paid dearly. What a horrible way to die. The only thing more powerful than an urban legend is urban truth, especially when it's this bizarre. In no time, the high school grapevine would spread to neighborhoods, workplaces ... and, of course, the media.

Speaking of the media, as you might expect, Flip Flanagan was the first to tap into that grapevine and seize the day. Remember, ethics and responsible journalism were not his hallmarks so, in spite of the best efforts of the authorities to keep a lid on things and reassure the public of their safety, he almost single handedly caused a panic to ensue. Flip couldn't believe his good fortune. The only thing juicier than a serial killer would be a serial killing animal with innate predatory skills and no sense of remorse or conscience. It was Jaws come to life, on land, right here in St. Louis County. As good as that was by itself, it wasn't enough for Flip. He had to blow away the competition. So he went back to his handy lunar chart and bypassed the ancient Algonquin and other Native American legends to find, to his delight, that March, according to the neo-pagans was home to the death moon. He didn't bother with an explanation which sounded like a bunch of unintelligible, pagan gobbledy gook but the name itself was journalistic gold. And, yes, Mike and Carol Sue had been slain under the gaze of a full moon, just like Merle Polk.

If there was any saving grace to be found in Flanagan's opportunistic, overblown coverage of the story, it was that it contained the panic a bit, in a strange way. People were actually buying into the notion that the wild beast in their midst was somehow driven by the lunar cycle. That meant, at least, that during the rest of the month, the ill effects of panic were more muted. But when the full moon approached, pandemonium set in.

Vernal Equinox ...
Love and Wolf's Bane
Blooming

CHAPTER 3

SEED MOON

COMING OUT OF WINTER'S GRIP can be a long, arduous process in central Missouri. It can be maddening to the point of infuriating because of the frequent teasers … eighty degrees one day in early April with the threat of snow flurries the next. It's a good thing that Phil the groundhog lives in Punxsutawney, PA because he would have been turned into road kill long ago by angry Missourians after some of his unfounded prognostications of an early spring. However, this year seemed to be shaping up as the perfect antidote to the winter blahs. Already two weeks into April, the cold, gray skies seemed to be a thing of the forgotten past. With trees budding, lawns greening and flower shoots breaking ground in gardens everywhere, spring fever was in full bloom.

Of course, the glorious start of many folks' favorite season was not enough to disperse that one dark cloud in an otherwise azure sky. At a time when a young man's fancy might blithely turn to thoughts of love ... when the prospects of romance might lure him to spend the day in a peaceful, secluded meadow, with a picnic lunch under a spreading chestnut with the object of his affection, an invisible specter dispelled such delicate pleasures with the haunting reality of a stalking, man-killing beast somewhere on the loose. But life goes on and with each passing day springtime's hypnotic pull grew stronger. This trend toward normalcy was aided by the press who, for the most part, turned their sights toward the annual rites of spring ... happy, light hearted fare like gardening, the coming close of the school year, family vacations and Cardinal baseball.

Flip Flanagan was never one to go along with the crowd. He satirized his sappy peers with a piece on spring proms that started out with a bouquet of fresh wolf's bane for the prom queen and ended with her date turning into a corny version of a teen wolf with plenty of titillating double entendre. It was utterly tasteless especially to the kids at Pattonville High and the parents of Mike and Carol Sue but it boosted ratings so Flip couldn't have cared less about his detractors. He took their criticisms for jealousy which just egged him on. He did an in-depth piece on wolf's bane and started seriously enough with beautiful images of aconitum's purplish petals, named its indigenous regions and even delved into its genetic make-up. But there was really no reason to put the spotlight on this flower so uncommon to these parts other than to play off its legendary mythical powers which Flip did unabashedly.

That in itself was not a ratings draw but it provided a great segue to something that was ... more lunar trivia. Shunning the Native Americans and their bland pink moon, Flip opted for the new age pagans again and the seed moon with its more exciting visions of fertility and adolescent coquetry. Capturing the imagination of people under the spell of blossoming buds and the percolating passions of a glorious, precocious season was easy. From there, it was a short walk to turn this lunar attention back toward the season of the wolf that still lurked in the back of so many minds. As much as people wanted to ignore that one blot on the otherwise clear, blue heavens above, haunting fears crept closer and closer with each passing night as the crescent moon grew in unrelenting proportion like a glowing, celestial tumor. Flip figured he could milk irrational fears for another two weeks leading up to the full moon.

Flip's intentions were purely self-serving and in no way good but they had the beneficial effect of keeping pressure on the local authorities. The distance between the two attacks was so great that the potential range generated by a logistical algorithm made the prospect of tracking down the beast seem like searching for a needle in a haystack. Nevertheless, with Flip's prodding amplifying the public outcry, Sloan had no choice but to sink precious resources into an apparent hopeless cause. It was a boon to local hunters and out-of-work survivalist crazies who received hefty government payouts to do something they would have gladly done for free … gain a license to kill with the likelihood of gaining a hero's status by ridding the area of such a menace. Only the most committed environmentalists and animal rights activists might object to taking out such a dangerous threat. Even though I was not part of that fringe element, I was no fan of the Rambo hunter types who were roaming local woodlands including some areas under our jurisdiction. Nevertheless, after seeing what had happened to Mike and Carol Sue, I was ready to take up arms myself.

The first time I encountered one of Sloan's *hit squads* on the prowl, it reminded me of that scene in Jaws where Hooper sees the folly of Amity's bounty on the man-eating shark as it draws a flotilla of fanatic fishermen rushing to their own peril. It was starting to resemble the Wild West around here. With so many loose cannons running around with happy trigger fingers, the Conservation Department had to issue warnings and restrictions to keep the spring turkey hunters from plying their trade in St. Louis County. They didn't want to see the situation turn from bad to worse by having some over-zealous buffoon mistake a hunter for a wolf or puma. The county bounty as it was called also proved harmful for other local wildlife. There was only so much supervision to go around, so many of the hired teams were operating independently. Naturally, they wanted to shoot something, anything. So when there was no big game to be found, they resorted first to a little target practice on trees, road signs and the like. When that lost its luster, they began taking out other *dangerous threats* like snakes and coyotes.

We wanted to cooperate fully with the county police since two of the deaths occurred in one of our parks. It wasn't just a public relations ploy. There was a genuine concern for the safety of our guests. Nevertheless, we had to set some limits. The first line of demarcation was to prohibit bounty hunters from accessing Park lands during normal operating hours. Park management figured the risk of an animal attack during daylight hours was much, much smaller than someone getting injured or killed by a stray bullet. Later, as nearby residents reported the sound of gunshots breaking the stillness of night and dead coyotes and such started turning up, we closed our doors completely. Sloan urged our management to reconsider but, with input from Wes, they said they would only lift the restrictions on a case-by-case basis if there was clear evidence of a need to track the beast on park land. Sloan could have applied insurmountable pressure by leaking details of the dispute to the press but declined since, in his heart of hearts, he was not thrilled with the shenanigans of some of the *death squads* either.

We all had something else in common. There was shared frustration over the fact that no one could find a hint of a large predator that was somewhere in the vicinity. In addition to Sloan's hit squads scouring the countryside, everyday folks were on high alert looking for any sign of the worrisome beast. We were taking extra precautions in all the parks and the police were on the lookout for anything strange during normal patrols even in highly populated areas. But we had nothing, not even a sniff. There was strong temptation to herald this as good news and float the prospect that the menace had been forced to move on by all the attention and intrusions into its habitat. However, Sloan and company resisted the urge to fall into that same trap again. Fool me once, shame on you ... fool me twice, shame on me.

If we were lax in any area, it was the way we spread our park resources. Every park in the system was subject to some kind of extra scrutiny but, to be perfectly honest, some parks got more attention than others. I wouldn't say there was anything pernicious or careless about our approach. It was a pragmatic way of utilizing scarce resources where we thought they could be of the most benefit. If you look at the system as a whole, some of the parks are far flung to the point where it didn't seem possible that they'd fall within a reasonable range of Missouri Bottom Road or Creve Coeur Lake where the attacks occurred. For example, why focus as much attention on Suson Park or Sylvan Springs way down in

South County? Some of the state parks were actually a bit closer. With that in mind, the State Department of Natural Resources joined us in taking extra precautions. Some of the closest parks like the first state capital in St. Charles were not really in play since they were historic sites in populated areas but some more traditional locales were within twenty miles of Creve Coeur Lake such as Babler State Park which was a popular camping site for county residents.

As much as I had been affected by the deaths of Mike and Carol Sue, my attention was thankfully somewhat divided. School work was still my primary concern, especially with finals only a month away. It was a blessing in disguise to have my focus diverted by the rigors of the classroom. Worrying about tests and grades seemed like child's play compared to the concerns which sometimes haunted me in nightmares featuring decaying zombies with mangled throats and hairy, four-legged fiends with dripping fangs. So I welcomed being engaged in lectures and discussions on campus, especially when we were fortunate enough to get off the subject on some lively tangents.

One day, during an archeology session concerning artifacts from ancient agrarian societies we somehow got Dr. Mosely onto the subject of genetically modified organisms (GMOs). With his mind clouded with the magical dust from our distant past, we trapped him into tasting a speculative delicacy called what if. We knew it would fascinate him to explore the catacombs of what might have happened if the ancients had had the benefits of GMOs at their disposal. The shared discourse on possible benefits quickly took the form of a debate on the pros and cons of GMOs; a hot, controversial topic in environmental circles.

Many, including me, were enamored with the thought of our distant antecedents being empowered to avoid the plagues of pestilence and famine. How might it have reshaped their world and ours? It seemed to me that it could have delivered longer, healthier life spans and helped to avoid some of the greatest sources of instability that plagued mankind. With less scarcity of resources perhaps it could have reduced our propensity to wage war on one another. Just think of the possibilities! Oddly enough, Dr. Mosely was at odds with me, the environmental science major who should have been deathly opposed to GMOs. Whereas I saw it as a potential boon to mankind he saw it as fraught with dangers.

Much more than half the class sided with Dr. Mosely even though their reasons were discordant to his. On the surface, Mosely was not at all opposed to GMOs in contemporary times in the context of transgenic plants. He was in favor of man using his intelligence to manipulate the genetic code of staple crops to improve their resistance to pests or drought. He argued that environmentalists should welcome something that helps avoid the use of herbicides, conserves water and produces higher yields without cultivating greater land masses. But, as the debate wore on, he demonstrated how environmentalists don't always exercise reason in pressing their pursuits. For example, he claimed, they denounce proposed investments in nuclear power even though it would greatly reduce the need for the fossil fuels they abhor. Likewise, he exclaimed, they enthusiastically promote ethanol in spite of the fact it requires more water and farmland, is less efficient than petroleum and natural gas and drives up the price of our food. He punctuated his argument with a dagger point, "So hopefully now you can see my friends that a common thread binds all of these nonsensical arguments which are counterintuitive to many of the environmentalists' favorite causes. That is, in every case, the hard core environmentalist must choose in favor of mother earth and the animal kingdom anytime they perceive a conflict between those interests and man's."

That last premise would have invited a firestorm had it not been for folks like me pressing the point of the prospective, long ago benefits of GMOs. The true believers, as Dr. Mosely called them, were fighting a two front war and he kept shifting to where it was hard to tell if he was friend or foe. Moments after throwing down the gauntlet, he launched a salvo against me and the other pro-GMO adherents, "Not so fast Mr. Seth, aren't you overlooking things a bit with your utopian view?" I remained silent with a puzzled look that begged a rebuttal. Mosely quickly obliged, "There are clearly some potential benefits as you say ... but let's not get too hasty without considering some of the risks as well. If we could limit this technology to simply tweaking the plants to produce healthier, more nutritious and plentiful crops, I might wholeheartedly agree with you. But since when is man able to harness technology for good alone? Isn't it always a two-edged sword? Take nuclear power for example. What about the internet? On the one hand, it has unleashed a positive information revolution beyond the wildest dreams of Guttenberg and his printing press but at the same time has given rise to vile pornographers, predatory pedophiles, identity thieves and all manner of techno-criminals."

Now things were getting really deep and far afield. How did we get from Mayan pottery to this? Many of my environmental allies-turned-opponents quickly switched allegiances back to Dr. Mosely temporarily forgiving his earlier transgression. How odd was it for the libertarian Mosely to be arguing against technology that expanded individual freedoms in favor of restrictions from, I supposed, big government? This was not making any sense but we didn't care because we were having a lot of fun winging it instead of getting bogged down with the study of farm implements from ancient Egypt.

Then the fog began to lift as Professor Mosely's seemingly divergent path got back on a more familiar course. He argued, "GMO technology is no different than others when it comes to the good news, bad news scenarios. Of course there are some good outcomes but I would suggest that the downside is much too dangerous for us to accept the risk. Taking advantage of this seemingly harmless technology to boost farm production is like playing with fire. What comes next? Well we've already seen what direction this is headed in. It starts with experiments on lab animals." Dr. Mosely was not opposed to this but many in the class booed at the very notion assuming that the professor was suddenly their champion. "Perhaps, as we've seen, this could lead to cures for terrible diseases or even the production of transplantable limbs and organs. Sounds good so far, right?" There were more boos of support as though the good doctor was speaking sarcastically. "Then things go further, first cloning and then all manner of human genetic engineering." This time there were neither boos or cheers as the mob was somewhat confused. They didn't like animals being sacrificed to achieve human benefits but were largely in favor of cloning. To them, it was a path to immortality. Some even had designs on cryogenics to freeze their heads until science could advance far enough to reanimate them at some future date.

Mosely ended any confusion and crushed the hopes of those who had mistaken him for their new standard bearer. "When you get right down to it, the problem is that we risk playing god. Of course, we should do everything possible to comfort the sick, feed the hungry and stamp out debilitating diseases which spread suffering and death. But we've got to ask ourselves if the things we do are meant to conform to God's will or supplant him. Unfortunately, we've already gone too far. Somehow, in our extreme arrogance, we've replaced God with evolution buying into the ludicrous notion that everything we see, including man, has come about by an impossible sequence of random chances. We deny the undeniable evidence of an infinitely more intelligent designer that is right in front of our faces while foolishly assuming we can somehow conquer all of our problems, including death, through our own meager, ego-inflated sense of intellect."

Here we had thought we were taking old Mosely on a senseless joy ride but he had seen it coming and used it as an opportunity to bring us around to a tangent of his own. He was, as he might have put it, quite a wise old bird. If this had been part of the curriculum or even a random discussion prompted by the professor, he would have been open to criticism and perhaps discipline for violating some convoluted taboo surrounding the separation of church and state although, as a private institution, Wash U was technically exempt. However, Mosely was just responding to a question raised by a class member. You couldn't punish him for responding to opinions with an opinion, could you? He had achieved another ulterior motive with his clever ruse. What better way to liven up a sleepy classroom and engage his all too dispassionate charges. Mosely didn't care so much that most everyone disagreed with his final hypothesis. The fact that they were listening and responding enthusiastically was enough to please him.

Although they didn't like some of what he had to say, most of the students were willing to give him some credit for keeping things interesting and allowing for an open exchange from all points of view. And, as always, he was entertaining. But there were a few hard core individuals who could see no redeeming value. One fellow in particular got way too serious in my opinion and took what Mosely said as if it were a personal attack against him. Even though I didn't agree with a number of Mosely's points, it bugged me to see someone try to take him to task in such a personal, mean spirited way as if his life were on the line. As usual, the jolly old soul didn't display any animosity or righteous anger but took the barbs and disrespectful behavior in stride and offered charitable good will instead of a strong tongue lashing that I thought might be more appropriate. I didn't know the recalcitrant fellow by name but recognized him from somewhere. Oh yeah, he was also in Professor Greene's environmental science course that I was taking. Now I remembered him ... the dude was always way too serious in that class too. I wanted to tell him to lighten up but, on second thought, decided not to waste my breath.

Mosely had his own way of peacefully restoring order. Instead of lurching all the way back to old world agronomics, he eased back with a more gradual transition, "Speaking of GMO technology, did you know that one of the current and early leaders in this field is located right here in St. Louis? One of our own most prominent local corporations, Monsanto, was involved in some of the early research back in the 1970s. They were also one of the first companies to graduate from the laboratory to viable commercial products with pest resistant strains dating back to the 1980s. Monsanto's focus has been on agricultural production whereas others have branched off into some of the more exotic areas we touched on earlier. It's been an amazing success story for Monsanto in that today they are the U. S. leader with roughly fifty million acres of their GMO products planted and over two hundred million worldwide. Well, let's get back to some other ground that should be just as familiar to us, ancient Mesopotamia and Egypt."

Coincidences are an odd thing. Not being a local boy, I was not really familiar with Monsanto but as luck … or should I say misfortune … would have it, I would soon get to know about them intimately. St. Louis had once been the home to a large number of noteworthy corporations. At one time it was the world's largest manufacturer of shoes and second largest producer of cars behind Detroit including its role as the exclusive maker of the legendary Corvette before GM absconded to Kentucky. The most famous of all was undoubtedly beer where Anheuser-Busch ruled the globe from this relatively small metropolis before the Brazilian invasion. Again, this I knew because of the *fortune* my dad had made in selling them brown boxes. Another biggie was McDonnell Douglas that helped put man on the moon and solidified our nation's defenses until it was swallowed up by behemoth Boeing. Even back then, Monsanto didn't have to take a back seat to anyone. It was a stalwart of the St. Louis economy and remains so today with a few others like Emerson Electric even though much of the city's commerce has fled to more favorable business climes or has been consumed by the leviathan of global consolidation.

Like many high tech businesses, Monsanto seemed to be dominated by relative youngsters, up and coming young Turks on the cutting edge of ever changing technologies. Brantley Earl had been one such fellow back in the early 80s when the beginnings of GMO research were taking root. He was a child of privilege, a local kid who had the advantage of a private prep school education before heading off to Princeton and later MIT. Brantley was an outstanding student who, like savory, sweet cream, always rose to near the top of the class regardless of the institution. He was a whiz in biology and chemistry and a natural born researcher. You might be tempted to call him a nerd but he was physically fit if not athletic. Brantley never wasted his time on sports but enjoyed being outdoors hiking, fishing, climbing, sailing and kayaking among other things.

While he didn't play football, baseball, basketball or run track, it didn't mean he wasn't competitive. He just preferred a different field of battle ... at first the classroom and later the laboratory and board room. His trophies were academic honors, scholarly publications, promotions, research grants and patents, even if the rights to the latter were owned by his employer. Brantley thoroughly enjoyed his life's work and was totally absorbed in it to the exclusion of family and friends. He was raised an only child and had a loving but somewhat distant relationship with his father who was consumed by a very successful career of his own. His mother doted over him but was a society maven who shared no interest in his scientific or career aspirations. She was wrapped up in her charitable causes and the necessary rigors of being an executive's wife. Thus, Brantley never developed a strong need for interdependence and this carried on to his school work and career where he tended to gravitate toward autonomous pursuits involving heavy, independent research.

Maybe that's why Brantley never took a wife to start a family of his own. He was a natural born loner and his parents certainly weren't clamoring for grand babies. Some suspected Brantley was gay but it wasn't the case. He enjoyed occasional female companionship and once was just a whisper away from getting engaged. Cheryl was a colleague at Monsanto who had a lot in common with Brantley. Her family was affluent and she attended the best schools. She preferred the arts and a good read over movies and parties and didn't give a hoot about sports. And she wasn't hard to look at either. However, that's where the similarities ended. She was daddy's little girl, shared a special bond with her mom and adored her two brothers. Family was at the top of her priority list and she wanted kids of her own someday.

Brantley didn't mind her family, even her younger brother who was somewhat of a jock, and tolerated mandatory attendance at the all-too-frequent functions that ate into his personal time. Other than family demands, Cheryl was independent enough to give Brantley plenty of personal space and alone-time to pursue his private interests. She was a great companion but not over bearing. He wasn't thrilled that her analytical abilities combined with her superior social and organizational skills led her down a path toward business management at Monsanto. But, while he considered management, apart from his research realm and top-tier decision making, to be a bit unsavory and beneath him, Brantley took some pleasure in the fact that her divergent career path would lead to less interference with his. All things considered, the pros far outweighed the cons when it came to Cheryl and, in time, he was actually prepared to take the leap and propose to her.

Brantley was too pragmatic to concoct some elaborate pretense to spring a surprise on Cheryl and far too reserved to turn his proposal into a brash, public display of sappy sentimentalism. He also didn't have enough of an appreciation for family ties to ask Cheryl's parents for her hand in marriage. It was a good thing. Also being a pragmatist, Cheryl had anticipated this moment and thought it through carefully. Her list of pros and cons gave a heavy edge to check marks in the plus column. However, being as analytical as she was, she went a step further and weighted each category for importance too. There was only one box left unchecked and it was at the top of her list … kids. Brantley didn't get down on one knee and Cheryl didn't get all giggly. It was more like two business people sitting down over lunch to close a big deal that had been in the works for a long time. They compared notes and everything appeared copacetic when Cheryl asked the defining question, "Brantley, I love you dearly and I feel like we could spend the rest of our lives together happily but there's one thing we need to get clear. It doesn't have to be right away but sooner or later I want to have a family. I want kids of our own. You've never really said much about this so I need to know how you feel about children, our children."

Brantley didn't get carried away by Cheryl's good looks, his physical attraction to her or even the genuine affection he had developed for her over several years. He didn't rush into something but thought for a long time and weighed his words carefully. "Cheryl, I came here tonight fully prepared to ask for your hand in marriage. We're a great match in so many ways. I've given it a lot of thought and there's no doubt in my mind that I'd like to share the rest of my life with you. I'm glad you brought up the subject of children because, honestly, I had not given it much consideration. I can see how close you are to your family and understand how much having a family of your own must mean to you." Brantley paused while Cheryl beamed with anticipation at the prospect of sharing this most precious desire together. She could sense the last possible barrier between them crumbling into dust. "I'm very sorry, Cheryl, but I can't come to grips with the thought of becoming a family man." She was absolutely crushed and wanted to let her eyes dissolve into tears but, ever the pragmatist, resisted the urge and accepted Brantley's pronouncement with stoic resolve knowing, deep down, that it was for the best.

That was the last time Brantley ever remotely entertained the thought of a serious relationship with a woman. They say that men cannot be just friends with women because sooner or later their thoughts will turn to amorous desires. For Brantley this proved to be false. He still dated casually on occasion but when he felt any hint of romance welling up that might turn into a binding commitment, the relationship was over. Nevertheless, he eventually found a few kindred spirits of the female persuasion with whom platonic friendship was not impossible. They were odd birds like him whose interests leaned more toward work and careers; who didn't want any part of a commitment that might deter them from their life's goals and solitary lifestyles. Call them selfish, self-centered, self-absorbed, ego-centric, workaholics or any other term that fits but, bottom-line, they were loners who only needed companionship and affection in small doses to get by.

Brantley's male companionships were similarly limited. He didn't have what you would call a best friend, wing man or a circle of drinking buddies. There was no poker night, Monday Night Football, clubbing or beers and shots at the local pub. If he attended a happy hour or joined the gang for a few pops after work, there was always some ulterior motive … pushing a pet project forward, career advancement, checking out the competition or fulfilling some perceived obligation. It wasn't that Brantley was heartless or calculating. He was just strictly business and a classic loner. He cared about people enough to devote his life to their betterment through research aimed, in his mind, at ending world hunger and advancing a higher quality of life to less fortunate people around the globe. Brantley would enthusiastically support charitable drives and team building exercises that he felt would advance Monsanto's efforts to achieve breakthroughs in cutting edge technology.

One such endeavor was right up Brantley's alley. Assorted members of associated research teams were invited to spend part of the weekend together on an overnight campout at Babler State Park along the outskirts of the west county area of Wildwood. Achieving true collaboration between research teams made up of staunch individualists like Brantley was no easy task. Overcoming their natural inclinations to the contrary meant generating more personal contact than what normally occurred within the sheltered labs and isolated offices across the company's campuses. Happy hours and other occasional social functions helped break down a few barriers but camping out overnight in close quarters would go a lot further, or so management supposed.

As much as Brantley loathed such contrived and forced socialization, he was still very attracted by the prospect of displaying his woodsman's skills. To him, it was a subtle form of competition where he could hopefully dispel nerdy notions with the outdoor talents that had been hone to a fine edge since childhood. This was a playing field where he could assert his leadership skills and, in his wildest imagination, perhaps even play the knight in shining armor to a distressed damsel or noodle-brained knave. He knew that most of his cohorts would be like fish out of water in such a setting and was almost giddy at the prospect of distinguishing himself as someone in command, in his element.

Most of his fellow campers were quite a bit younger than Brantley. At this point, he was senior to most in age, rank and reputation. Though he was not the loveable sort, he was kind of a father figure to the young lions and lionesses who were being groomed as the next generation of researchers and leaders. At work Brantley was so serious that he came across as solemn, staid and sometimes even grim. You just couldn't get close to a guy like that. But still he was well respected and almost revered for his work, achievements and superior mind. In many ways, he was a founding father of GMO technology at Monsanto. Thus, it surprised most everyone to see a different side of bookish Dr. Earl. Out there, he was like Meriwether Lewis, Jack Hanna and

Jeremiah Johnson rolled into one ... a regular Tarzan of the Apes in a white lab coat. He took on a whole new persona and there was a discernible glow about him.

Unlike his sometimes churlish behavior in the lab, Brantley was very accommodating and approachable out in the wilds of Babler State Park. It seemed he was genuinely trying to be helpful and wanted everyone to have a good time. Babler was only a stone's throw away from *civilization* but it still offered a good chance to rough it a bit. The campgrounds were well appointed and maintained but, for this crowd, presented worthy challenges ... setting up tents, building fires, cooking and the like. It was close enough to home that it didn't provide a true sense of taming the wilderness but was surrounded by a large expanse of woods and natural habitat to transport your mind away from the rat race to another, more primitive world. The puppeteers who contrived the exercise considered it perfect. It was convenient yet rustic and would force a camaraderie that couldn't be fostered back in the office.

No one had given much thought to the killings back when arrangements for the campout were in the works. Babler was far enough away from Bridgeton and Creve Coeur that it seemed a world apart. However, since twenty miles was not what you'd call an impassable barrier, park officials under the guidance of the Missouri Department of Natural Resources had taken extra precautions and done a nice job of offering up a good PR campaign with just the right assurances to help the public feel secure without making them skittish with too many red flags. Of course, Monsanto, like any overly cautious big corporation did a formal risk assessment before giving the green light. It was deemed a safe venue and the activities were considered low risk under a worst case scenario since there would be a large group of people staying in close proximity to one another.

It was just coincidence that the moon was in full bloom that Friday night during the overnight campout. No one would have given it a second thought were it not for Flanagan's flipping news flashes ... sorry pun intended ... that provided daily updates of the impending advancement toward the apex of the lunar cycle. Flip's unrelenting, insensitive ranting about monstrous, marauding wolves and their bloody fangs got to some of the tenderfoots whose ignorance of the outdoors made them prone to irrational fears. Of course, Flip's motives were strictly altruistic; aimed squarely at public safety with no eye toward ratings ... yeah, right! In any case, it made everyone, especially the real city slickers, feel secure to have someone like Brantley along to lead the way and dispel any worries.

If the troops were surprised to see the more human side of Brantley the outdoorsman, they were completely blown away by the charming, playful demeanor he exhibited around the campfire. Something about the crackling, popping fire with its shining embers wafting into the night sky to magically mingle with the stars made the kid come out in the older man. Nothing brings the Peter Pan out in a guy like grilling hot dogs on a stick, toasting marshmallows to a bubbly, crispy golden brown and washing it all down with an ample supply of frosty, cold Budweiser. It was a sight to behold as the stuffy, prim and proper scientist's scientist regaled the entranced audience with Bunyanesque tall tales and warbled his way in leading a chorus of upbeat campfire songs. The only thing that might have pleased the team building architects more would have been a few stanzas of Kumbaya.

As the hour grew late, blithe banter, mirthful merriment and general joviality gave way to a tried and true staple of campfire entertainment. It started with talk of movies which led to lively chatter about the greatest horror flicks of all time. After debating the merits of Psycho, Exorcist, The Shining and the like, it was time to swap ghost stories and tales of campfire terror. Brantley proved to be a master of the craft and had the group eating out of his hand with his own rendition of the classic hook man. He skillfully brought his fellow campers to the edge of their seats with his dire expressions and barely audible, raspy whisperings before lowering the boom with an explosive, jolting conclusion that made everyone jump out of their skin. After hearts stopped thumping and the effect of all the booze and food set in, everyone retired to their pup tents which were grouped in somewhat of a circular fashion around the campfire. The arrangement mirrored the social order with workplace cliques here, couples paired off there … and the reclusive loner seeking privacy furthest from the center.

Brantley was too keyed up from the night's festivities which were so far from the norm for him that he couldn't sleep yet. He sat outside and peered into the heavens rattling off the names of constellations in his mind and pondering the vastness of the universe. Then his thoughts drifted back to our insignificant corner of the cosmos as his gaze was drawn to the luminescent moon that dominated the bespectacled, inky black sky. It wasn't hard to see why such an April moon could be dubbed the seed moon. Its beams seemed to carry some unseen force with the power to draw shoots and sprouts from seedlings nestled in the warm, moist soil. The moonlight also seemed to carry tiny grains of soothing, therapeutic sand which caused him to involuntarily rub the gritty corners of his eyes. Finally, peaceful rest beckoned Brantley as he stared at the dwindling fire. That gave him a final, altruistic urge to gather a bit more wood to stoke the fire before retiring for the night. With lantern in hand, he quietly made his way down the dark, still path leading toward the shelter containing the campground's well-seasoned wood supply. It was the last time the uncharacteristically lively Dr. Brantley Earl would ever be seen alive.

Once again, I was woken up much too early for a Saturday by a call from Wes Woodson, "Sorry to call you so early Seth."

This time I was not so polite, "You're kind of making a habit out of this, aren't you?"

"I know Seth but there's been another killing and Detective Sloan would like you and me to visit the scene right away."

I resisted the urge to say something snarky, "Did he say why?"

Wes postulated, "I guess he thinks my background may be beneficial to shedding some light on the investigation. As for you, he wants your eyes since you were the one who found the two Pattonville kids. Maybe he thinks you're in the best position to notice any similarities or contrasting elements. Whatever his reasons, can you be ready in fifteen minutes if I swing by to get you?"

I couldn't resist one jab even though I didn't want to appear insensitive, "Sure thing Wes, as long as you don't mind seeing me without my make-up." At this point, I needed to keep things as light as possible to avoid a melt down from the paralyzing fear that continued to haunt me with visions of Mike and Carol Sue.

When we arrived we had to navigate the Monsanto folks who were nervously milling about. Thankfully for them, no one had actually seen Dr. Earl's mangled body. Once they noticed him missing, they had followed a logical progression of calling out, searching the immediate area and contacting park security who discovered the remains and contacted the county police. They were kept in the dark initially since, according to standard procedure, everyone in the vicinity was considered a potential suspect. That didn't last long though after Sloan arrived and took note of the obvious parallels. It was undoubtedly another animal attack with the characteristic trauma to the throat and odd posture of the reclining body.

After questioning people to trace Earl's final actions before everyone went to sleep, Sloan urged the group to pack up and leave but some folks hung around longer than others. The police informed them that their colleague was dead, apparently as the result of an animal attack but left them hanging otherwise. They wanted more details to satisfy their morbid sense of curiosity and allay dread fears but it would not be forthcoming. Gradually, they all gave up and retreated back to their homes. The team trip had started out as a roaring success but ended as a miserable failure with morale dropping to an all-time low. If there was any consolation, Brantley's death served to encourage more collaboration of sorts as folks networked to glean new details about the demise of their fallen comrade. As *scoutmaster*, Brantley had started to win over many converts to the great outdoors that night but his death nailed that coffin tightly shut. No one from this team of Monsanto researchers would consider camping out again for a long, long time.

Sloan may have been a fish out of water but he was quickly learning to navigate the animal kingdom and the strange circumstances it was producing. This time he had the area cordoned off and carefully controlled and called in a forensic team to fully process the scene of the attack and surrounding woods. Blood and tissue samples were taken and they went over the grounds with a fine tooth comb. The detective wanted to end the speculation once and for all regarding what type of animal was involved. Every inch was scrutinized meticulously for DNA, tracks, hairs, droppings … anything that would help solve the mystery and track down the rogue killer. A photographer snapped endless shots that would be used for comparisons to the other two attacks. No stone was left unturned.

Sloan meant business. With a third killing and this one only one month apart, he knew he had a tiger by the tail. The most seasoned tracker from the teams he enlisted earlier was already on the scene to try to pick up the animal's trail. Wes and I were allowed full access and encouraged to follow the tracker. Seeing Dr. Earl's body brought back shocking, deeply disturbing images of Mike and Carol Sue. The similarities were freakishly identical. Earl was prone, on his back as if laying down for a nap. His arms were at his sides with no apparent defensive wounds. The rest of his body was fully intact and the beast had killed for reasons other than hunger. There was no sign of a struggle, only sheer horror registered in a death mask that said he was fully aware of the swift, violent departure he faced. Just like with the young teens and old Merle, it just didn't add up.

Wes helped to point out several other anomalies that the rest of us would probably have missed. "Look at this, how this Coleman lantern is several feet away sitting upright. How did that happen? This man was taken by surprise so why didn't he drop it? What prevented it from breaking and starting a fire that might have scared off the animal? The only explanation is that Dr. Earl set it down himself. But why would he do it here before reaching the wood shelter? If he heard something approaching, wouldn't he have held onto the lantern and pointed it in the direction of the sound? I can tell you what I would have done. I'd have flung it at the monster with all my might to try to burn up the bloody bastard." Sloan, tracker Joe and I nodded in agreement as if it had been obvious to us too. Wes continued, "Now we've seen this before … the odd posture for someone that just suffered such a violent death. But what else is wrong with this picture? It's not just how he's laying but where. If something like a giant wolf was leaping up to grab your throat, wouldn't you try to flee? Even if you were caught completely off guard, wouldn't the impact have knocked you off the trail? He's laying smack dab in the middle of the path as if he volunteered to make it as easy as possible for the attacker."

Wes turned to our tracker, "Tell me Joe; does anything about the tracks strike you as odd?"

Joe peered back at the ground which he had already been inspecting between Wes' interruptions, "I guess you mean other than the fact that this is one huge wolf we're after." Wes nodded knowingly and Sloan felt a little foolish realizing how much he was spending on forensics to establish what Joe and Wes figured out with one glance at the large paw prints. "We need to follow the tracks further but I can already tell you from here that it looks a little too pristine for me … it ain't normal."

This caught Sloan off guard, "What do you mean, Joe?"

Joe waved his finger so as to not destroy the tracks, "We can all see the paw prints clearly but what don't we see? That's right … we don't see anything else. It's like someone swept the path clean for Mr. Wolf so he wouldn't catch a thorn in his big, honking feet. With the wood shelter, park office and bathrooms down at the other end of the trail, there should be all kinds of foot prints too. It would take a pretty good rain or one heck of a wind to smooth things out like this."

Sloan was taking copious notes and instructed the staff photographer to get plenty of shots of the prints. Joe cautioned, "Now follow along with me but stay behind me and off the path so we don't mess up the trail." We inched along behind as Joe narrated, "Yep, this is one big animal … just look at the stride on this thing. It was awful nice of Mr. Wolf to stay right in the middle of the path to make it so easy for us to follow him." No sooner had he said this when he stopped suddenly with a dumbfounded look on his face. He stretched out his hand back our way to caution us not to move then tip toed gingerly around the path, off in every direction. Wes noticed first, then all of us, how the paw prints halted abruptly as if the wolf had been beamed up to an alien space ship. After a long search with help from Wes, Joe declared, "This is the weirdest thing I've seen in all my years of tracking. There is absolutely no sign of this wolf turning from the path to high tail it off into the woods."

Wes beat Joe to the punch on the next oddity, "Look up ahead here. From here on down to the end of the trail, normal foot traffic resumes."

Joe punctuated the aberration with his own home spun wisdom, "I ain't ever seen a rain or wind that does spot cleaning on a dusty trail."

Earlier Detective Sloan had been starting to get his sea legs. His confidence was boosted by all the resources at his disposal along with the clear confirmation that the culprit was a large wolf. But his sense of security and resolve were obliterated by the unexplained, almost impossible set of circumstances we faced. All the progress we seemed to have made was thrown for a loop. Sloan looked to the sky as if seeking divine intervention then dropped a bomb on Wes and me, "I'd like the two of you to join the investigation and be part of my team, assuming I can clear it with County Parks." I just looked at Wes, since I'd be following his lead either way. I assumed Wes would not want to get involved and take time away from our park duties but I misjudged how much he had been affected by the deaths of the two teens and having their young lives cut so tragically short.

Wes consented without a hint of drama, "If the boss man agrees, you can count us in partner." Wow, this was more than I had bargained for. First my internship had been extended indefinitely and now I was officially part of the investigative team assigned to the most bizarre string of killings St. Louis had ever seen. I couldn't wait to tell Walt and Gretchen.

We worked our way back to the campground where another surprise awaited. Sloan did the honors, "Fellas, I'd like you to meet the other newest member of the investigative team, Zeb Greene."

Wes shook his hand as I confessed, "I already know Dr. Greene. He's one of my instructors at Wash U."

Sloan laughed, "It's a small world, eh Seth? As you know, Dr. Greene knows a thing or two about animals and their behavior. I asked him to join the crew at the suggestion of a friend who serves on the Zoo's board. He should be a big help in tracking down our killer. Now that we're sure we have a wolf on our hands, Zeb's work with the wolf sanctuary should prove useful too." We took Dr. Greene down the trail to revisit the scene and get him up to speed. He was as perplexed as the rest of us but just as determined to solve the mystery and restore safety to the region.

When word got out about the Babler State Park incident, the happiest man in town was Flip Flanagan. His initial reaction was that it was too good to be true. His bombastic, callous assault on the sensitivities of St. Louisans had been wearing thin. In spite of his audacious flare, there didn't seem to be any mojo left in his brazen attempts to mine ratings gold from the misfortunes of others. But Brantley Earl's vicious death was like a set of retreads that added fresh mileage to an otherwise dilapidated vehicle. His lunar links didn't appear so far-fetched now with killings taking place during three of the last four full moons. And while the satirical wolf's bane bit was still considered over the top, the menace of a confirmed, real, live, rogue predator lent credence to his heretofore irrational ranting juxtaposed with serious journalism. Unexpectedly, under the glow of reputational vindication and an injection of new life for his signature story, Flip showed that he was human after all. It started to sink in that four people, his *neighbors*, had died a horrible death. Shattered loved ones were left behind to mourn. And worst of all, a clear and present, four-legged danger was on the loose. As these thoughts hit home, Flip decided it was time to take a more serious turn with his story and play up the safety angle. He would lead the charge to bring the devilish monster to its fitting end and restore peace and security to our shell shocked city. Yes, as local media coverage exploded, sensible Francis Flanagan would ride herd over his peers as elder statesman and crusading sage.

CHAPTER 4

FLOWER MOON

APRIL SHOWERS BRING MAY FLOWERS. Everyone knows that ... including the Algonquin tribes who deemed May the month of the flower moon centuries before. The name seems out of place though, almost an oxymoron. It's the sun that brings the spring blooms. Who knows what they were thinking. Maybe they ascribed magical powers to the phosphorescent orb radiating in the night sky. Maybe they were paying tribute to some variety of cereus flowers that only blooms at night under the moon's glare then wilts with the break of day. No matter the reason, one thing is clear ... they ascribed powers to the moon that have been proven irrational. Their folklore has no place in a high tech society that has placed a man on the moon.

Don't try to tell that to the inhabitants of our town. Although Flip Flanagan had toned down his newsroom rhetoric and ceased exploiting the lunar cycle, it was too late to turn back. We had all been conditioned by his earlier harangues and the clockwork killings of the elusive predator to pay close attention to the changing moons. It seemed childish and superstitious to fear the full moon but still it was the elephant everyone pretended not to notice in homes and offices all across St. Louis. It was a ticking time bomb and there wasn't anyone living in the area who didn't know when it was set to go off. Lest anyone forget, all we had to do was look into the night sky at the reminder that expanded with each passing day.

It was foolish not to be on guard continually, especially at night, but many people felt like there was no need to be on high alert before the full moon. The only thing that might change their minds was an attack during some other phase of the moon or, preferably, to catch and kill the beast. While this irrational thinking persisted, very few were foolish enough to think that only north county residents needed to be on edge. Brantley Earl's death in the outer reaches of Wildwood put an end to that notion. The wolf showed us all that its range stretched far and wide … no one was safe. The police and county authorities tried to preach calm and invoke a sense of security with constant reports of all the precautions and proactive measures that were under way. But nothing could stop the panic from spreading when a pilfered picture of Merle Polk and his mutilated throat made its way across the internet. Sloan was incensed over the leak, especially when he was raked over the coals by his superiors for lax control. It was so unfair since he was such a pedantic control freak but, shoot, that's the way it goes. The buck stopped with him.

I too was tangled up in the figurative fangs that gripped the metropolitan St. Louis area. How could I not be? I was part of the police's investigative team. Okay, so I was not much more than a tag-along. However, Sloan was not the kind of man to keep me around for grins or the furtherance of my education. He still held out hope that my direct link to the second attack, my first-on-the-scene, eye witness experience would prove valuable along the way. It was a good thing I was Wes' right hand man because he was much more valuable to Sloan.

What bothered me was the way the killings preoccupied my thoughts when I was away from the investigation. The wolf stalked me within my own four walls. One night when I couldn't keep my mind on my studies, I turned on the tube for some inane relief from the torment. A cable movie channel was in the midst of an all-nighter featuring classic horror flicks. I caught the end of Frankenstein then, after Dracula had successfully started to numb my brain, the 1941 version of The Wolf Man came on. It held up as great entertainment after all these years and Lon Chaney Jr. was still the consummate man-beast.

I must have dozed off somewhere around the time the old gypsy fortuneteller, Maleva, recited the fateful poem.

> *Even a man who is pure in heart*
> *And says his prayers by night*
> *May become a wolf when the wolfbane blooms*
> *And the autumn moon is bright.*

Even sleep did not bring peace for I had one of the freakiest, most troubling nightmares imaginable. I found myself inside the old Disney cartoon version of the Three Little Pigs and we were locked away within our brick house as the big, bad wolf pounded on the door. He was somehow mortifying in spite of his cartoonish pants, suspenders and rumpled top hat. I should have felt safe and secure within the solid, stone confines but I was gripped by terror nonetheless. Then things really got weird. I turned to my two piggy companions to find they had morphed into ghastly, Mike and Carol Sue zombies. I opened the door to make my escape and they held me tightly in their clutches as the wolf entered to devour me. As he crept nearer and nearer with saliva dripping from his fearsome fangs, Mike and Carol Sue laughed maniacally as blood gurgled from their severed throats. Their ridiculous, falsetto voices wheezed with bloody mist as they repeated the song over and over, "Who's afraid of the big, bad wolf?" as the ghoulish creature inched closer and closer. I woke up in a heavy sweat with my chest heaving … in the nick of time.

Yeah, the rogue wolf was getting to me … at all hours … really messing with my world. I needed a diversion to let my mind escape and relax for a while. It dawned on me the next day in Dr. Greene's class that the best possible diversion was right there in front of my face. What better way to forget your troubles than to drown them in two limpid pools of crystal blue set within the heavenly visage of a girl that had to be the prettiest one on the entire campus. It wasn't like I hadn't noticed her before. How could you help it when she was absolutely stunning in every way? Still I had never talked to her or even tried to find out her name. Maybe it was because I was so focused on my studies I wanted to avoid an unnecessary diversion. Okay, to be honest, it was more likely that I was intimidated by her drop dead, gorgeous good looks. In my current state of mind, unable to concentrate anyway, I found myself trying to muster the courage to approach her after class.

Through a Herculean effort, I forced myself to hang near the exit after class ended. I was going to just come right out and say hello as she left the classroom and go from there. Why was I sweating? Was it so difficult to form the words, "Hi, how are you? My name is Seth, what's yours?" What was taking her so long? She was the last one to leave the room. I had cast my lot and was fully committed. It was now or never. She was half way toward the door when Professor Greene stopped her, "Faith, are we still on for some coffee this afternoon?"

"Yes, count me in." What a punch to the gut! I turned and hurried away to hide the shame of the embarrassment that flushed my face as if she would somehow know that I had been ready to make my play moments before.

At least there was a side benefit to my near blunder. I was so crestfallen that I completely forgot about the killings for the time being. Now I was faced with another mystery. I had an hour before my next class to nose around and quizzed a few classmates about the unlikely couple while trying not to reveal my true motives. The few puzzle pieces I slapped together with the help of the campus grapevine told an interesting story. Associate Professor Greene was not violating any formal policy because Faith was not a Wash U student. She was enrolled at Lindenwood College in neighboring St. Charles and was here only temporarily for two extension courses not offered at her school. It was hard to get the scoop on the budding romance without sounding like a creep so I was able to glean just enough to get a feel for the situation. One guy who was not really in the know passed along some lurid but hopefully incorrect rumors about the nature of their relationship. Two better sources informed me that it was something casual, more of a friendship than anything else. Still, I fretted that it would be tough for someone like me to compete with an accomplished, older man like Greene. Would I want to anyway? I mean, the guy was now a colleague of sorts since we were both members of the investigative team. I'm ashamed to say it but I basically decided to give up without a fight.

I didn't have long to put Faith out of my mind because the other course she was taking at Wash U was Professor Mosely's archaeology class that same afternoon. I hadn't really taken notice of her there before because it was a large class in an auditorium with stadium seating and I normally sat right up front to keep up with Mosely's Aussie-speak. Things had changed though. With her lovely, alluring image burned indelibly into my gray matter, my radar spotted her the moment she stepped into the room. I tore my eyes away and took my seat up front. Mosely was his interesting, entertaining old self but, for the first time, I couldn't concentrate on a word he said. Even though I couldn't see her all those rows behind me, I couldn't get her out of my brain. Like any show business professional, the good doctor didn't betray his thoughts during his performance but he took notice of my absent-minded behavior and uncharacteristic lack of participation. When class was over, he tapped me on the shoulder before I could escape, "Seth, do you have a moment mate?"

All I could think was, "Crap, I'm busted. How do I get out of this one?" I wasn't about to reveal my true feelings, "Sure Dr. Mosely, my classes are done for the day. What can I do for you?"

We weren't what I'd call close friends then but I had developed a fondness and appreciation for the Aussie and I think the feeling was mutual. Thus, he caught me off guard with a blunt bolt from the blue, "What's the matter with you today my boy? Have you got a case of the spring fever?"

It was just an amiable shot in the dark, no more than an ice breaker, but I was rattled that his volley hit the bull's eye. My awkward, defensive response didn't do much to hide my secret, "What do you mean by that?"

"Oh nothing really; I just couldn't help but notice that you seemed to be distracted today as if your mind was someplace else. Is there something bothering you?"

His courteous, non-invasive tone helped me to regain my composure, "I guess I have been a little flustered by the investigation."

What an idiot I was! Dr. Mosely didn't have a clue about my involvement. I was successful in throwing him off the scent of my romantic tragedy but opened the door to a long explanation of something I preferred to keep to myself. "Whatever do you mean? What investigation are you referring to, Seth?"

I mentally tried to back away, "Oh, I'm sorry Dr. Mosely. Here I am talking as though you should be able to read my mind. I'm sure you've heard about the animal attacks, right?"

He perked up right away, "Yes, of course I've heard about them. You'd have to be living in a cave not to know about those killings with the constant media barrage. I can't say that I appreciate the continuous, ghastly reminders; very tragic really. So what's bothering you about the investigation into those bizarre, unfortunate deaths?" My body language must have revealed my reluctance. "I don't mean to push you Seth but you really should talk about it if it's bothering you to the point of disrupting your studies."

I acquiesced, "Well, you see Doctor I became involved through my part-time job with the County Parks Department. Unfortunately, I was actually the first one on the scene at Creve Coeur Lake and discovered the bodies of those two dead teenagers."

Mosely gasped and his eyes grew wide "My word; that is unnerving."

"Now, I'm involved in the ongoing investigation. The police asked me and my boss, Wes Woodson, to assist them."

My explanation must have satisfied the professor because his shoulders relaxed and he reached into one of the multitude of pouches in his canvas vest and began fiddling with an unidentifiable treasure. "I can certainly see how your mind might be cluttered under such serious circumstances. I understand that one of my colleagues has also been tabbed to assist the police."

"Yes, Dr. Greene was added to the team about the same time. I'm currently enrolled in his environmental science course. Do you know him well?"

Mosely smiled, "I'm familiar with young Doctor Greene but couldn't say that I know him well. I don't think I'm his cup of tea. He tends to keep to himself as far as it concerns dealing with me. If I didn't know better though, I might think he's keeping tabs on crazy, old Professor Mosely through one of his acolytes."

My memory sprang back to the lively discussion we recently had on GMOs and the outspoken fellow from Greene's class who had rudely taken the professor to task, "I think I know who you mean. That guy's a real pain in the ... uh neck."

Dr. Mosely took a more conciliatory view, "I don't mind too much really. It's hard to carry on a conversation and have a friendly disagreement with people like that but I'd rather see someone who is committed to a cause rather than another bump on a log drifting aimlessly with the current."

Then I made a bigger mistake than the first. Perhaps I was too at ease with Dr. Mosely and didn't think before engaging my tongue, "What's that you're holding?"

That opened the flood gates and I felt like I had been baited into one of the professor's favorite sermons. Before going too far, he offered a welcome suggestion, "How about if we get out of this stuffy old classroom and grab some grub and a Foster's?"

I grinned, "That sounds good … as long as you don't mind me having a real beer … and the daily special isn't one of those Vegemite sandwiches." He laughed heartily and we took off for one of those quaint, comfy university haunts with juicy burgers and cold brews. At least if I had to listen to a lecture, it wouldn't be so bad over a few cold Buds.

He liked to drink his Foster's straight from the over-sized, bold, blue and gold can whereas I preferred my Bud on tap in a chilled pint glass. "So where was I mate? This here is a piece of ordinary tree bark. Well not so ordinary … perhaps extraordinary would be more appropriate. I had to travel all the way up to your neck of the woods to get it."

Now he had my attention, "Really, where did you get it?"

"Oh, it was maybe fifty miles from your home in Portland," he toyed with me. "Ever heard of a place called Mt. St. Helens?"

"Of course, I've taken several field trips there. Why would you keep a piece of tree bark from there?"

He wasn't done teasing me along, "You weren't too moved by my arguments favoring a young earth, were you? That really surprises me, what with such compelling evidence right in your own back yard." Now he had me hooked so I just leaned back, took another swig of beer and went along for the ride.

He handed me the sample of bark and let me examine it, "Do you notice anything different about this?"

"It's not very soft. In fact, it feels more like stone than wood."

"You might almost say it's a chunk of petrified wood, eh? Well, you'd be right because that's exactly what it is; or was becoming when I took it." I wanted to see where he was headed so I didn't object. "Since you're from Portland, I'm guessing you know when the mountain blew its top even though it was before your time."

"Yes, everyone around Portland and Seattle knows it was 1980."

"Then tell me, how could the process of minerals replacing organic matter occur in such a relatively short period of time?"

So far, I was on solid ground, "That's easy Doctor. The eruption at Mt. St. Helens was such a cataclysmic event that trees were uprooted and buried under tons of sediment in the blink of an eye."

"Good answer my boy! And as you probably know, under more normal circumstances petrification only takes about 100 years rather than eons. But could you say the same for say coal formation or the build-up of the geological column?"

I still felt on solid ground, "Of course not, as everyone knows those processes took millions of years."

"Ah, I see … then my eyes must have been playing tricks on me when I visited your neighboring state of Washington."

I tensed a bit sensing I had tripped into some kind of trap, another one of the professor's clever illusions. "So I must be the only fool in the whole world who doesn't think it takes millions of years to pressure cook coal or build up many layers of stratified earth. Do you know why that is? I'll tell you. Because I've seen otherwise with my own two eyes. The problem with evolution and such fantastic lengths of time is that it's impossible for anyone to observe them firsthand. You're studying to be a scientist so I'm sure you know the definition of science. You and I as scientists are both on a quest for knowledge and we each entertain certain hypotheses. But the only way a scientist can prove or disprove one of his theories is to witness repeated observations and conduct controlled experiments. It's the most objective discipline in the world because everyone who claims to be a scientist agrees with strict, universal rules and procedures and checks their biases at the door. Outcomes are what they are and facts are facts. It's the beauty of science."

We were in complete agreement until he pressed further, "If I argue on behalf of a young earth, a literal six-day creation, on the basis of my faith in the God of the Bible, then I'm exhibiting bias rather than practicing science, correct?" I nodded at the obvious. "You're right; I am biased in that regard. I cannot look at the facts and evidence objectively because it would go against my conscience and faith to accept evolution or anything else so diametrically opposed to what I see as God's absolute truth: the Holy Bible." I stared blankly as he made his case for me. "Now, when you express your belief in evolution, you're doing so on the basis of objective, scientific fact; right?"

This was easy, "Yes, that's right."

Dr. Mosely smiled in a friendly way that worried me, "All right then, tell me when and how you've observed evolution."

It took me a while to respond, "Everyone agrees with evolution. It's an accepted fact."

He smiled some more, "Seth, that's not what I asked you. Please tell me how and when you've observed evolution at work. Just one good example will do. Let me get another round of beers while you give it some thought."

This helped; not only having time to think but keeping it friendly and non-confrontational over beers. "The most obvious evidence is in the fossil record. We have thousands of bones from apes and early man right up to today. They're laid out in chronological order. The evidence dates back millions of years."

He calmly pulled a fossil bearing stone out of his pocket, "What does this look like to you?"

"It looks like a dragonfly."

"How old do you think it is?" Before I could hazard a guess, "According to carbon fourteen dating, it's over a million years old. I found this one myself. I have hundreds of others like it; from ferns to frogs, apes to dinosaur bones. It's really easy to dig up fossils, they're bloody everywhere. And you don't have to go anyplace exotic. I've uncovered dozens here in and around St. Louis. Anyway, here's my point. What's the difference between this fossil and the dragonflies we see flitting about today other than the size?"

"I don't know … I guess they look pretty much the same."

Then in an encouraging, not an I-told-you-so way, "Exactly; if we're to believe the carbon fourteen, the dragonfly hasn't changed in a million years. It's stayed the same. If you look at the fossil record objectively it repeats this lesson over and over; things don't change but stay the same."

He had a point but I could see through this one. "What about mutations? That's change that we can observe all the time."

"Now you're talking like an objective scientist, Seth. But the question is what causes mutation? It's typically defective DNA or DNA that has been damaged by some harmful, outside effect like radiation. That's not evolution but degradation. How can lower life forms evolve into higher forms through degradation or the removal of genes?"

I countered, "But what about all the changes in species that are so evident everywhere around us … look at all the countless breeds of dogs … lizards and fish that have developed camouflage to avoid predators … reptiles that developed into birds?"

Mosely didn't attack but rather just questioned, "What do all those breeds of dogs have in common? Yes, they are all still dogs. Not a one of them have turned into cats. As for protective coloration, you are absolutely correct in your observation. But is that evolution or another, much speedier process called natural selection, the survival of the fittest? Can you imagine a chameleon running away from a hungry bird yelling, 'Please wait for a few million years while I evolve my cloaking genes'? You know the answer. If the gene pool of moths living in the forest consists of white and brown ones, which will survive? The white ones will be spotted by birds easily and devoured while the brown ones blend into the tree bark and are spared. But is that evolution? They are still moths and the so called change in species is brown ones thriving while white ones become extinct."

From there, things took a sharp turn and got very deep. I had the feeling that somehow, Doctor Mosely was following a script as if he had known how the conversation would unfold. "All this talk of species brings me back to my original point. The theory of evolution is no more scientific than creation; it's a matter of faith, a religion of another sort." I blanched at the mention of religion, a taboo subject in polite conversation. "Please, hear me out Seth. All I'm saying is that, if you look at the history, the motives behind evolution are clear. Did you know that the original definition of the terms species and genus in the Latin were not meant to be part of a classification system like we have today? The father of modern taxonomy, Carl Linnaeus, back in the 1700s used species in a much broader sense than today in something akin to the biblical word kind. Yes, the great Swedish scientist was a Christian who found no contradiction in being a man of faith and a scientist. To him, a dog was a *kind* and all the breeds were just evidence of variation within a species, not new and separate species. Although it's a little more complicated, a species or kind was basically defined by its ability to reproduce within the classification or grouping. So to Linnaeus it would not seem odd to breed horses and zebras to produce zorses. The same would be true for the zonkey, that is, a donkey mating with a zebra or the more common mules. They were considered all the same kind; just different varieties of horses. This is also why highly educated scientists like Linnaeus, Farady, Newton, Pasteur and Mendel didn't take issue with Noah fitting all those *species* into the ark. He took two of each *kind*, a much smaller number of maybe 1,600."

My aversion to religious talk waned as Professor Mosely piqued my interest in history, "So then, when did the definition of species change?"

His exuberance showed by the twinkle in his eyes, "Excellent question my boy! And not only when but, more importantly why? It started before Charles Darwin published On the Origin of Species. The modern notion of evolution had its roots at least as far back as ancient Greece but more formally in the French Revolution through philosophers like Descartes in the seventeenth century and Rousseau in the eighteenth. They promoted a belief system that removed God from French thought. With such motivation, the French Legislative Assembly burned the Bible and renounced belief in God in 1793. That's quite a difference from the American Revolution, isn't it? England's Protestant beliefs were more steadfast than France's with their Roman Catholic roots but cracks eventually formed nonetheless. It started in the late 1700s when a small group of fourteen men formed a mysterious group called the Lunar Society of Birmingham which met each full moon." My mind snapped back momentarily to my bizarre big, bad wolf dream but I quickly shook it off. "Like their French predecessors, this influential group was driven to find ways to reduce the influence of the church in England. The founder of this group was Erasmus Darwin, the grandfather of Charles. His writings, which later became a guiding force in Charles' work, included the term evolution."

My rapt attention was shattered by the image of fabulous Faith who entered the place with Doctor Greene. As they passed by toward a table behind me, Greene offered an obligatory nod of acknowledgment to Mosely but appeared ready to keep silent until Faith offered a warm greeting to Dr. Mosely. I tried my best not to appear rattled by this brush with the youthful Greek goddess. Thankfully, once they sat down my back was to the couple or I wouldn't have been able to hear a word from the doctor. Mosely continued quickly so as to not lose momentum, "The two fellows who really pushed the fledgling idea forward were James Hutton and later Charles Lyell who postulated the theory of uniformitarianism which stated the present is the key to the past. More fully formulated, this led to the belief that the earth was molded by a long, slow process and ruled out cataclysmic events like the biblical flood or a six-day creation by God, the ultimate intelligent designer."

"This is why it's so important to study history and understand motivations. Darwin was human like you and me and not some saintly, altruistic scientist in an objective search for the truth. Darwin's father, unlike his grandfather, was a medical doctor who held to some Christian beliefs. Before taking that fateful trip on the HMS Beagle, Charles studied medicine in an attempt to follow in his father's footsteps and then quit in favor of pursuing a life in the ministry. Something happened to derail his theological pursuits and change his mind-set completely. Before disembarking on the HMS Beagle, Darwin once commented that he in no way doubted a single word of the Bible. How things changed on that trip! He later was quoted as saying about his influential predecessor, 'Lyell is most firmly convinced that he has shaken the faith in the deluge (flood) far more efficiently by never having said a word against the Bible ... he insists strongly that direct attacks against Christianity produce little permanent effect; real *good* seems only to follow slow and silent side attacks.' The great evolutionist was bent on replacing one system of religious beliefs with another."

Mosely tried to conclude and move on, "The theory of evolution did not originate with Darwin but he helped to wrap it up in a nice neat package and popularized it with his books. He lamented in his later years that the fossil record did not yield the boon of evidence he expected. If anything, he noted that it tended to poke a lot of holes in his theory. But it lived on and thrived to the point of ascendency and dominance today not because of the science but the motivation behind it. Men like Huxley and Marx picked up on Darwin's views and embraced the philosophy which gave rise to political systems in the twentieth century ... with the influence of a divine creator abolished it made way for the primacy of the state for the socialists and the communists had the party to make everyone equal since God had not created them so. That is why the mention of teaching creation in our classrooms is met with such fierce opposition. It's not science versus faith but two diametrically opposed faiths, systems of belief locked in a death struggle."

I had never heard anything like this before and didn't know whether to be curious, skeptical or turn and run away as fast as possible. Mosely didn't breathe fire or try to shove his odd claims down my throat. He questioned, proposed and gently prodded in a disarming fashion that didn't seem threatening at all. But still, it was just so foreign to me ... completely different from everything I'd been taught. Before I could drift away, Mosely, with his elephant's memory, back tracked, "Before I forget, let's wander back to that big mountain in Washington. We were talking about coal formation and the geological column. I've observed firsthand in various places around the world that these processes seem to occur much more rapidly than we've been led to believe. Rather than boring you with stories of far off places that mean nothing to you, I thought it would be best to compare these findings to what we can both witness right there near your home town. Before we do this, we need to talk a little bit about the dating methods used to determine the fantastic lengths of time that have come to be accepted for the age of our earth."

This seemed logical and appealed to the scientist in me … you need to calibrate the gauge before you start taking measurements. "There are several methods used by scientists to determine the age of our world and the things in it. Probably the most well-known is carbon fourteen dating. The first thing to keep in mind is that it only works for organic matter like plants and animals that contain carbon so it has its limitations. Next we need to understand how we get C-14. In brief, C-14 is formed in the upper atmosphere when cosmic rays bombard N-14. The atmosphere also contains a lot of C-12 that is contained in the carbon dioxide which cycles through plants and animals through photosynthesis and breathing. C-14 enters our bodies in much the same way but is different in that it is radioactive and decays back into N-14 at a constant rate or half-life. It's like uranium decaying into lead. As scientists, we can measure the ratio of C-14 to C-12 in the atmosphere and compare it to what we find in dead plants and animals. Measuring what's left after the decaying process can tell us how much time has passed since the organism stopped processing C-14."

It seemed logical and I was able to follow but didn't get the point, "So what's the problem?"

Mosely was patient and nonjudgmental, "As scientists we need to check and verify our assumptions. It's fair to assume that the ratio of carbon in our bodies is the same as the atmosphere since we take it in from there when we breathe. But it gets a little sticky because we must also assume to know what the carbon ratio was thousands of years ago ... many more for the evolutionist. Evolutionists and creationists alike agree that this ratio has not remained constant as can be seen by studying the rings in trees and other evidence. Also, the amount of C-14 in the atmosphere changes as it decays into N-14. Like filling a leaky bucket with water, you can't achieve equilibrium until the bucket is filled and the inflow matches the outflow. Since the creation of C-14 in the atmosphere is not constant even over the small amount of time we have been able to observe it, there are potentially significant variations in the constants used to employ C-14 dating that can throw things off exponentially. Scientists question if and when we've achieved carbon equilibrium in our *bucket*."

Mosely was methodical in his explanation ... like a scientist, "A more common dating method that can be employed with inanimate objects like fossilized remains for a much greater length of time than C-14 dating is gauging age through the use of sedimentary rocks. This is the approach commonly used to establish the fantastic lengths of time assigned to our so called ancestors and extinct species of every kind. It is much simpler than C-14 dating in a way. If you find the fossil remains of an animal encased within a sedimentary rock, all you have to do is establish its position within the geological column of time and voila! For example, if you find a primitive reptile encased in Permian sediment, it's 200 million years old. Likewise, a trilobite in the Cambrian layer must be 450 million years old. It's all so simple, right?"

Oh, oh ... I could see it coming so I held my tongue. "Isn't this circular logic of the worst kind? First we come up with a theory of evolution that claims simple forms have turned into more complex beings in a steady progression over the eons. From there, it stands to reason that the simpler, earlier life forms would have died out before the more complex ones with the former's remains deposited into the sediment at the bottom of the geological column and the latter's coming much later after ages of gradual build-up of new sediment. We assign ages to the layers of sediment with the *science* of pulling them out of thin air because we've been told by a bunch of philosophers that, in the absence of a divine creator ... a wholly unacceptable and therefore impossible myth ... the world we see today had to come about through random chance taking place over millions of years. Then with our time scale neatly established in perfect vertical fashion, when we find a fossil we date it referring back to the same monolithic column. It's very dangerous to use unproven theories to establish historical references."

Mosely was not deterred by the perplexed look on my face, "There are a few problems with this column as you might expect from its origins. First of all, we're able to discern many things today that were hidden from science back then. The supposedly simple trilobite is not so simple after all. Studying the structure of their eyes under an electron microscope is a marvel to behold revealing amazing complexities that baffle our best engineers and designers. Also, we've found that the column is not as set in stone as we've been led to believe. Pardon the pun, please. We're constantly finding complex creatures at the bottom, simple ones at the top and every mixture in between. I even have pictures I've taken personally from my own treks where human and dinosaur tracks are nearly side-by-side in the exact same layer of sediment. I've also seen dinosaur finds, supposedly eighty million years old, that are amazingly well preserved with bones containing flexible blood vessels, connective tissue, blood, intact proteins and red blood cells. You don't hear much about it because evolutionists know these things can't survive for millions of years. It presents quite a dilemma. Nevertheless, I've seen it with my own two eyes. It's true … what do they say here, 'I'm from Missouri; so you've got to show me'? Like doubting Thomas said, 'to see is to believe' no matter where you're from, right Seth?"

You can't wipe out twenty some years of learning in one conversation so I was still skeptical, "I guess so but there's probably a good explanation."

"You're right again, mate. How do we get these fossils that are so well preserved in sedimentary rock? Have you ever seen a dead animal lying by the side of the road? What does it look and smell like after just a few days?"

I reluctantly went along, "It starts decaying and smells to high heaven."

"Exactly my boy; we know from common sense that animals can't be fossilized in sediment that is laid down slowly over thousands and millions of years. They must be buried swiftly, completely encased in mud before the oxygen and bacteria can take their toll. Speaking of good explanations, doesn't it make sense that a worldwide flood like Noah's would result in all of these fossils being formed everywhere? And wouldn't it help solve the mystery of sharks' teeth being littered all over Nebraska and fish fossils that are deposited on the highest mountain tops?"

The old man was on a roll, "Let's go back a moment to your lizards turning into birds. The fossil record contains evidence of what was once thought to be a transitional form called the archaeopteryx. It possessed many bird-like characteristics such as fully formed feathers; strong, light, hollow bones and perching feet but also a few reptilian features like teeth and claws on its wings. Evolutionists, driven by their belief system rather than pure science, immediately assumed it was a half bird, half reptile that showed evolution in progress. They ignored the obvious such as modern birds like the ostrich that also have claws on their wings. Eventually they were done in by their own geological column when another fully formed, fossilized bird called the protoavis was unearthed. It was discovered in strata that made it 75 million years older. Today, the archaeopteryx is considered just another rare, extinct bird rather than a transitional form since *fully evolved* birds were present in the fossil record long before the archaeopteryx appeared on the scene."

Mosely tried to bolster his point, "When the pure science raises questions about the validity of the theory, why won't the evolutionists consider other alternatives, especially if the alternatives fit better with the evidence at hand? It's because both are trying to prove something scientifically impossible. Our origins cannot be observed or subjected to controlled experiments with repeatable results. Both creationists and evolutionists are clinging to incompatible belief systems, competing philosophies. As the dearth of transitional forms and the fossil record in general undermined the theory, the evolutionists could not abandon the underpinning of their entire belief system. Instead they had to come up with new explanations to fit within the model that is taken as a given. For example, Stephen Gould dreamt up something called punctuated equilibrium to explain the discrepancy between theory and anomalous observations. He didn't give up on the timetable with its millions and billions of years but suggested species go for long periods of time without changing, as we see today, but go through step functions where the changes in forms occur rapidly within a short time span due to the introduction of powerful, outside influences like radiation, meteor showers, visiting aliens, etc. That would help explain why we don't see a progression of transitional forms in the fossil record but still doesn't show how a monkey can suddenly turn into a man or any lower life form would evolve upward rather than devolving or dying out due to mutations or other degradations of the genetic code. It's like claiming that an orderly progression is evolving from the chaos and disorder we can observe in the universe around us. Evolutionists choose to see that the clock is advancing forward rather than winding down."

Dr. Mosely was distracted from his seemingly singular purpose by something at the nearby table of our cohorts, Zeb and Faith. Apparently he had been keeping an eye on them while expounding on our origins and paused to eaves drop at that critical moment. I had been so engrossed in his elaborate explanations that I missed everything else prior to his momentary silence where I caught this snippet from Faith, "I don't think it would be a good idea, Dr. Greene. I hope you understand. It's great the way you've made me feel so welcome here and I really appreciate everything you've done to help me with my studies. Since I'm only here one afternoon out of the week, I really haven't gotten to know anyone at Wash U so it's good to have a friend like you." Shortly thereafter they left and Faith offered a cheerful farewell to Dr. Mosely but it seemed to pain Dr. Greene to be bothered with bidding him adieu. He barely acknowledged me but would be much more civil when I saw him away from Dr. Mosely during our next meeting with Sloan and company. I didn't catch the full drift of Zeb and Faith's conversation but Dr. Mosely must have been able to pick up much more from the gestures, expressions and body language that preceded it. He didn't reveal it to me then, preferring to get back on topic.

"I apologize for continuing to wander but there was a reason for bringing up Mt. St. Helens. Since a picture is worth a thousand words, your hometown volcano can shed more light than I could ever hope to bring to bear with all of my travels, explorations, stories, pictures and fossils. You've seen what happened at Spirit Lake, haven't you?"

This really got my attention, "Once, it was so cool. My dad arranged for me to ride along when he and some fellows from work hitched a ride on the company helicopter to visit one of their recycled paper mills on the other side of the state past the mountain. Along the way, we could see the huge cavity in one side of Mt. St. Helens where the blast had occurred. The evidence of the power was amazing. We flew along the valley toward the missing side of the mountain and there were still miles and miles of devastation where the pines on one side of the slope looked like massive, burnt out match sticks. On the other side there was new growth where they had hired college kids to replenish the forests by planting thousands of saplings but after all those years they still looked stunted compared to the old growth forests nearby. I imagined that a nuclear bomb would not have had such far reaching effects."

Mosely was sincerely enjoying the experience I was sharing and let me go on, "Closer in to the mountain, the terrain in the valley looked like the surface of the moon. The dirt, ash and lava had paved over everything and gave it a surreal look that seemed more bizarre as a huge herd of elk traversed the barren scape. Then we did something that I imagine only a few people have experienced. The pilot took us right over the top and descended down into the crater just above the dome. It was thrilling and scary at the same time because we could see the vapors that were still escaping and wafting skyward. Part of me wanted to stay there for as long as possible, taking in the magnificent view, but a little voice kept saying we better get out of here before she decides to blow again and make toast out of us. As we departed, we got a grand aerial view of Spirit Lake and the pilot told us all about how it had been changed so dramatically. I remember him talking about how it was completely littered with trees that had been jettisoned from the mountain like a hail of arrows from a legion of English long bowmen."

My last comment struck a chord with Mosely, "What a perfect segue, Seth. It's those very trees I wanted to mention. I've seen the after effects before but Mt. St. Helens provided a glimpse into the process while still in progress. When the mountain blew its top, the branches on those trees were incinerated and the trunks were launched into the sky with hundreds landing in Spirit Lake. They floated row-upon-row and side-by-side until the water seeped in and they sank to the bottom. Since trees are bigger and heavier at the base, when they sank they tipped to the vertical position and dropped into the sediment as if planted upright. This showed how the petrified forests can be formed and helped to explain how a single, upright tree could appear to be buried in layers of sediment that supposedly represented millions of years of evolution. Mt. St. Helens was proof positive that trees can be stripped bare and left standing vertically and rapidly become mineralized almost like living fossils. It also showed how deep, layered sediments can be deposited in one fell swoop in the blink of an eye rather than thousands or millions of years. I'm guessing that none of your Portland teachers ever presented this evidence to you in such a context." He was right and I had to agree.

I was exhilarated but fatigued as was Dr. Mosely. He heaved a sigh of relief and I thought we were ready to leave when he said, "It's getting late and we should be getting on our way. However, perhaps we should tip one more brew mate."

I wasn't about to turn down another beer even though I was feeling a bit of a buzz already, "Hey, whatever you say Doc."

He returned my silly grin in kind, "Not to change the subject but there's something I've been meaning to ask you."

He didn't need my permission but nevertheless I offered, "Fire away Doc."

"Okay, well, it's about that lovely lass; Faith."

My buzz evaporated and my defenses immediately went up, "What are you talking about, who's Faith?"

He laughed and smiled a Cheshire grin as if he were toying with a mouse, "Don't be silly, Seth. You know exactly whom I'm talking about. Do you think I don't know why you were so discombobulated in class today?"

This guy was amazing. He didn't miss a trick. All that show of concern over my troubling behavior was completely contrived. And he had spent over an hour offering a discourse on creation and evolution apparently just to throw me off course and lower my guard. I marveled at how Professor Mosely always seemed to be several steps ahead of me as if I was trying to compete with Bobby Fischer in a chess match. What could I do? He had me dead to rights. I didn't try to fight it. I laid my elbows on the table, clasped my fingers together and, with slumped shoulders, bowed my head in resignation. Not one to rub it in, he tried to let me off the hook, "Seth, there's no shame in it. If I were thirty years younger, I'd be panting after her like a lap dog. She's quite a looker ... a stunning bird she is. I'm just surprised you hadn't noticed her before."

I completely caved in at that point after taking a long draw from the fresh beer that had thankfully just arrived, "Actually, I noticed her before, in Dr. Greene's class weeks prior but, to be honest, I was kind of gun shy about approaching her."

He smiled and offered a toast, "Why, a strapping, good looking, young fellow like you? I'd say that's balderdash but I know what it's like. Someone that beautiful can be quite intimidating. But you really shouldn't be worried. She's not the snooty type with a big ego."

I shook my head as that one sank in, "What do you mean? You act like you know her."

"That's because I do."

I blinked and shook my head again as if trying to shoo some gnats, "How did you get to know her so well from one class in a large lecture hall setting?"

"Oh, I have my ways," he teased.

"C'mon Doc, be serious."

"Okay, I didn't get to know her through class. I met her over a year ago outside of class. Actually, I helped make the arrangements for her to be able to take a couple of classes here at Wash U. Right now, I'm helping her to obtain the proper clearance to sign up for two more classes this summer including mine."

Now he really had my full attention, "Tell me more Doc. Where is she from and how did you meet her?"

"She's attending Lindenwood University in St. Charles. I met her at a church near there where I was invited to lecture on creation."

That one floored me. The last thing I expected was for such a hot babe to be some kind of junior church lady. My bubble wasn't burst but it was deflated. "What was she doing at a creation lecture?"

He looked at me with raised eyebrows in mock indignation, "I'm surprised at you, Seth. So you think that no one in their right mind would waste time in one of my lectures, eh?"

"C'mon Doc, you know I didn't mean it that way. She just doesn't strike me as the church going type."

I was digging the hole deeper because he feigned exasperation and chided me, "So only ugly people can go to church? I didn't take you for a heathen. What have you got against the church?"

"Hey, you're twisting my words. I don't have anything against church. I go to church … as least I do when I'm back home."

Mosely was champing at the bit to ask me more about my church but didn't want to get off course, "Believe it or not, that pretty little thing is a devout Christian and is very involved in her church." The professor paused and waited for my reaction but I did my best to conceal my disappointment. I wanted to know more about Faith. He rewarded my patience, "I met Faith Harper and her parents along with a bunch of other people during some food and fellowship after the presentation. During the chit chat she told me about her studies at Lindenwood and expressed a desire to take a course in environmental science to satisfy her science requirement but said they didn't offer it at Lindenwood. I offered to help look into the possibility of her earning transferrable credit at Wash U. Of course, I suggested she might want to try one of my courses too while at our campus one day a week. I didn't say anything at the time but wanted her to get both sides of the story instead of solely the indoctrination into secular humanism. It worked out perfectly that my archaeology class followed Greene's environmental science course on the same day of the week. She seemed so nice, I decided to pull a few strings and help her out."

My curiosity was running high, "So, that doesn't explain how you got to know her personally."

"Be patient my boy. There's more to the story. I had been looking for a good, temporary church home. It's not easy to do these days especially when you're far away from home like me. I really took a shining to Faith's church. The people are very friendly and everyone seems to take the Bible seriously. The pastor is rock solid with his doctrine rooted completely in the word. So I started attending there off and on and it grew on me."

Now it was my turn to have some fun so I rolled my eyes and said, "Oh great, I knew she was too good to be true!"

"Be thankful she's much more than just a pretty face."

Then my tragic revelation came rushing back to me and I lamented, "Who am I kidding? It doesn't make any difference anyway."

Now Mosely was puzzled, "What do you mean by that, Seth?"

"I'm man enough to admit I don't have a chance with Dr. Greene in the picture."

The professor stroked his scrubby beard and looked heavenward, "Ah, I see … it's a case of the other man … opportunity lost … too little, too late." I nodded not recognizing the facetious nature of his volley. "Cheer up mate, Greene hasn't staked his claim to your beauty."

I perked up a bit, "So, what is the story with those two?"

"It's not really a story … it's more like a few sentences or a paragraph at most. You can't blame the young associate professor for being smitten by her. As I'm sure you heard, he's been trying to make her feel welcome and helping her to adjust to the odd situation of being a bit of an interloper on our prestigious campus. I must give him credit for helping her to overcome the feeling of inadequacy she must have treading our *hallowed grounds* after having hailed from such humble academic surroundings as Lindenwood. But don't get me wrong, he had ulterior motives too. I'm sure he hoped his acts of charity would pave the way for more amorous pursuits. Call me old fashioned but I found the age difference and violation of the teacher/pupil pact to be a bit disgusting. I didn't fret though because I knew it didn't have a chance from the start."

My interest soared at his last remark, "How can you say that? It looks like he's doing just fine if you ask me."

He guffawed good-naturedly, "Are you blind man or just dense? Didn't you see her give him the brush off a few minutes ago?" He gathered from my blank stare that I missed the obvious, "I can excuse your cluelessness since you had your back to them and didn't see the little drama that played out in front of me. He was trying his level best to take things to the next level but she would have none of it. Trust me; it was the kiss of death when she said she appreciated being just friends. As I said, it was over before it started. Greene is a nice fellow and all and quite good looking but he is her polar opposite. She's a committed Christian and he's, well, just as committed to secular humanism to put it politely. They say that opposites attract but oil and water doesn't mix."

I don't know if I was more exhilarated or depressed. It felt like having a new lease on life to know that Faith was unattached. Her Christianity was another matter. Mosely quizzed me, "Why so glum, Seth?"

"I don't mean this to sound the wrong way but I wonder if it's dead in the water for me too."

"Seth, I thought you said you attended church regularly at home. Aren't you a Christian too?"

"Yes Doc, that's true but … I don't know … I'm just not a fire and brimstone kind of guy."

"Oh, so that's it. Faith will only go for a guy who parades around wearing his faith on his sleeve?"

"I don't know. I just wonder if we're not oil and water too."

"There's only one way to know and it's not by sitting here jawing with me. I'll tell you what. Let's call it a day and you think about it. If you decide you'd like to check it out for yourself, you let me know and I'd be happy to introduce you to Faith."

"That's a deal, Doc, thanks." I was pleased with the way we left things and excited by the prospect of getting to know Faith better but I had a creeping feeling that the Doc was way ahead of me again. Could it be that he had had designs on playing Cupid all along?

If I had any doubts about his intentions, he subtly but quickly laid them to rest. "Seth, I know this is of no interest to you since I'm sure you'll be very busy this summer with your park internship and the investigation."

He paused to dangle the lure in front of me and, like a fool, I took the bait hook, line and sinker, "Not interested in what?"

He knew he could reel me in but decided to toy with me first, "Oh, it's nothing. Finals will soon be over and I'm sure you need a break from school and have all kinds of adventures to pursue this summer."

I was getting peeved, "C'mon … not interested in what?"

"Well Greene and I are both offering extensions to our spring classes in environmental science and archaeology. It's a chance to dig deeper into these subjects and earn additional credit hours along the way."

My impatience turned to agitation, "I know that! You and Dr. Greene have been promoting your summer classes for the last three weeks ad nauseam."

Mosely knew it was time to let me off the hook, "Oh, I just thought you'd like to know that Faith has signed up for both courses this summer." The son of a gun had me again. I left immediately for the registrar's office. It didn't matter to me that this would totally change my summer plans.

Before I could get out of ear shot, the jolly old sage chuckled and cautioned, "Seth, make your hay while the sun is shining. Faith's time at Wash U will be done when the summer comes to an end."

CHAPTER 5

STRAWBERRY MOON

T HAT WEEKEND, WE WERE CALLED together by Sloan to reconnoiter and adjust our strategy going forward. April's seed moon had left us grasping at straws. The tension leading up to the full moon had led to a fit of near hysteria followed by relief and anxiety after it passed without incident. Everyone in the area was happy that the beast had not struck again but frustrated by the lack of predictability and our inability to uncover any sign of the wolf's whereabouts. As for our team, the strain was beginning to show with Sloan as the fount of all stress. Although we were volunteers, he treated us as if we were as fully obligated as him to accomplish the task at hand. He was under tremendous pressure from higher ups and the media. Sloan only made it worse by going all in with this poker hand by expending such a high level of unbudgeted funds on manpower and resources including Professor Greene, Wes and I. Wes and I were not paid extra for our time but the county police still had to reimburse the parks department. It was just slopping money from one county bucket to another but it didn't seem that way to Sloan since he was accountable only for his budget and judged accordingly.

His sniping and criticism started to wear thin. Under normal circumstances, we would have all given into the urge to tell him to take the job and shove it. Things weren't going very well and we didn't expect accolades but we felt he should have been more appreciative of our time. After all, we were volunteers not hirelings. Sloan was toughest on Tracker Joe because the trail had gone completely cold. A humongous, bloodthirsty gray wolf does not disappear into thin air. Joe was on the hook more than the rest of us since he was getting paid along with his staff of trackers and compensated for the use of his dogs. Consequently, he bit his tongue as Sloan unloaded on him in front of the rest of us. I could see the hairs on Wes' neck standing up as Sloan piled it on Joe until he couldn't stand it anymore, "Hold on Detective, that's enough. We're all put out by the lack of progress but it's not Joe's fault. If you want, you can blame me too because I've been out there tracking with him on several occasions to no avail. Do you realize how much ground there is to cover in St. Louis County? If we had one hundred times the people it would not be enough to guarantee we could find that wolf."

Sloan stared back at Wes matter-of-factly, not defiantly, as if to say okay I deserved that without conceding one inch of ground. When he got no verbal response from Sloan, Wes added, "I don't know about the rest of you but I've had about enough of this. If it weren't for the fact that four people have died I would probably have been out of here a long time ago. I'm still here though because people remain in danger and we might be able to help. But we've got to start pulling together if we're going to make this work."

Sloan didn't change his expression much, just enough to dial back on the tension a bit, "Okay, good enough. Let's circle back and see what we've got. Where do we go from here?"

Zeb Greene spoke up to break the deadlock between Wes and Sloan, "Do you gentlemen remember not too long ago when all those exotic animals were turned loose just before the owner committed suicide?" Everyone nodded having recalled the national media attention it drew. "There's something we can take away and apply to our situation, I think. Among all those dangerous, deadly beasts, there was one, solitary, very large, alpha male gray wolf in the bunch. With lions, bears, monkeys, tigers and other such animals on the loose, do you remember the one that was hardest to apprehend?"

No one else ventured a guess so I volunteered, "Let me take a shot in the dark and say the monkeys since they have the highest level of intelligence and can travel through the trees."

Zeb replied, "That's a good guess and your logic is sound, Seth. However, the monkeys were only second best in eluding the trackers after they caught the lions, tigers and bears." I badly wanted to say lions, tigers and bears, oh my but thought better of it. "The last animal caught was the gray wolf and it took much longer than all the others."

Sloan grew impatient thinking Greene was only making excuses for their failure, "So what's your point?"

"My point is simply this. They had a difficult time tracking down that wolf too … but they eventually got him. Maybe we can take a lesson. Do you know how they finally caught and killed him? They couldn't find the wolf so they lured him to them ... with live bait."

This made sense to Sloan and he perked up, "Joe, Wes, what do you think of this idea?"

Joe responded first, "The darn thing has gotta eat. It's worth a try if we can figure out what it wants for dinner."

Wes added, "I think we can come up with the right kind of *snacks* to appeal to his palate. The bigger issue will be where. We still have a lot of ground to cover. Those folks up in Zanesville had a big advantage because they knew exactly where to start and began tracking almost immediately. It narrowed the hunt considerably. Our trail has grown cold and we don't really have a clue about where to start."

Sloan tried to stay upbeat since we needed some kind of momentum working in our favor, "Yeah, it might be a long shot but it's better than no shot at all. Let's keep up with tracking and all our other efforts but add this to the mix. It can't hurt and it might help."

I felt like I had to chime in to justify my existence, "We better be careful in setting our traps far away from populated areas. The last thing we need is to draw the wolf in closer to unsuspecting people." Sloan rolled his eyes as though I had wasted his time stating the obvious but I still thought it was a worthwhile caution.

We implemented Greene's idea quickly after plotting our strategy on the map. Our first impulse was to place our traps near the sites of the previous attacks but resisted that urge since there was no real pattern to follow and Joe's trackers had hit those areas the hardest. With the trail more than cold, basically non-existent, we used simple logic. We took the number of traps we could effectively administer and set them out around the county at roughly equal distances that allowed us to loosely cover the

entire area. Wherever possible, we located them near a St. Louis
County Park so Wes and I could manage them with the help
of the other rangers on duty. Even though they didn't give me
credit, they apparently heeded my warning and placed the bait
far enough away so as to not endanger park guests. We used a
variety of live animals such as wild deer and smaller mammals
tied to stakes, reminiscent of that poor goat in Jurassic Park. At
least our victims had a better chance since the perimeter was
surrounded by carefully hidden steel traps that would snap shut
around the leg of any unsuspecting predator. These things were
way off the beaten path but we still marked them all clearly with
warning signs just in case some idiot wandered way out in the
middle of nowhere.

We struck pay dirt faster than anyone anticipated, two weeks
later or half way toward May's strawberry moon. Our strategy
worked because our wolf took the bait at a brand new location,
far from any of the earlier attacks, way down in South St. Louis
County near George Winter Park. It's similar to Creve Coeur Park
in that it has a large lake on the property. I was with Wes when
he was contacted by the ranger on duty at George Winter. To the
untrained eye, you'd never know Wes was excited but I knew him
well enough to gauge from his muted but unusual reaction that
he was super excited. "Seth, get the truck and pull around front.
We're headed to Winter Park." I didn't bother to ask why. I could
tell something big was up and didn't want to interrupt Wes' phone
conversation.

Wes jumped in and motioned for me to go while the phone
was still glued to his ear. I learned what was going on by listening
to half a conversation between Wes and Sloan, "Detective, I just
got a call from our man down at George Winter Park. It looks like
there's been some activity at trap five near there." Wes paused as

Sloan spoke then continued, "At this point, I don't really know but Seth and I are already on our way. Yes, I'll contact Joe and you can touch base with Zeb Greene and we'll meet you there in thirty minutes." My adrenalin pumped at the prospect of finally getting the killer wolf and didn't notice how my foot was getting heavy on the gas pedal. "You better keep it under seventy Seth. I don't think Sloan likes you well enough to fix any tickets for you."

Once inside the Park's boundaries, we took the one lane, gravel road that gave us access through the deep woods surrounding trap five then left the truck on foot to cover the last half mile. Ranger Carson met us just this side of the warning signs. He didn't look nearly as excited as we felt, "I don't understand it. How could a wolf big enough to kill and haul off a deer work its way through this virtual mine field without tripping one of the traps?" By the time Sloan, Tracker Joe and Greene arrived, we were already down in the dumps.

Sloan noticed something was wrong right away, "What's the matter Wes?"

"The damn thing got away scot free with a nice meal courtesy of St. Louis County."

Sloan was still keyed up, "Hey let's keep our chin up. We may not have the wolf but now there's a fresh trail we can follow. Joe, give it a look see and let's get after him." Joe began to do his thing but Wes already knew the outcome from his own inspection of the area with Carson. It looked like the same wolf judging from the size of the tracks near where he slayed the deer and there were prints all over inside the perimeter. But outside there was nothing; clean as a whistle as if he had vanished into thin air again.

Joe summed up our failure in his homespun style, "That's one smart wolf, fellas. Look at the way these traps are laid out. He must have tip toed through here on his hind legs, back and forth like a damn water bug. Maybe the sum bitch knows how to read these signs."

We didn't give up immediately. We couldn't find any visible trail to follow so Joe called in the dogs. At first, our spirits leaped as they picked up a scent outside the perimeter leading back in the direction toward the gravel road but dead ended leaving the frustrated hounds turning circles and moaning in high pitched whines. Wes stood there with hands on hips, "Joe, have you ever seen anything like this?"

"Not for the life of me, Wes."

"How about you Zeb … have you encountered a wolf like this before?"

The normally self-assured Greene was perplexed, "This is bizarre. It doesn't make any sense."

Once again I had to throw my two cents worth in to point out the obvious thing that everyone seemed to have missed, "What about the deer?" Everyone stared at me dumbly and Sloan looked perturbed. "I mean, where's the trail from the body being dragged away? Is the wolf big enough to pick a full grown deer up off the ground and carry it? And, even if he is, where's the blood from the deer? Did the wolf devour it whole before slinking away into nothingness?" I could tell from their expressions that my questions hit home. Hey, maybe I was starting to pull my own weight.

Sloan mulled the latest setback as his grumpiness returned, "Okay then, do any of you *experts* have any suggestions?"

Wes bit his tongue but Joe just rolled with this latest punch to the gut and kept going, "I guess the first thing I should do is call my boys and have them shift their focus down south here. This son of a gun has a heck of a range but there's no use tromping around North St. Louis County and Wildwood right now."

Sloan nodded and looked down at his feet as if to gather his emotions before going down the wrong path again, "I agree. Good idea Joe."

Dr. Greene, ever the calm, detached, practical one, offered, "This thing still has me baffled. I think we need special help … that is, if you think you can afford it, Detective."

Sloan was desperate so this piqued his interest, "Money is no object if it will help us capture the damn wolf. I'm already so far in the hole; I might as well dig myself in a little deeper. What do you have in mind?"

Green laid out a new strategy, "I realize that Wes, Joe and I know our way around the woods and have had personal experience in dealing with wolves. But our experience is limited and in most respects conventional. We need someone who can get inside this animal's brain and think like it. We need someone who eats, sleeps and drinks wolves."

Sloan had an inquisitive look, "Where might we find this man who dances with the wolves?"

Greene didn't even crack a smile as the rest of us grinned, "We're in luck. The best guy in North America happens to be right here in St. Louis. He's on sabbatical from the University of Ottawa while writing his latest book. I know him from the zoo where he is, in a manner of speaking, on loan part-time. His name is Mingan Muraco. He's Native American and is considered by many to be the foremost expert on the gray wolf."

Sloan pondered, "He sounds interesting. I'm okay with it if you think he can help us but I want to meet him personally before adding him to the team." Sloan had to maintain tight control or a least the appearance of the same. The rest of us had to break. We all had things to do. I needed to get my head back into my studies and get my butt to Wash U.

It was a little weird going to Greene's class now. I was starting to almost feel like a colleague away from school during our work together on the investigative team. That quickly evaporated in the classroom. He was very good at putting up that high wall that separates professors from students. There was no inkling of any kind of personal relationship on any level when he was teaching. It was almost a Jekyll and Hyde type of transformation even though away from the university he was never quite what you'd call the warm and fuzzy type. The only exception to the rule had been Faith Harper but now even that had changed. There seemed to be a distance between them; imposed by Greene and not Faith. Maybe Dr. Mosely was right and Faith's pledge of friendship had been the kiss of death. At least that's how it seemed to me in trying to interpret Greene's aloofness. I had bigger problems than trying to figure out Greene and his invisible walls. I was erecting some barriers of my own, trying to keep Faith Harper from invading my thoughts and breaking my concentration.

Knowing how perceptive Dr. Mosely could be, I was determined not to lose focus in his class again. As I listened to his lecture, my brain was fully engaged but my heart wasn't in it. It was kind of like being so tired that you begin to nod off. No matter how much you fight it; you keep finding yourself being jolted back from a momentary slumber only to feel your eyelids growing heavy and chin drooping over and over. Her image kept squeezing its way into my head like water bubbling through a tiny crack in a dike. Like the proverbial Dutch boy, I kept patching the holes but new leaks sprang up everywhere. Mosely must have sensed my dilemma because he decided to take matters into his own hands after class. I was closest so he tapped me on the shoulder as everyone headed for the exits and, then with me immobilized, quietly skittered up toward Faith before she could leave, "Ms. Harper, may I see you for a moment?" What was he doing? I wanted to crawl into a hole.

The professor must have known panic was setting in as he approached me with Faith in tow so he struck with lightning speed before my fight or flight reflex could kick in. "Faith Harper, I'd like you to meet someone. This is Seth Lomax." She smiled and extended her hand but I was dumbfounded. Dr. Mosely rescued me before my paralysis could become awkwardly apparent, "Have a go at it my boy. I assure you her hand is quite sanitary." I forced a laugh and thrust out my hand. It's hard to explain but there was something about her hand … it was warm, soft and gentle … that put me at ease even though high voltage currents were shooting up and down my spine.

"It's a pleasure meeting you Faith." I was so captivated by her easy, inviting smile that I forgot to let go of her hand.

Thankfully, Dr. Mosely came to the rescue again in his bold, brassy, no nonsense, Aussie fashion, "I'm sorry Seth but you'll have to give that back to Faith." I laughed but my compulsive Cupid didn't trust me to maintain the momentum, "Now I have work to do so you'll have to take this elsewhere. May I suggest to Hannigan's for a cup of coffee? Faith, you should ask Seth to tell you about a special project he's on for the county. I think you'll find it very interesting. Now you two run along. Go ahead and scoot."

Talk about your shotgun weddings! Forget tact, diplomacy or anything resembling subtlety. Dr. Mosely had used a sledge hammer rather than a gentle shove. I'm not complaining though because his over-zealous meddling paid off. He left us no chance to demur, defer, decline, postpone or gracefully back out. My head was spinning and I was completely off balance but I had to hand it to him. There I was headed to Hannigan's with a Greek goddess who had been haunting my thoughts. "I'm sorry about that Faith. I want you to know that I had nothing to do with putting Dr. Mosely up to this. He's just … well … very different and has a mind of his own." I was thrilled to find out that the goddess was just as uncomfortable as me. Her manner was shy and humble and not at all like the self-assured, super model, persona I had pictured.

"You don't have to be sorry, Seth. I know how he is. I hope it's not too awkward being put on the spot like this. If you'd rather not go to Hannigan's right now, I'll understand. It can be just our secret if you want to buck the Doctor's orders."

I almost pinched myself because this seemed too good to be true. "There's no way I'm backing out of this since I know it would get back to him somehow and I'd never hear the end of it. I guess I'll just have to suck it up and suffer through it." She laughed which put me at ease knowing that she had a sense of humor. "Seriously though, I'd love to have a cup of coffee with you. I'm honored, Faith."

She blushed a bit, "The pleasure's all mine." We were off to a great start but were in danger of hitting a wall. We settled into a booth and kept busy stirring creamer and sugar into the coffee. Before an awkward silence could descend upon us, I started asking about her studies and we shared small talk for almost an hour getting to know each other's backgrounds … home, family, friends, school, outside interests and the like.

The time passed quickly because we were enjoying each other's company so much but then awkward silence lurked again. One of the best proofs of a great relationship is the ability to weather silence without panic but we were light years away from that so I grew nervous thinking of ways to fill the time. I could have taken the easy way out by asking how she met Dr. Mosely but feared getting on the subject of church and religion. It turns out I had nothing to worry about because Faith had a good memory, "Seth, what was this about a special project that Dr. Mosely mentioned?" That led to another good hour of conversation which flowed easily because Faith was genuinely interested in hearing what I had to say and I enjoyed recounting how the mystery was unfolding … except for some of the disturbing images that I down played for her sake and mine.

Finally, Faith looked at her watch and I worried that I had bent her ear to the point of boredom. "Seth, this has been great but I really do have to go. I'm glad that stinker, Mosely, prodded you into taking me here. I don't mean to sound too pushy but I'd love to do this again sometime. In any case, I look forward to seeing you in class next week."

I was on cloud nine. The only lame thing I could utter was, "It's a date!" I could have kicked myself for sounding like such a dork but Faith just smiled her pleasant, soothing smile and I didn't give it another thought.

I had a tough time putting Faith out of my mind but did my best that Friday night in order to get ahead of my studies and free up the weekend. Saturday stood to be an exciting day with a team meeting to introduce Mingan Muraco. We started at Sloan's office in Clayton. It was earlier than I preferred but I was helped along by adrenalin and the hot rolls, steaming coffee, donuts, cream cheese and fresh fruit Sloan provided courtesy of St. Louis County. The detective, several of his officers and technicians, Tracker Joe, Wes and I were seated around the conference room table filling our faces when Greene strode into the room with Mingan. The big man filled the entire doorway. With his long, straight, raven black hair; coarse, shabby clothing and unkempt appearance, he reminded me of the big Indian who tore the sink out of the floor at the end of One Flew over the Cuckoo's Nest. He seemed to have a mystical air about him that was aided by a single feather that hung loosely from a beaded latchet entwined in a small braid on the side of his big, bronze head.

Greene did the honors, "I'd like you all to meet my friend, Mingan Muraco." We all shook hands and I was amazed at how his giant paw swallowed up my larger-than-average mitt like a child's.

He spoke slowly in a deep baritone that made him seem wise, "Please, my friends call me Michael." This Anglicized version helped him fit in but didn't do justice to the literal meaning of his real name: gray wolf silhouetted against a white moon. In any case, his imposing and intriguing presence seemed to completely change the dynamics in the room. It made me think back to Richard Dreyfuss as Matt Hooper in Jaws … it was like the cavalry had arrived just in time. With the help of Sloan's staff, we took plenty of time to carefully review the facts of the case to freshen our memories and help Michael get up to speed. He quietly took in all the information without jumping to any conclusions and we collectively held our breath waiting to hear his diagnosis of the confounding situation that confronted us. He held his tongue as we embarked on a field trip to see the actual sites at Missouri Bottom Road and Creve Coeur Lake.

Standing around the wooded site where Mike and Carol Sue met their grisly end, he uttered his first words of analysis, "From everything I've seen and heard today, I am very concerned." This was nothing new, nothing earth shattering but, coming from him, it sounded grave and foreboding. Sloan was not impressed and maintained a skeptic's visage while Greene held a smug, self-assured expression as if, through his wise foresight, we were listening to an oracle. Sloan cut Michael some slack since he was new and withheld his wisecracking thought … so tell me something I didn't know.

In trying to be gracious, he still found a way to be offensive and insensitive, "Go on, Chief."

This incensed Greene who had an ingrained sense of political correctness, "His name is Michael, Detective."

Michael quickly displayed a hearty sense of humor that cast him in a new light, "No, that's okay … I kind of like the sound of it … Chief." He reared back and cut loose with a deep, bellowing, infectious laugh that had us all in stitches. From that time forward, in our lighter moments, we all referred to him as the Chief. Well, almost everyone did except for Greene who refused to stoop to the level of such antics.

Things got quiet and serious again as Michael continued with his brief, direct assessment, "I am concerned because you're dealing with something very unusual. I've lived with and around wolves my entire life and know how they survive, their very essence and spirit. In all those years, I've only encountered something like this once before. What you have here is not a hunter or pack predator. This animal is driven by something other than normal instincts. This wolf lives to kill … it lives to kill the one natural enemy that other wolves fear and avoid … it stalks with an evil purpose … it seeks its pleasure in killing man."

We all felt chills from this description except for Sloan, "Yes, we have a killer, no doubt. So how do we track it down and kill it before it kills again?"

Michael was not finished, "The wolf is a most cunning creature and highly intelligent. This is exhibited in the way the pack skillfully collaborates in seeking its prey. Nevertheless, if we were tracking a pack, they would be easy to find. Not this one though. He is a loner … and a breed apart … much more intelligent than normal … which makes him almost impossible to track … and so much more dangerous"

As usual, Sloan was focused, strictly business, "So what do you recommend in terms of next steps?"

Michael offered a brief outline, "First, I would like some time to go over all the evidence you have in Clayton with a fine tooth comb. Then, I would like to visit the sites in Wildwood and Winter Park to see for myself."

Sloan persisted in pressing, "How long do you think this will take?"

"Oh, it should take only a day or two or three at most."

Sloan wanted something nailed down, "Great, then by mid-week we should be in a position to develop our strategy going forward."

Michael stopped him in his tracks, "This is something we cannot rush. It will take more time than you suggest."

Sloan's knickers were starting to twist, "And why is that?"

Michael offered the worst kind of answer. It was what Sloan might refer to as mystical mumbo jumbo, "I need time to think. I need to get into the animal's head."

Sloan threw up his hands at that one, "We need to do better than that!"

Michael defused the situation immediately before Greene could rush to his defense. He dead panned in exaggerated Indian-speak, "How?" There was a moment of stunned silence while his clever, self-deprecating satire sunk in and then we all doubled over laughing, even Sloan … but, of course, not serious sour puss Greene. It was a good way to end the meeting and Sloan suggested we reconvene in a week or so when the Chief deemed he was ready.

Sloan was such a proud pragmatist and realist that he would never admit to such superstitions, at least not publicly, but in the back of his mind he was concerned that we were in the latter half of the month creeping toward the next full moon. The strawberry moon was set to appear at the end of the next week. The public held mixed emotions. The killings seemed intertwined with the lunar cycle but the pattern was not fool proof as evidenced by the uneventful snow and flower moons in February and May respectively. Flip Flanagan had been burned by this unpredictability before so he offered conditional warnings leaning more toward the laudatory public safety angle. Most people would have preferred a clear cut trend. It wasn't that they were disappointed that no killings occurred in February and May. They just longed for certainty. What they really wanted was for someone to eradicate the elusive killer and get their lives back to normal.

Hanley Wilson was nothing if not opportunistic but missed the chance to take advantage of the strawberry moon. It wouldn't have taken much effort or money to seize upon the media's attention and public's preoccupation with the strawberry moon. Why not try to lighten the mood and give everyone a much needed distraction? Enjoy the strawberry moon with a hand-picked quart of juicy, red, ripe, delicious strawberries from Wilson's Farm! Liven up your dull cereal, spice up your salad, turn your ice cream into a dreamy, frozen confection, put some bam in your jam or just savor their sweet, succulent, natural goodness as God intended … straight from Wilson's Farm to your mouth. The possibilities were endless with a little bit of initiative. But Hanley Wilson had grown tired of the family business long ago, before his folks died and brothers moved away leaving him the sole heir to the Wilson *empire*.

There was a time under Hanley's grandfather, Vernon, when Wilson's was a working farm with a fair share of livestock too. The rich soil of far Northeastern St. Louis County reaped a generous harvest and open land was still fairly plentiful back then. That was before heavy development occurred. Then the squeeze began. Large manufacturers like McDonnell Douglas and the Ford Motor Company brought good paying jobs that attracted thousands of families. Developers followed with subdivisions popping up everywhere. This attracted shopping malls and other businesses that boosted the tax base which led to an amazing growth in the local public schools. Faced with such encroachment on every boundary and competition from corporate agricultural combines, old time farmers sold out to close up shop or moved further out to the wide open spaces.

Vernon was an industrious, hard-working farmer but not much of a businessman. As demand waned and price competition put the hurt on him, he sold parcels of land one-by-one to survive. Unfortunately, his strategy was to downsize to survive rather than making a killing. He never envisioned leaving the farming life and was too set in his ways to relocate and start over. Thus, he received bottom dollar to sell off his land bit-by-bit to other farmers who naturally drove a hard bargain given the depressed farm economics they were suffering through. They were in most cases much shrewder than Vernon and not at all as encumbered as he was by emotional or family ties to the northeast corner of the county which was under siege by the invading *barbarians*. After they increased their holdings for pennies on the dollar from poor, old Wilson, they turned around and sold out to the developers for hefty profits that allowed them to kiss farming good bye.

Hanley's father, Tanner, was sharper than Vernon in many ways but had the same loyalty to Wilson tradition. The plot of land he inherited was too small for a true, working farm and certainly couldn't support a profitable livestock operation. The thought of expanding was out of the question because he wound up being the last man standing and his corner of paradise was completely surrounded by two-stories, split foyers and ranches with tidy patios and manicured lawns. He was not one to throw in the towel and found a way to turn his sow's ear into a silk purse. Tanner figured these suburbanite escapees from the big city might enjoy a slice of Americana right in their own back yards. All of the Oliver Douglas wannabes could satisfy their occasional Green Acres longings without driving more than ten or fifteen minutes. Hop in the car with the wife and kids and head on over to Wilson's farm for some good, old fashioned family fun out in the *country*.

Tanner was right. He turned his old family farm into a direct consumer business. It was like a roadside produce stand on a grand scale. The only way to get fruit and produce fresher than what they offered at the roadside stand was to get out there and pick it yourself … and it sure beat that grocery store stuff with all the preservatives. In addition to his business savvy, Tanner had great foresight and could already see the environmental trend picking up steam by the time the early 1970s rolled around. Wilson's farm was country before country was cool and green before the color turned into a philosophy. On top of it all, Tanner Wilson had the heart of a showman. Picking your own goods fresh from Wilson's farm was not only healthy and environmentally friendly but it was fun. There was an element of entertainment down on the farm when you went to Wilson's.

They weren't getting rich but under Tanner's guidance the Wilsons made a good living. They had everything they needed and were able to squirrel away some modest savings too. In the fall, it was apple picking time and people came from miles around to trudge through the orchards and provide free labor while paying the going rate for their apples. Tom Sawyer couldn't have topped this racket. In October, they opened the pumpkin patch. There were hayrides, haystack castles and gigantic pumpkins that you'd never find at the local stand or grocery store. So you paid a little extra. It was worth it since you got so much more than a jack-o-lantern. The kids could be entertained for at least a half day at Wilson's Halloween extravaganza. Winter was slow but Christmas trees and decorations helped them get through. Spring brought strawberries, flowers and garden supplies and summer was chock full of all sorts of veggies and the highlight of the season, water melons. Wilson's Farm became somewhat of a local landmark and enjoyed esteem from the community along with the popularity of its customers.

If Tanner had a failing, it was that he may have spent too much time on the business and not enough on his three boys. Or maybe there was just something missing from their character. They never learned to appreciate getting their fingers down into the soil. Of course, everyone had to work on the farm but the boys gravitated toward the retail side preferring to work a cash register over anything else. Tanner didn't press them and was happy to hire outside help as long as the bottom line was healthy. As the boys got older and into high school they lost any pride they might have had in the family farm. They resented being different from their suburban peers; too often viewed as dumb, backward farm boys. Also, they were jealous of the other kids who seemed to have plenty of time for fun and games while their weekends and summers were consumed by work.

As Tanner grew old and eventually lost the capacity to run the business, the boys stepped into the breach but only half-heartedly. When their mother died and Tanner was homebound and finally bed ridden, things got worse and the farm deteriorated further. When Tanner died, Hanley's brothers bolted before he could raise an objection and headed off to pursue their own dreams. As you might expect, they never amounted to much of anything. By circumstance rather than choice, Hanley was left holding the bag and thrust into the unenviable position of managing an operation he loathed. He hired outsiders and did his best to keep the farm running smoothly, not out of a sense of obligation, pride or family loyalty but simply survival. Hanley never saw a future in the business but needed its sustenance as a bridge to a different path. If he would have spent as much time focused on growing the business as he did plotting his exit strategy he might have done quite well.

The best and easiest option for Hanley seemed to be to buck the tradition laid down by his father and granddad and sell out to the developers. At one point, after years of rejection, it appeared his ship had finally come in. A large developer with a new idea took interest in Wilson's Farm. They intended to drop a pre-fabricated, self-contained community right into the middle of suburbia. It would feature single family homes around the perimeter surrounding condominiums with a small group of retail shops in the center. With the fat profit their business plan afforded, Hanley would have been set for life. He was delirious with excitement and anticipation as they worked toward closing the deal. Then the bottom fell out leaving Hanley a bitter, broken and desperate man.

When the Wilson's first settled the land long before, they had specifically chosen the site for the creek that ran right through the middle of the property. It provided much needed moisture and ensured their fields would be rich and fertile without expensive, artificial irrigation systems. The topography was basically flat and it mattered little that everything sloped gently downward toward the creek in the middle of the farm. It didn't matter that the water occasionally escaped the creek bed in those few years where heavy flooding occurred along the Missouri and Mississippi Rivers. It didn't come close to their house or barns and left behind rich sediments when the flood waters receded. It had been years since the last occurrence so Hanley never gave it a second thought when he shook hands with the developers. But grief and panic hit him like a tsunami when the inspectors designated that Wilson's Farm was centered on a legal flood plain. The developers still could have built on two thirds of the land but the economics crumbled without all the condos and retail center.

Hanley's dream of living the good life was shattered to bits. He came to see the family farm house as a prison and the surrounding land as a hostile, uninhabitable island; his own personal Alcatraz. As you can imagine, it wasn't too much fun working for Hanley and with his sour outlook on life, Wilson's Farm lost the theme park cachet it had developed under Tanner's leadership. Hanley was trapped like a rat and began to think like one. As the business shrank, a good forty percent of the land lay fallow and began to get lost in undergrowth and neglect. Hanley did just enough to get by and focused all his attention on wild, get rich quick schemes. In an ironic quirk of fate, Hanley found his gold mine in being the anti-Tanner. Whereas his dad had recognized environmental awareness early on and took advantage of it by being a good corporate citizen, Hanley took up with the creeps who bent the rules and basically raped the earth to turn a profit.

Hanley found that there were some unscrupulous business people who would do anything it took to beat the competition, including ducking those pesky EPA regulations regarding the disposal of hazardous wastes. Proper disposal of such by-products was essential to a healthy environment but very, very expensive. In some cases, you could save hundreds of thousands of dollars by beating the system. And Hanley was more than happy to provide the loop hole. Tanner and Vernon would have turned over in their graves if they could have seen how Hanley turned the center of Wilson's Farm into a poisonous dumping ground. Hanley didn't think about this much because his conscience was buried so deep but sometimes in his sleep old Vernon would come to him wagging his finger saying the love of money is the root of all evil. During his waking hours though, he only had one thought. A few more years at this pace and he'd be able to escape this horrible, painful place forever. That was a good thing for Hanley because the clock was ticking. Rumors had begun to circulate about his nefarious deeds and environmental groups on the trail of his corrupt clientele began to piece the puzzle together. It wouldn't be long before federal inspectors might take notice and bring the heat down on wayward Wilson.

Normally, Wilson slept like a baby, partially due to the heavy doses of hard booze he polished off regularly but mostly because of his aforementioned dormant conscience. Occasionally though, his peaceful slumbers would be interrupted by the darned high school kids making late night incursions to swipe a few pumpkins or water melons. They didn't do so for profit but rather the thrill of avoiding mean, old man Wilson and his dogs. Now that June had arrived and the kids were off for the summer, the late night raids had picked up in frequency to where Hanley was not startled by the intrusions. It was a perfect night for interlopers with the shine from the full moon to light their way through the strawberry patches. He was so conditioned that he didn't bother to get dressed. Hanley just trudged out of bed and let his two hounds loose to drive off the drunken teens.

As they bounded off into the night baying under the moonlight, Hanley slumped back into bed to wait for the noise to cease.

In a few minutes, they would be at the back door whining and scratching to get back in and he would be able to slide back into a soothing slumber. However, this night was different. Off in the distance there were faint yelps then nothing. Hanley could have tolerated some noise but not the unanticipated silence. When the dogs didn't return, it unsettled Wilson to the point of sleeplessness. He sat up and then began to pace. Maybe the dogs had found some critter to dine on … or, heaven forbid; maybe the dang kids had hurt his precious pooches. After another five minutes, Hanley couldn't take it any longer and threw on some clothes, grabbed a flashlight and ventured outside to investigate. He muttered under his breath as he trod the soil that Vernon and Tanner had tilled for so many years. Like the dogs, Hanley never returned to the old farm house.

The next morning, Hanley's hired hands showed up for work faithfully and got things running without the boss' guidance. It wasn't unusual for him to get a late start especially when he imbibed a little more than normal. When noontime approached, they thought it was odd not to see hide nor hair of him but no one complained about the absence of the grumpy task master. It was a customer who literally tripped over Farmer Wilson while plucking juicy delicacies in one of the farthest flung patches of strawberries. It was such a shocking revelation that the horrified woman turned tail and ran toward the exit screaming at the top of her lungs. Needless to say, it created quite a commotion and several employees hurried out to see what had caused the babbling customer to suffer a near nervous breakdown. When they came upon Hanley's prone body they were momentarily paralyzed by what they found and failed to keep many unfortunate, curious berry pickers from gathering round. Then they realized they needed to shoo them away, close down the farm and contact the police immediately.

By the time Wes and I arrived, Sloan and his team already had the scene well secured. Greene and Michael Muraco arrived together a few minutes later just about the time Tracker Joe showed up with his favorite hound in tow. I dreaded seeing another mangled victim but hid my angst so as to not lower my standing among the team members. The others were seasoned professionals who could view the disturbing scene analytically in a clinical fashion but I couldn't remain so detached. Thus, it took a while for the stunning impact to subside so I could let my brain catch up with everyone else. At first, the only thing that registered were the similarities to the other four victims ... horrified expression; odd, prone posture; lack of defensive wounds and, of course, the shredded, gaping, blood spattered hole where there once was a human throat. Then I finally focused in on the stark difference that had floored Sloan and everyone else. Hanley Wilson's shirt was torn open and a bloody pentagram was crudely carved into his bare chest.

There was another key difference. Not far away, in the thickets where the strawberry patch ended, we found Wilson's two dogs. One had its throat crushed and torn, silenced by violent suffocation, while the other was cleanly slashed as if by a razor sharp knife. Neither dog was eaten, not even partially. It was as if they had been executed. Beyond these new revelations of the pentagram and dead dogs, the crime scene was a major disappointment. The area around Hanley's body had been totally compromised by the tracks of berry pickers and the foot prints of employees who rushed to find Wilson. If the killer, or should I say killers, left tracks, they had been eradicated. So Sloan had us search the area between Wilson's body and the dogs for other clues but, unfortunately, the ground cover was so dense there were no prints left in the soil beneath. Joe's dog picked up the scent of the wolf but, once again, it ended in a frustrating dead end. Nevertheless, Sloan knew there was new evidence to be found so, for the second time, ordered a full forensic analysis to be conducted.

Later, after everything was fully wrapped up, Sloan asked us to meet down in his office in Clayton to compare notes. He had an I-told-you-so look on his face as if to say, you see, animals just aren't that smart. "One thing we know for sure now is that this is more than an animal attack. We don't have a rogue wolf on the loose. A crime has been committed … there's a murderer at large."

Greene objected politely, "We can't discount that a wolf is involved. We have the forensics to prove it."

I thought Sloan might grab him by the neck and shake him but he kept his cool, "Do you think I don't know that Einstein? Of course there's a wolf involved. I'm just saying it's not some super wolf with magical powers. There's a human brain behind these murders. It's a twisted, demented one but human nonetheless."

Greene didn't back down, "How do you know there's a human being involved in all four attacks?"

Sloan snapped back sarcastically, "The last time I checked, wolves don't have opposable thumbs so I'm guessing a wolf didn't carve that pentagram into Wilson's chest."

Greene persisted, "You're right about that but how do we know this killing isn't isolated from the other attacks? And how do we know that some lunatic didn't come along and slash Wilson after the wolf had already killed the man?"

Sloan rolled his eyes, "That would be one hell of a coincidence. This poor guy became a victim of our rogue wolf then, just by chance; some roaming lunatic came along, found the dead body and decided to add a little artwork … yeah, right!"

Wes, Joe and I were at a loss to stop this debate from escalating into a full-fledged argument but Michael jumped in at just the right time, "Did anyone else notice the artwork? There was some thought put into it." He pointed to a picture tacked up on Sloan's bulletin board. "It's not just any pentagram. It's a pentangle or five pointed star with strokes through the center. Notice how it is bound by a double circle surrounding the star. Most importantly, the orientation is upside down with two points facing up and three down below. This is the work of a Satanist. The two points of the star facing upward represent the horns of a goat … the symbol for the place where fallen angels dwell. The three points facing the other direction reflect the rejection of the Holy Trinity. Someone is sending us a message."

Sloan let that sink in for a minute so I took the opportunity to interject a question, "What would cause the killer to reveal himself like this? Wouldn't he want to remain anonymous with us chasing after a rogue wolf?"

Sloan had a thoughtful look now with curiosity overtaking his frustration with Greene, "I was thinking the same thing. Maybe it's a cry for help … you know, the guy wants to be caught. Or perhaps it's his way of taunting us. Sometimes these serial killers get tripped up by their inflated egos thinking they're too smart to get caught. I'm intrigued by what Michael said. Maybe the guy is just plain evil."

Michael added, "It's not just an evil person. The beast is just as evil. The two may be inseparable in their diabolical work."

Sloan scoffed, "I think you're right that the two are working together. That would explain how the wolf was able to navigate through all the traps we set out near Babler State Park. But I don't believe this nonsense of a diabolical tag team working in tandem."

A mystical look came over Michael's face, "I never said anything about a team."

Sloan was exasperated by this parsing of words, "Then tell me, what exactly did you mean, Chief?"

Michael said in a matter of fact, somber tone that was a little bit spooky, "Maybe the two are not two but only one."

Summer Solstice ...
Loup Garou

CHAPTER 6

BUCK MOON

SLOAN WAS IN HIS ELEMENT now ... this was a homicide investigation. He knew how to track a two-legged killer and this helped him to further assert his authority. I think he would have preferred to dismiss us, his band of misfits, but still needed our expertise since, in some form or fashion, there was a wolf involved in the killings. He lost respect for Michael when he alluded to ... to what? Sloan didn't even entertain whatever nonsense he was proposing. The last thing he needed was someone on the inside stoking the crazy werewolf fires that were being fanned well enough by Flip Flanagan and other irresponsible members of the media. If Sloan had his way, he would have withheld the new information regarding Wilson's death from the public. He would have preferred to maintain the story that a lone killer wolf was on the prowl. He could have justified withholding information about the pentagram as a detail best kept confidential to help identify the perpetrator. Unfortunately that was not a choice since there had been so many witnesses that saw the satanic carving in Wilson's chest.

The detective called us all back to Clayton once the forensic work was completed. "Gentlemen, I'm going to do you a big favor and give you a brief synopsis of the stack of paper in front of me. What it boils down to is this. We have indisputable evidence that a human and a wolf were present at the Wilson crime scene. There is wolf DNA on Wilson and one of the dogs. Fortunately, the other dog was apparently able to nip the killer before he slashed his throat. We found human blood on the dog and on Wilson. We don't know who's blood it is but there are definitely two sources of blood found on Wilson; his own and the killer's."

I blurted, "Can they identify the killer from the blood sample?"

Sloan's smart aleck retort was swift, "This isn't CSI New York, son. Anyway, there isn't a universal database of criminal DNA at our fingertips and if there was it wouldn't help unless our killer was a convicted criminal who was processed somewhere along the way."

I didn't like being the butt of his criticism and tried to regain my footing and reputation, "But now that we have a sample, it could help us screen any suspects down the road, right?"

"Yeah, that's right Sherlock."

Greene took the lead next sounding like he was in the classroom delivering one of his lectures, "We know from the DNA forensics that the same wolf was involved in at least two of the attacks. Based on

Michael's analysis we can take it a step further and state unequivocally that it was responsible for the other two attacks too."

Before Sloan could launch a counter strike against Dr. Green, Michael thrust forth into an explanation, "While I was visiting the other sites and reviewing the pictures and remains of all the victims, I took some careful measurements. The bite radius is perfectly identical on all five bodies and, from what I could gather; the teeth marks reflect a pattern of remarkable consistency. We are without a doubt looking for one wolf that is responsible for all the deaths."

Sloan conceded as little as possible, "I agree that there's a wolf involved; one big, damn wolf. But we also have forensics and the pentagram that tells us a man was involved at least once for sure and more than likely in all five murders. The key to solving this crime and ending the killing spree is to focus on the man … we've got to catch the murderer."

Michael pleaded, almost apologetically, "I beg you. Do not discount what I am about to say. My ancestors taught me a most valuable lesson; that is, to see beyond what meets the eye. There is a whole other world that can only be seen through spiritual eyes. It is a realm possessed by both good and evil … a terrible, powerful evil that can infect both man and beast. If we insist upon wearing worldly blinders to ignore the spirits all around us, we do so at our own great peril."

I'm also a realist and not the superstitious sort but Michael's sobering words sent a chill down my spine. I think everyone felt the same tingle except perhaps for Sloan who remained combative, "So what exactly are you trying to say, Chief? Are you trying to tell me you believe in ghosts, goblins and werewolves?"

Michael offered a calm, serious response, "I understand that I'm out of touch with the mainstream."

Sloan barked, "Boy, that's the understatement of the year!"

It didn't deter Michael in the least, "I come from a different culture where stories have been passed down from generation to generation across a millennium. My people were much more in tune with nature, the spirit world and animal kingdom. As such, I was raised to have an open mind and heart. I see things that others cannot. I knew from the moment I joined this team that we were dealing with something unknown, other worldly ... unlike anything you've ever come across in your white man's world."

Sloan remained as feisty as ever, "Oh, now I see ... it's a race thing, is it?"

Michael was as calm as Sloan was fiery, "No, it's a cultural thing. You can only see what you want to see. Your mind cannot comprehend what escapes your eyes because you fear the unknown."

Sloan laughed derisively, "Okay, I'll call you Chief and you can call me Helen Keller, blind as a bat. What is it that you see that I can't?"

Michael's calm masked his frustration in knowing that Sloan was hopeless, "There is no use in me trying to convince you right now. You have your mind made up. I would only ask that you try to keep your heart and mind unfettered. Someday when the time is right, I will explain the legend of Loup Garou. For now, we must find our killer before he strikes again. As my ancestors knew, since this is July, by the time the full buck moon appears, the new antlers of the male deer will push out of their foreheads in coatings of velvety fur. We should beware this moon because it will bring more than maturity to the buck deer. I fear the horns of the great goat will spring forth again under the influence of the evil one; beneath the hellish aura of the full moon."

Sloan settled down a bit, perhaps feeling sorry for Michael who, to him, was steeped in a backward culture that made him a slave to irrational, delusional beliefs. "We can agree on one thing, my man. We all need to get our butts in gear because things are going to get crazy by the time the full moon, buck moon or whatever you want to call it moon appears. The media is having a field day with all this lunar nonsense and werewolf crap. All it does is make our jobs ten times tougher. This isn't all a bunch of unfounded hysteria though. The body art left on poor Wilson tells me one thing. We have a nut case on our hands that likes to kill during the full moon. I don't know why yet but he does. Perhaps he wants to cause a panic." Then he closed with a final smirk, "Or maybe the guy has spiritual eyes ... wooooooooooooooooo."

Sloan didn't want us to leave on a sour note so he actually offered an apology of sorts, "Hey, I'm sorry guys. I don't mean to make light of the situation. I'm just saying what I think we can all agree with. We have our work cut out for us and really need to move ahead and pull together in order to stop the killer in his tracks. I don't know about you but I'm beat. What do you say we take a break and get back together this evening under better circumstances? You guys know where Hannigan's is, right? It should be convenient for all you Wash U guys. Meet me there at 8:00 and the department will spring for dinner and beer." That was a winner. Sloan had finally found some common ground.

Everyone scurried off quickly with much to do. I'd see Greene and Mosely soon enough since I had their classes that afternoon. But that wasn't my top priority. I'd be seeing Faith Harper again and planned on taking her up on her offer to share another cup of coffee. I steered her away from Hannigan's since I didn't want to hit the place twice in one day and also feared we might run into Greene or a nosey classmate. I offered to follow Faith out to her stomping grounds in St. Charles and she took me to one of the quaint, old spots on historic Main Street. It was perfect. There was no way I'd run into anyone from Wash U there and we were basically all alone in a private booth tucked away in a back corner of the joint.

I felt like having a beer but Faith wasn't quite twenty one yet so I opted for a coffee too. It didn't matter because I fell under the spell of her lovely gaze and got a natural buzz just being with her. Being in a remote place like St. Charles that was far removed from campus and where no one knew me made me feel incognito and thus comfortable in the laid back setting and I was at ease with Faith. I wanted to broach the subject of Zeb Greene with her but she beat me to the punch on the topic of conversation, "Seth, I've been hearing so much on the news about that poor man who was killed. Are you still helping the police?"

"Yes, I was actually called out to the crime scene when the body was first discovered."

"Tell me about it. Was it exciting … kind of creepy … were you scared?"

I was so at home with Faith that I opted for honesty over some macho routine, "I guess I'd have to say yes to all of the above. There was no immediate danger but it brought back the same really bad vibes I felt when I saw the bodies of those two dead teenagers."

"How much of what we hear on the news is true? I mean it sounds so crazy with all the talk about wolves, full moons and even werewolves."

"I'm not the superstitious type but I've got to be honest. There's something really strange about these killings; there are things that just don't add up. We were sure the culprit was a savage wolf on the loose until what happened at Wilson's Farm but even before that we were facing a bizarre situation. There are a lot of details that haven't come to light in the news that would blow your mind. Now we have clear evidence that a human being was involved; at least with the last murder. And not just an average, run of the mill murderer, if there is such a thing, but a satanic maniac that carved his calling card into his last victim."

Faith's face grew almost grim under a furrowed brow, "That sounds horrible Seth. Where did this werewolf talk come from? Is it just something the media has fabricated to get ratings?"

"Normally, I'd say yes but some of the evidence is pretty weird … it lends itself to wild speculation. There's someone new on the investigative team, a big, Native American fellow who doesn't think the idea is so far out."

Faith seemed amazed that I had so much inside information and was fascinated to learn more, "That sounds so peculiar. How did someone like that wind up as part of the police's investigative team?"

Ah, I thought, here's my chance to broach a touchy subject, "He was recommended by our own Dr. Greene. Did you know that Professor Greene is on the team too?"

She looked genuinely surprised, "No, I didn't." Now the gears were turning in my head. Were they not as close as I thought? Perhaps Greene preferred to remain tight lipped when it came to the investigation for confidentiality's sake.

I thought, oh well, here goes, "Really, I'm surprised because I thought you and Dr. Greene were somewhat of an item."

Faith blanched at the notion but kept her composure, "Oh no, not at all. We're just sort of friends, I guess." There was a pregnant pause as I tried to hide my skepticism. For some reason, Faith felt compelled to explain further, "We share a cup of coffee now and then but Professor Greene is just trying to make me feel welcome at Wash U." After more silence from me, "C'mon Seth, you've got

to be kidding! He's way too old for me and we're polar opposites."
She wrinkled her nose and squealed, "Gross ... do you think I'd
get involved that way with one of my instructors?"

Of course, that's exactly what I thought but could tell this was
headed for trouble so I laughed loudly to feign my innocence, "I'm
just kidding you. Sorry Faith ... sometimes my sense of humor
can be kind of twisted."

She relaxed but was still a little exasperated by my veiled
accusation. Yet, Faith was able to display a little humor of her
own, "That's lucky for you mister. I'd hate to waste this coffee by
pouring it over your head." I played along and pretended to duck
for cover and we both laughed.

After having narrowly escaped disaster you'd think I would
have had more sense but my curiosity got the better of me, "What
did you mean when you said you and Professor Greene are polar
opposites?"

"Oh, it was nothing really. When I thought you were serious,
it just struck me how little we have in common outside the
classroom." I should have left well enough alone but gestured for
her to go ahead. "We just have different backgrounds. The biggest
thing is that I'm a Christian and ... well ... let's just say that I think
Professor Greene holds to some different beliefs."

Oh boy, I thought, now I've done it! I had to go and open my
big mouth. I really painted myself into a corner. The last thing I
wanted to do was kill our budding friendship in the cradle. I must
have had a look of concern on my face if not outright panic because
Faith picked up on it as if she could read my mind. She tried to
back me off the ledge with a little teasing, "Is there something you
need to tell me Seth? Are you an atheist or something? If you are,
you might as well let me know now because there'll be no more
coffee breaks for you, buddy."

Her light hearted sense of humor and that dazzling smile helped me relax to where I decided to spar with her, "So, are you telling me that you will only date Christians?"

"Hey, I just thought we were sharing some coffee. Are you asking me out on a date now? If you are, you better be a Christian … or thinking seriously about converting."

I was having fun with our jousting and a huge, silly grin invaded my face, "You better believe I'm a Christian … hallelujah and amen!"

"Okay then, it's a date. What did you have in mind, big boy?"

That was enough fooling around. It was time to get down to business. I was really smitten with this girl and had a feeling unlike anything I'd experienced before. It was more than her gorgeous looks. She was special in more ways than one. I had a sense that I needed to come clean and build a good foundation from the ground up. "I was serious about being a Christian."

I hesitated and Faith had to break the silence,

"But …?"

"Well, to be perfectly honest, my church is different. It might not fit in so well here in the Midwest." It was her turn to apply the pressure of the silent treatment. "We're just not as outspoken. People don't quote from the Bible and all that." She held her tongue as if to say, what else? "I wouldn't blame you for changing your mind about me but, frankly, I've been pretty lax about going to church lately." There, I said it and threw myself on the mercy of the court, expecting the worst.

Faith gave me a sly smile. "You must think I'm pretty shallow … and judgmental." Before I could offer a denial, "Seth, you haven't told me anything that would change my opinion of you. I've yet to meet a perfect Christian, myself included." She paused before dropping the bomb on me, "Besides, Dr. Mosely already told me all about you … that you're a real reclamation project." That son of a gun was way ahead of me again but apparently still paving the way for me! Faith's smile radiated brightly, "You promised me a date and I'm holding you to it. Again, what do you have in mind, good looking?"

I was back on cloud nine, "You can name the time and the place. Your wish is my command, my fair lady."

Faith was not quite done having fun with me. I was momentarily distracted as a waitress walked by. "Seth Lomax, how dare you?"

I truly was caught off guard, "What, what did I do?"

"That's the third or fourth time I've caught you glancing at that waitress! Do you have a wandering eye, Mr. Lomax? I guess I can't blame you for being distracted by Miss Bouncy in her Daisy Duke hot pants with half her rear end hanging out."

This time I really was innocent, "I was not checking her out, honest!"

Faith poured on the mock indignation, "You most certainly were staring at her." Then another smile, "But I really don't think you were ogling her caboose. You never paid a bit of attention to her when she passed by with food. It was only when she had a tray full of cold beers. Maybe you're subconsciously trying to tell me you've had your fill of the coffee."

I was still a little unnerved but laughed off her joke. "You know Seth; you could have ordered a beer. I'm not a Baptist! Believe it or not, I have had a beer before."

I decided I'd get the last word in on my little comedienne, "Well, that settles it then. How about a home cooked meal at my palatial estate on Friday night and I'll supply the beer?"

"Hmmm … do you think I can trust you alone?"

"I'm making no promises." When we got to our cars and I offered a good bye, Faith gave me the most pleasant surprise. To a casual observer it would have looked like a rather innocent, inconsequential kiss, the briefest of encounters with her provocative, supple, pursed lips. But she packed the punch of a neutron bomb. Even before our mouths met, every electron in every cell of my being stood at attention and flipped its orientation toward Faith when she leaned into me and brushed her body, ever so lightly, up against mine. If I hadn't been preconditioned by this partial sampling of her amazing power, the full force of her electrifying kiss might have knocked me clear off my feet. I'm sure I had fantastic gas mileage on the ride home because I was floating on air.

That night at Hannigan's, the team seemed to take on a different personality. Everyone let their hair down including Sloan who dropped some of the formalities. Even Greene tried to be more cordial instead of his stuffy, oh so serious self. The beer flowed along with some good natured ribbing. Sloan cranked it up, "So Chief, tell me, what's the English translation of your name, Lon Chaney Junior ... or Benicio Del Toro?"

Sloan busted up over the Chief's retort, "Wouldn't you like to think so, white boy."

Next the detective turned his sights on Greene, "How about you college boy? Do you believe in werewolves too?"

I was waiting for Dr. Greene to kill the mood by launching into some diatribe or hyper-intellectual explanation but he played right along, "I didn't use to until I saw Woodson without his shirt on." That even got a laugh out of normally stone faced Wes whose excessive body hair was on display on his arms and the thick tuft protruding from the top of his t-shirt. No one was safe from the flying barbs. Joe was portrayed as a backwoods hillbilly and they skewered my youth by asking several times if I was ready for a diaper change.

It was hard for me to fight back since I was at such a disadvantage constantly deferring to my elders. Maybe it was the beer but they eventually took pity on me and tried to make me a full-fledged member of the team by allowing me the honor of putting them on a first name basis. It started when I referred to Detective Sloan, "Hey Seth, why so formal? You can call me Stan here."

Everyone chimed in except for Greene who was obviously reluctant but finally caved, "Feel free to call me Zeb. Don't forget though that on campus or whenever your classmates are around; no first names please." I would have never referred to him as Zeb in a formal setting anyway but it said something about his personality that he felt it necessary to state the obvious. I nodded quickly but before the moment could turn awkward we were interrupted. Doctor Mosely had dropped into Hannigan's and was shuffling by on his way to the bar for a night cap and overheard our conversation.

He stopped and put his hand on my shoulder, "And you can call me Doc." He smiled and introduced himself to everyone and said, "You can all call me Noah ... or as Professor Greene likes to say, that crazy, Aussie bastard." Everyone laughed and immediately took a liking to Professor Mosely except for Greene who was barely able to utter a forced laugh.

Since we had already squeezed in most of our business in between the various comedy routines, Sloan thought it would be okay and asked, "Noah, would you care to join us for a beer?"

"Are you sure I wouldn't be interrupting anything?"

"No, not at all ... this is mainly just a bull session anyway."

"Well then mates, I'd be honored." After a couple more beers, the conversation drifted back to the investigation. It didn't matter that informality and juvenile humor had taken us well off course. In spite of all his frivolous banter, Sloan was still Sloan and the detective in him was never too far from surfacing, "Tell me Noah, do you believe in werewolves?"

Mosely made a steeple of his fingers indicating the seriousness of the question, "I'm familiar with homo sapiens, the genus Canis and considerable subspecies variation thereof, including Canis lupus the wolf, but I've never heard of homo Canis, Canis homo, homo lupus or anything of the sort. No, I don't believe in myths, legends or transitional forms."

Sloan clapped, "Bravo Doctor, well said! Maybe we should add you to our team." Mosely let that slide on by assuming correctly that it was said in jest.

I peeked at Michael who seemed to take Mosely's comments in stride but Greene's countenance took on a stern look as if he was struggling not to respond. Sloan couldn't resist probing further, "Do you have any suggestions for the team, Noah?"

Mosely knew better than to poke his nose in where it didn't belong, "I haven't really followed the investigation closely. I'll leave that up to you and your team of professionals." The Doctor finished his beer and politely excused himself. It took the edge off of Greene who relaxed noticeably after Mosely's departure.

Sloan tried to get a rise out of Michael, "Chief, what did you think of Noah's take on things?"

Michael must have felt that Sloan was still not ready to fully open his eyes and thus offered a curt reply, "There are things that science cannot explain." Sloan let it go, not wanting to ruin the mood and the team camaraderie we'd achieved.

We relaxed to enjoy one final beer and everyone, including Greene, appeared well at ease that is until a smoker at the bar fired up a big stogie. Hannigan's was one of the bars that qualified for a waiver from the area's smoking ban because of the ratio of bar versus food revenue. It was perfectly legal to smoke but relatively few people did so, probably due to the campus influence. As luck would have it, the plume from the man's cigar wafted directly toward Greene's sensitive nostrils. Isn't that the way it always works? If you're in a restaurant with smoking and non-smoking sections, the fumes always have a way of drifting toward the non-smokers. Maybe it's because our lungs are healthier and naturally pull in more air. In any case, Greene wouldn't let the intrusion pass unnoticed even though the man was perfectly within his rights. He strode over to the bar and quietly confronted the surprised man who was quite a bit larger than the fit, wiry professor. We couldn't hear the words that were exchanged but I paid close attention to their facial expressions. Somehow Greene convinced the bigger man to back down and snuff out his odorous cheroot. Just as he turned toward our table, a split second before he had his mask of cordiality in place, I caught a glimpse of the menacing look in Greene's fiery eyes. It was the look of a true, committed believer who was prepared to take up arms for his favorite cause. As we finished our beer and prepared to leave I wondered about Greene and made up my mind that I'd have to dig a little deeper into why Faith referred to him as a polar opposite.

Meanwhile, the media machine was winding into high gear as the full buck moon approached. Once again, unscrupulous, flimflam Flip Flanagan was savvier than the rest of his counterparts at the other stations and in the local press. They were going off on so many tangents that it was hard to discern anything more than that they were pressing a lot of panic buttons. Many of them tried to span the entire spectrum of possibilities from a satanic cult run amok to some kind of Canis lupus Maximus stalking the area. Flanagan played the werewolf card now that there was some basis in forensic evidence and he stayed on message. It was quite a stretch from human and wolf DNA at the scene to conjuring up a mythical creature but Flip chose the long shot and was determined to ride this horse for as long as possible. It was no longer pure entertainment; tongue-in-cheek reportage aimed at garnering ratings along with a few laughs. He was seriously playing upon hidden fears, superstitions and people's worst instincts. Flanagan didn't come right out and propose something so preposterous but let subtle doubts and suspicions creep in by posing questions, dropping hints and sprinkling in a few anomalous facts … just enough to keep people off balance.

In the midst of this three-ring circus with the likes of Flanagan and his cohorts fanning the flames higher and higher as the buck moon approached, Sloan did his best to counter them with the facts and sound reason. It was nearly an impossible task because, in spite of his measured tones and constant reassurances to the contrary, no one felt safe. The public had been living with an unrelenting, unknown terror on their doorsteps for six months and the police didn't have a clue and seemed helpless to stop the killings. Nevertheless, Sloan had to continue to wage the battle in the public relations war we were losing badly. He had no choice because people were skittish to the point of bedlam. For Sloan and the authorities there was a bigger fear of what frenzied people might do to one another than the danger presented by the wolf and/or some crazed killer. All it would take is an accident with one fearful citizen killing another out of self-defense to blow the lid off of this pressure cooker.

There was at least one small segment of the population that was blissfully oblivious to the wolf mania that gripped the rest of us. July is the time when preparations get under way for the high school football season. From summer camps to touch-only passing leagues to jamboree interschool scrimmages to dreaded two-a-day practices, this is where fall heroes and team glories find their genesis. Without July's heat, dust, sweat and soreness, there would be no November ballyhoo for Pirates, Cadets, Spartans, Jaguars, Flyers, Wildcats, Comets or Crusaders. Toiling under the summer's brutal sun was a hard sell for coaches who were competing against all the more pleasant distractions available during the break in the school year.

At least one team needed no extra motivation in making the necessary sacrifices. Tradition alone was enough for the Hawks of Hazelwood but there was much more at stake. The perennial powerhouse of North St. Louis County had a state title to defend with a plethora of returning starters and lettermen hungry for a dynastic double dip. They knew that everyone would be gunning for them and were prepared to take the necessary steps to meet the challenge of trying to repeat. The Hawks were well equipped with seasoned veterans returning at most of the skill positions and their stout defense lost only two players to graduation. Yes, about the only thing missing was the alchemy of hard work and dedication necessary to gel as a team. This was an ingredient that everyone was eager to add to the mix as two-a-days approached.

Team chemistry was usually a big advantage for the Hawks. They enjoyed the type of camaraderie that only comes from the torch being passed on successfully from one class to the next for many years. Rich traditions were so well engrained that they stood the test of time. One such ritual was said to have started back in the early 1970s by the group that brought the first state title to Hazelwood. According to Hawk lore, a gritty bunch of sophomores refused to collapse under the weight of a terrible two-win, eight-loss season. To show their spunk and give the beleaguered coaches hope for the future, they decided to pull a Halloween prank in honor of an assistant coach known affectionately and fearfully as the Great Pumpkin. He was a cement block of a man with a colossal noggin topped with a shock of bright, orange hair.

That Halloween night, some twenty or so adventurous members of the team gathered in the high school parking lot at close to midnight with cars, trucks and station wagons. They plotted their strategy and fanned out to the district's seemingly endless neighborhoods. At midnight, the costumed kids had all long since been put to bed after calming down from their treat induced sugar highs and the parents were fast asleep too. It really wasn't stealing, they figured, since most of the jack-o-lanterns were destined for the garbage anyway. They rationalized that they were kind of performing a public service. A mechanized army of snickering Hawks collected hundreds of pumpkins that night and gathered back at the school parking lot to take inventory and map out the next steps in depositing their gleaming, orange treasures. They visited all of the coaches' residences and left each with a lifetime supply of carved pumpkins in their yards and blocked their front doors and the cars of those unfortunate enough not to have parked in their garages. Those founding fathers of fun paid a dear price the next day at practice but it had the desired effect. You wouldn't know it from the harsh discipline they meted out but the coaches' spirits were buoyed by such a collaborative act of rebellion and they rewarded the players after their last game in a miserable season by offering the ludicrous promise to that group of sorry sophomores that they would be state champs one day.

Those words proved to be prophetic and that group of young men grew into quite a team and, in fact, produced Hazelwood's first state title two years later. With such miraculous results, the legend of the Great Pumpkin became larger than life and the annual pumpkin-fest grew proportionately. As the Hawks filled their trophy cases with new hardware, there were ample stories of late night Halloween adventures. At one point, there were more than fifty vehicles involved in the annual fright night operation and so many pumpkins were collected that the players were able to spell out mammoth words like "Go Hawks" on the coaches' lawns with bunches of jack-o-lanterns. The coaches kept up their end of the bargain by doling out the punishment at the next day's practice. To keep anyone from missing out on the fun, they issued an announcement over the PA system that no excused absences would be allowed, regardless of notes from parents or doctors. Everyone had a blast taking their medicine even though some puked up their guts along the way from all the wind sprints and burpies. Nature seemed to have its part in the fall melee too by somehow always providing a steady rain that soaked the practice field in mud. The players were caked from head to toe and it was said that a coach might occasionally take a dip in the slop courtesy of deliriously happy players.

The Great Pumpkin eventually retired and the grand Halloween tradition faded under the heavy hand of party-pooping administrators and board members who deemed such tomfoolery as politically incorrect. Young football players are resilient though and the Hawks were not about to relinquish the edge in team spirit that had taken years to develop so new traditions cropped up, ones that often were conducted in a manner that would not come under the gaze of the kill joys in charge of running the district. The one unit on any football team where cohesion is paramount is the offensive line. They must operate in lock step as if performing a brutal choreography for the team to succeed. The great offensive lines at every level; professional, college and high school have always been blessed with a special type of togetherness. Practice is not nearly enough. They study together, eat together, and hang out together … six peas in a pod when you include a blocking tight end. In order to win, they have to get to a point where they can basically read each other's minds.

The only potential vulnerability for this otherwise stacked team was the inexperience of the offensive line. Both tackles were returning but the center and left guard were spot players with limited playing time and the right guard was a rookie starter as just a junior. Size was not the issue since Billy Schmidt was six feet and two inches tall and weighed in at just around two hundred fifty pounds. Heart was not a problem either. Billy had built a reputation as a tenacious blocker on the junior varsity and had earned the nickname Armadillo for his ability to get down low to the ground and plow his way through the defensive line. It was also fitting since he had a large proboscis that was bent from being broken on more than one occasion. No, the Armadillo was deemed as a potential asset to the offensive line but the proof had to be in the pudding. It would take more than experience. To fit in with such a tight knit group, you had to earn their respect and trust.

This is where tradition came into play again. Hazelwood High School is located not too far from Wilson's farm. Like the kids at Pattonville and Parkway North who frequented Creve Coeur Lake, the Hawks have Sioux Passage Park. There's a large expanse of playgrounds, athletic fields, campgrounds and picnic areas surrounded by many acres of thick woods replete with numerous hiking trails. At the back end of the Park, you can make your way to the Missouri River on foot and gain a panoramic view of the muddy waters flowing past the northern perimeter of Sioux Passage. The body of water nearest to the bank is actually a chute that cuts across a huge bend in the Missouri River to form Pelican Island. The Chute is named Car of Commerce after one of the river boats that sank while using the popular short cut of that time in history. Pelican Island is a misfit of sorts since it is under the authority of the Missouri Department of Conservation even though it butts up to Sioux Passage which is one of our St. Louis County Parks. It's a large, natural river island about six miles in length and over a half mile in width in some spots.

The history goes back quite a ways with Pelican Island being named for the migratory white pelicans that frequently rest there during their long journeys. Ancient Indians camped along the banks nearest to Sioux Passage Park in an area considered favorable for hunting and fishing. It was believed that tribes from the Woodland Period inhabited the area as long ago as 100 A. D. and considering the rich Native American history made me think of Chief Michael. Much later, many explorers passed by these lands as they trekked westward up the Missouri River. In an odd coincidence, Greene's namesake made reference to camping in close proximity to this area in his Journal of Zebulon Pike.

Pelican Island was about as wild and isolated as you could get in St. Louis County so near to a heavily populated area. It was perfect for a rite of passage unique to the modern day tribe of Hazelwood Hawks. The idea was this. In order to be fully initiated into the tight knit clan known as the Hawk offensive line, rookie members had to spend the night alone, camping on Pelican Island. In most Julys like this one it was not an impossible task to reach the island. In the heat of summer, the water level would typically drop to where the Car of Commerce Chute was narrowed to a veritable trickle of maybe thirty yards at only two to three feet deep. Late in the day when the coast was clear of any rangers, the O-line would gather at the back end of the Park and make their way out on top of the rock jetty that jutted part way across the chute near the eastern bend of the river. Then, with provisions for the night in hand, held above their heads depending on the river's depth, they'd cross the water over to the island.

Since the Armadillo was the only rookie, he'd have to go it alone but his buddies stayed until well after dark to keep him company … and make it easier to elude any park personnel on their way out of Sioux Passage. It was against the law and certainly afoul of the coaches' rules but nevertheless the boys shared a few beers. It was flashlights only until 9:00 to avoid detection then everyone helped Billy start a fire to keep the bugs and critters away. As part of the ritual, the veterans regaled Billy with war stories about great Hawk victories past and other significant conquests of high school rivals and hot cheerleaders. It all helped to bring the Armadillo into the fold and cement the bond that would hopefully help them lead the way to another Hawk championship season.

All good things must come to an end and finally the boys had to make their way back and leave Billy to the task of proving his manhood. They cautioned him to clean up his mess in the morning. Everyone was so touchy about the environment these days there was no tolerance for any littering or disturbing of nature in any way. Last year's illicit campout had raised a few eyebrows and they didn't want to risk losing another tradition to over-zealous watch dogs. Billy couldn't help but concentrate on their fading voices and dimming flashlight beams as they made their way back across the water to the far bank. It was his last lifeline before a long night of solitude. He cracked another beer and fiddled with the fire to occupy his mind.

Billy was not only a big kid but strong as an ox too, especially for a high school junior. He had a thick chest and arms that helped him to bench press three hundred fifty pounds and tree trunk legs that made him look like he could squat a Volkswagen. Yet he was only seventeen years old and, if the truth be known, still a bit of a momma's boy. He didn't let on to his pals but he was really nervous about his man versus nature challenge. He had only been camping a few times in his life with his dad and under the tamest of circumstances. Pelican Island was the real deal. It was home to deer, muskrats, raccoon, snakes and who knew what else. He was stuck out in the middle of nowhere on an island that was technically off limits to people, certainly to overnight campers. There was no TV to occupy his mind, only a small battery powered radio. The Cardinal game was over and he wasn't much of a music fan so late night talk radio was his only companion. That's when he picked up on all the crazy talk about wolves, killers and the magical powers of the full moon. He looked over head and there it was illuminating the night sky, encircled by a haunting halo of ominous clouds.

The solitary moon surrounded by a tight circle of *friends* in an otherwise dark, clear, cloudless sky made him seem so far away from everything. There were no sounds of civilization; no voices, cars, trains or airplanes. The only symphony was composed of crickets, bull frogs, buzzing bugs, lapping water and the faint whisper of the wind through the trees. The clearing he occupied was surrounded by thick trees and vines that seemed to form a living wall. The flickering flames cast eerie shadows that performed a freakish war dance around him. He popped another beer to induce welcome sleep but still remained on edge. The news reports were unsettling so he flipped the radio off and entertained himself by grilling another hot dog on the end of a stick. After scarfing down that morsel, he toyed with the fire some more to maintain his sanity.

Another hour passed and sleep was nowhere in sight. To Billy's dismay, the fire was burning down and, as the flames dwindled, darkness advanced and the surrounding trees appeared to creep closer and closer, choking him with claustrophobia. He only had two choices. He could sleep or gather more fire wood. Billy chose the latter but failed to heed the advice of his peers who had told him to pick up more driftwood near the river rather than cutting down any trees and possibly incurring the wrath of Johnny Law. He took his hatchet and lopped off a few branches before felling some small saplings. This green wood didn't burn very well and started to shroud his campsite in smoke so he mustered the courage to venture out to collect some dead, dry wood by the river bank. Near the water's edge, his flashlight beam caught the eyes of a busy raccoon and the glowing reflection startled him as though he had seen a demon. He summoned enough resolve to gather some driftwood while staying well clear of the furry menace. On the way back to his campsite he heard something that was definitely larger than a raccoon. He froze in his tracks with his body completely still except for his right hand which waved the beam of light back and forth. Then his heart jumped into his throat as the light came to rest upon a very large animal. Thankfully for Billy it was only a deer doing a bit of night time foraging. Still it took several minutes for him to gather himself and start making his way back to the fire.

By this time, he was so rattled that his ears started to play tricks on him. As he walked, he could have sworn he heard footsteps coming from the darkness behind him but, when he stopped, there was nothing but the hum of crickets and the belching croaks of bellowing frogs. Billy probably thought that maybe he was losing it because he heard it again every time he started walking. He tried to ignore it and refused to look back any more and picked up the pace like a frightened child scurrying back to his bunk from the bathroom before the boogey man under the bed could grab him by the ankle. Enough was enough and, like any sane person, Billy must have seriously considered making his way off the island and heading back home. Yeah, that's the ticket … he'd get a few good hours of sleep then sneak back to the Park and his campsite before anyone was the wiser.

Then it must have struck him that he might be playing right into the hands of his pals. Yeah, maybe the guys had quietly returned to scare the ever living daylights out of him. That was it … that was probably the punctuation mark on this initiation rite. He got back to the fire just in time to add the dry wood and replenish the flames. As he sat down, he probably couldn't help but smile at the image of his line mates thinking they'd get the drop on him. Billy would show them. He'd remain awake and at attention and give them a good scare of their own. He bundled up some clothes and provisions inside his sleeping bag to make it appear he had bedded down for the night and then snuck a few feet outside the campsite's perimeter to wait for his buds. He'd let them gather around his tent before flying up behind them to scare the crap out of them. It's too bad that Billy didn't follow his first instinct and get off the island. It was the worst and last mistake the Armadillo ever made.

Wes was scheduled for duty at Sioux Passage that weekend. He was filling in for one of his guys who had put in for vacation. My normal responsibility was to shadow him wherever he was serving so, like a good sidekick, I offered to open up that day. I didn't really take notice but my first guests of the day were five hulking, high school football players who made a bee line for the back end of the park. I was too busy with my morning routine to know that they had made their way across the chute to Pelican Island. It wasn't long thereafter that I found out. Luckily, I had forwarded the phone at the ranger station to my cell number so I picked up their frantic call immediately. It was unusual to receive a call to the ranger station that early in the morning with so few guests in the park. Occasionally there'd be a real emergency involving an accident or injury but mostly the calls involved complaints, silly disputes between guests or panicked snake sightings. This one was unlike any other. The caller was so distraught and completely discombobulated that it took over a minute to calm him down to where I could make sense of his dire plea for help. I told them to stay put by the jetty and I'd meet them there pronto.

I heard enough to know that I was heading toward our fifth crime scene so I shot a call to Wes as I headed to the jetty. He said he would contact Sloan and the rest of the team and cautioned me not to touch anything. When I got down to the river bank I was met by five quivering towers of jelly. There was nothing imposing about them in spite of their size and muscular builds. The color was drained from their faces and they were visibly shaking. One boy was able to talk coherently but his speech was interrupted by a sudden stutter the shock had brought on. One thing was clear though ... their teammate had been killed on Pelican Island. I asked their spokesman, Pete, to lead me to the scene and instructed the other four to stay put and wait for Wes Woodson and the police to arrive. In order to keep my guide from wigging out on me, I tried to keep his mind off his fallen friend by offering distractions such as explaining why we had to be careful to preserve the crime scene.

I had been around enough crime scenes now to know how to keep a keen eye out for evidence. As we made our way through the woods to the campsite, I looked for tracks, blood trails or anything out of place that might help identify the killer. Unfortunately, there was nothing on the path we followed other than footprints from the five big lugs that preceded me. When we approached the clearing, I asked Pete to stay back behind me and cautiously stepped forward heeding Wes' warning. As my mind raced to take inventory, I clicked off all the familiar signs. The Armadillo's body lay prone, his face was a horrid death mask of frozen fright, there were no signs of a struggle and his throat was a bloody, gaping mess with flesh torn to shreds around a massive, jagged wound. Otherwise, the body appeared to be perfectly intact. How did such a big, strapping boy succumb without putting up any kind of struggle?

I stepped a bit closer taking care not to erase any tracks or footprints. Even with my untrained eye, it was easy to tell where the frightened footballers had trod near the corpse. I slowly surveyed the area seeking any differences from the previous crime scenes. There were clear paw prints surrounding the body. I would need help from Wes, Joe and Zeb later to ascertain that only hind prints were left in the dirt. The most obvious difference was something we had never encountered with any of the five other victims. There was a gigantic, bloody paw print stamped on the Armadillo's chest, soaked into his tee shirt as if the wolf intended to brand his victim. Then my eyes roamed toward and around the perimeter until they froze looking at a spot farthest from our entry path. There appeared to be another, much smaller clearing matted down just off the edge of the campsite. The leaves, grass and underbrush were freshly tamped down as if the killer had laid down to rest there only hours before. I took a wide route so as to not disturb anything and noticed as I approached the spot that there were another set of prints in the dirt. We were in luck because Pete and his friends had not adulterated this area. No wait, maybe I was wrong because there were some shoe prints near the matted area only they were leading away back into the woods where they disappeared with the ground cover that hid the soil below. I peered intensely and pivoted my head back and forth to try to determine if these prints matched any of the five boys' shoes. Just then, my concentration was shattered and I nearly jumped out of my socks as Wes' voice boomed from the distance, "Seth, where are you?"

I carefully made my way back to the path where Pete and I had entered the site, called out to Wes and waited for him and the rest of the crew to make their way. Wes smiled grimly and Sloan nodded approvingly as I reviewed my initial findings with them. The photographer snapped pictures of the bloody paw print and a forensic investigator swabbed it for DNA testing. Eventually, we made our way over to the matted area. With the extra eyes to help, we quickly determined that the shoe prints leading away from the clearing did not belong to any of the football players. The prints were large like theirs, at least a size twelve or thirteen, but the shoes were a different style. There were no heel prints. They appeared flat, smooth and uniform like maybe a sandal of some sort. Several people picked up on the biggest oddity but it took Michael Muraco to state the obvious. It was a conclusion Sloan despised but couldn't deny. The only tracks leading to the matted down area were made by a wolf. The tracks leading away were human. The only thing Sloan could do was to instruct the forensic experts to collect hair and other evidence from the area where someone or something had apparently bedded down for a while before escaping to the far side of the island.

The Hawks didn't repeat as champs that year. They couldn't quite recover from the devastating blow they had been dealt on Pelican Island. As times changed and memories faded they would recover and return to dynastic form again but another tradition bit the dust. This time it was not at the hands of pesky administrators or over bearing board members. It was imposed by the players, starting first with the five poor souls that witnessed the bloody aftermath of the moonlit madness that claimed their fallen comrade, the Armadillo. The story would be repeated over and over again in hushed tones until some wondered if it was reality or just another urban legend inspired by teenage imagination. The five surviving line mates knew though. Anyone who heard their eye witness testimony had no doubts about what happened on the island. It was something that would haunt them for the rest of their lives.

Sloan preferred to let people believe what had happened was only the stuff of legend. This time he tried his best to clamp down on public disclosure, at least until the forensics came back. He was worried that the werewolf rumors would gain momentum and lead to an unmanageable situation. He hoped the test results would somehow conclusively disprove what seemed hard to deny based on the crime scene. If nothing else, he wanted something solid on which to base a different, more reasonable theory. I could tell right away when he called us all in for the results that he was not pleased. "Gentlemen, I hate to say it but this case is getting more rather than less confusing. The latest results make it as clear as mud. First, the bloody paw print on the kid's chest contained a mixture of human and wolf DNA. They broke it down and kiss my butt if it isn't the same damn wolf and the same damn person that was at the Wilson scene." Michael and Zeb did not seem at all surprised like the rest of us. Sloan was clearly frustrated and at a loss for explanations but continued, "If that wasn't enough, there was more DNA evidence from the matted down area that revealed the same presence of both our wolf and killer. We still can't tell who it is but we know for sure that it's the same son of a gun."

Sloan was still completely skeptical but, as a trained professional, had to follow the evidence. "Okay Chief, the white boy is ready to have his mind expanded. I think it's time for you to try to explain what's going on here."

Michael spoke in measured tones, "What I'm about to tell you will be very hard, perhaps impossible for you to comprehend. The modern mind cannot grasp a concept that is so foreign. But in my culture, where the legends have been handed down from generation to generation back to a different time, a different world where the spirits dwelled side-by-side with the living, it is much easier to accept. It is a way of life that seems normal to us." Sloan made quick circles with his hand as if to say okay, okay, get on with it. "As a small child in Canada, I was raised by parents of a mixed culture; part French, part Indian. Both shared the same legend but it was best captured by the French term Loup Garou."

Michael had a way of telling a story that transported the imagination to another place and time. Although we were in a conference room on a bright, sunny day, his words made me feel like I was sitting outside by a campfire under a starry sky in the Great White North. There was something authentic in his voice and mood. "The word Loup means wolf and Garou refers to a man who turns into an animal. My father told me what his father and father's father passed along down from the ages. It was not just his way of scaring some sense into me to keep me in line. He spoke the truth as he was told, as I believe to this day. First, it is most important to know that the Loup Garou is not a werewolf; nothing like the Hollywood version. In the movies, when a man turns into a werewolf he becomes a beast. This is not so with Loup Garou. He is much more dangerous because the man takes on the physical characteristics of the wolf with great strength, prowess and ultra-keen senses but retains many human attributes … cunning, intelligence; the ability to reason and … most disturbingly, the propensity to perpetrate evil with malice."

Michael paused to let this sink in. We were glued to our seats like kids hearing a ghost story for the first time. "There are other ways in which Loup Garou is as much human as animal. Unfortunately, they possess many of our flaws. They typically know their victims personally and attack with some purpose in mind, a grudge or vendetta … perhaps jealousy over a love turned sour. They kill for a reason and intend to inflict pain, sorrow and terror."

I blurted, "What about the full moon?"

Michael mused, "Yes, like with the imaginary werewolf, there is a common connection to the way the moon's power holds sway over the Loup Garou. But it is not the same. Loup Garou can also change at other times without the moon's command." Michael paused to reflect on the past, "I remember my father's words well. He told me that Loup Garou is a magnificent creature to behold and should be held in awe. Father also gravely cautioned me to respect and fear the Loup Garou. You see they are not like mythical werewolves that lose their human identities as if in a temporary trance. They maintain their full awareness as human beings while gaining an animal's enhanced powers and senses. Because of that, he warned, they are extremely difficult to destroy."

What Michael said closely fit with our situation so much so that Sloan didn't offer any of his characteristic objections. Michael laid out the parallels in case any of us had missed the connections. "Loup Garou can explain why it seems we have a man and beast working in tandem. It also makes sense that we have not been able to apprehend it. Now it does not seem so odd that it was able to navigate around our traps or that the wolf's tracks appeared to evaporate into thin air, does it? Also, Loup Garou does not eat the victims. He kills for a purpose but not hunger."

Sloan lurched into regaining a modicum of control, "There are still some things that cannot be explained by your Loup Garou. Where did he come from and why is he here? Why did he carve the pentagram? What reason would he have for killing all these disparate people … an old derelict, a lab geek, a farmer and three, innocent teenage kids? Something still doesn't add up."

Michael offered a cunning, self-assured smile, "You raise some good questions my friend but I can tell that you are at least considering all the possibilities."

Sloan huffed, "Yeah, yeah … I'll tell the boys to list your pal, Lew Carew, as a person of interest." Sloan's off-the-cuff, sarcastic play on words had a ring to it that tickled him in some perverse way. He was overhead using this moniker more than once to express his frustration and disbelief but only within a tight circle of people involved in the case. Sloan would never utter anything publicly that might feed the werewolf frenzy further.

CHAPTER 7

STURGEON MOON

F LANAGAN AND HIS MEDIA MATES were operating in high gear. The strange, otherwise unexplainable and ample evidence that the police were unable to contain along with the clear lunar connection provided great fodder for the modern werewolf tale they were weaving. The idea that a preponderance of *responsible* journalists and a good portion of the viewing public were actually buying into the possibility that a serial werewolf was on the prowl in greater St. Louis was ludicrous ... or was it? Lots of people still believe in Sasquatch, yeti and the Loch Ness Monster and those legends aren't supported by a fraction of the hard evidence that pointed to the werewolf of St. Louis. In any case, the police reports and public support gave literary license to Flip Flanagan and his colleagues and they ran with it. Opportunistic business folks didn't miss a beat either. A rather tasteless cottage industry sprang up with souvenirs and keepsakes aplenty to satisfy the most morbid curiosities. It was August so they were already pushing the collectible of the month, little sturgeon moons. It commemorated the Algonquin practice of fishing for these river monsters late at night during the summer solstice.

As much as I admired and was fascinated by Michael Muraco, I had been closer to Sloan's camp up until the death of the Armadillo. I'm not as much of a skeptic as the detective but was certainly much more of a realist than a spiritualist like the Chief. But it was hard to deny what I had seen with my own eyes. Some of the conclusions we reached were remarkable but the forensic evidence did nothing to dispel them. I couldn't help it. I found myself wondering if it was somehow possible. Myths and legends like the Loup Garou were unacceptable in my world but I couldn't resist the urge to question if there wasn't some scientific explanation behind it all. Could there be a genetic mutant lurking about with amazing transformative powers? Could it be some kind of chameleon effect to the nth degree … the ability to realign gene sequences with DNA nucleotide pairs shifting back and forth to pull off an incredible metamorphosis … caterpillars on steroids … a living transformational form … a missing link? One thing was clear from the results we had seen. The Loup Garou was no harmless butterfly.

I tried to put this out of my mind and concentrate on my work and the start of the new semester. My two summer courses were nearly over and I was facing a normal, heavier load for the fall. I'd miss my classes with Greene and Mosely for several reasons but most importantly because I'd no longer be seeing Faith on a weekly basis, at least not at Wash U. I'd still see Greene as part of

Sloan's team and, thankfully, I had classes near Dr. Mosely that would give me a chance to stay in touch with him. Yes, things were changing and getting very busy with my internship and the way the investigation was heating up but my mind kept drifting back to the puzzling werewolf conundrum. I needed a confidante and Greene was a more likely candidate since his scientific chops were more in tune with my understanding of the world ... but he was too aloof and unapproachable for me to bear my soul to him. Mosely was quirky and seemed to come out of left field more often than not but there was something reassuring about him. He always seemed to have my best interests at heart and never came across as judgmental or vindictive regardless of our differences. With that in mind, I decided to share my burden with him.

"Hey Doc, have you got a few minutes?"

"Sure Seth my boy, what's on your mind?"

I tried to shed my reluctance and embarrassment, "You know I'm still part of the murder investigation." Mosely nodded and listened intently. "I don't know quite how to say this but I'm really troubled by the last murder."

He encouraged me with his understanding, sympathetic eyes, "Yes, go on Seth."

I must have sounded apologetic, "I'm a realist; really I am. I'm not into myths, legends, wives' tales or the boogey man." He gave me a reassuring nod to help me along. "Shoot, why am I beating around the bush? Doc, I never thought I'd utter these words. I'm starting to wonder if there isn't something to this werewolf stuff." He didn't say anything but it wasn't necessary. The look on his face spoke volumes. "I know; I know ... it sounds crazy but all the evidence is pointing that way. I just wanted to bounce this off you and see if there's something I'm missing. Could there be a scientific explanation for something so bizarre?"

Good old Doc Mosely was true to form. He didn't hesitate or equivocate in the least but instead dispatched the notion like the morning's garbage, "Gawd, blimey ... Don't be a dill my boy!"

I shook my head, "What did you say?"

"I think you're a chop short of a barbie, bloke."

Obviously I had touched a nerve and sent him into an Aussie frenzy, "Doc, I'm still not following you."

He exhaled loudly, "If you listen to these illywackers in the media, they'll make an arse out of you." He looked skyward, "Hughie, please send down some understanding to my poor cobber." All I could do is shrug and lift my palms skyward. He took a minute to catch his breath and composure, "Seth, this isn't like you. You know better than to embrace such rubbish. Do you remember when we talked about the meaning of science? We both agreed on the basic principles. This is not science. It's the worst kind of paranoia."

"I hear you, Doc. But what about the evidence; what about the DNA? Could this be the result of an evolutionary, one-in-a-zillion genetic mishap that produced a freak-of-nature misanthropic monster?"

Mosely shook his head while extending his lower lip to try to shame some sense into me. "Listen to yourself, Seth. Am I really hearing this from your mouth?"

"Doc, I know it sounds absolutely crazy but, for the life of me, I can't come up with a better explanation. It's not just me. A lot of people, serious people are wondering the same thing."

The professor took on the patient, understanding air of a father figure once again, "I admit this is quite confusing. But it goes back to what we discussed before. A lot depends on your world view, where you're coming from in the first place." I started to feel more at ease. "One view is that of the evolutionist. In that belief system, it's taken on faith that this world came into being out of nothing more than a big bang. No one can say what existed before that or caused that big bang … only that it couldn't have been God. From there random chance has taken us on a long, mysterious sojourn to arrive at where we are today. No one knows quite how but we're afforded billions of years to make statistical impossibilities seem more than reasonable … settled science as they say. Evolution helps us to suspend our common sense in interpreting everyday observations all around us. In that world, who's to say that random chance might not have produced the man-monster that's wreaking havoc upon us?"

I waited patiently for the inevitable other side of the coin. "My view is a different one … one that starts with the existence of God the creator. Things didn't come about by chance but rather are the direct result of God's providence and thoughtful, loving, omniscient design. Yes, since we brought the curse of sin upon ourselves and the whole creation it's a different world but it still bears the marks of the perfection and goodness God intended. The universe and our earth are descending into disorder and chaos but there is still clear evidence of the orderliness of God's handiwork. Mutations and mishaps have occurred since the fall into sin but they have never produced different or higher life forms. When genetic material, a building block of information is destroyed or is missing it always results in degradation and devolution not progress. We can see defects and even extinction occurring but never new life forms, never a higher order coming from chaos. I can't offer you a better explanation for your *werewolf* either but I do know one thing. God did not create a world where one kind turns into another. There may be wolf DNA commingled with human DNA in blood and hair samples but that simply means this … there is a wolf and a man somehow involved in these killings, not a wolf-man."

Evolutionary theory was hard for me to discount. It was part of my DNA so to speak. I had never known it as anything other than accepted fact, not only in school but also in our church. It wasn't really questioned in our church. I could think of a lot of reasons why it didn't jibe with many of the other beliefs we held as Christians but we all kind of went with the flow. Almighty science had trumped religion and we had no choice but to embrace some rather confounding logic if the two were to coexist. Thus, no one challenged the notion that God was omniscient and omnipotent but somehow couldn't have created the world and man without the aid of a process called evolution. And, of all things, God elected to use a horribly bloody, violent and cruel method to bring about the human race. Did killing, death and sin exist before man ... an imperfect world ... or did man fall into sin and corrupt God's perfect creation? It has to be one or the other ... you can't have it both ways. Furthermore, it never occurred to us that God had apparently been kidding about all that stuff in Genesis but somehow that didn't undermine what the Bible had to say about the other, more fantastic things it taught that we took on faith and held dear such as Jesus' resurrection from the dead, eternal life after death and our salvation. It's just the way things were. And in any case, thinking about such imponderables might give you a terrific headache. It was a lot easier to go along with what everyone else assured was accepted fact no matter how many inconsistencies this created.

In the case of the St. Louis wolf-man, I didn't have the option of letting my brain take a vacation from reality. I had to face up to the fact that this was not going to go away no matter how much I tried to ignore it. So, in spite of my upbringing to the contrary, I forced myself to try to see things from Dr. Mosely's perspective for a bit. If you stripped away all of my preconceived notions about evolution and focused solely on the facts rather than conclusions, it did make a lot of sense. Wasn't it more reasonable to think, as Mosely had proposed, that both man and beast were involved in the killings? "Doc, I guess you're right about the DNA. If we have human and lupine blood at the scene, any reasonable person would conclude that there were both a man and a wolf present."

Then Mosely surprised me by playing devil's advocate. "That still leaves us with a lot of strange mysteries, doesn't it?"

I was perplexed, "What do you mean?"

This crazy old man was hitting on all cylinders. Once I got past his religious beliefs and unorthodox view of origins, I couldn't argue with his down to earth conclusions. He was absolutely right. It was much more reasonable to accept the obvious, that a man and wolf were involved, even though the Loup Garou story seemed to fit hand-in-glove with the curious, peculiar circumstances of the case. It made me wonder if we had the right chemistry on Sloan's investigative team. We were slanted in two directions; Sloan's ultra-skeptical, close-minded approach and the Chief's mystical imaginations. The slopes were so steep that there didn't seem to be a chance for anything to settle in the middle. The notion crept into my mind that perhaps we needed someone like Dr. Mosely to stir the pot and provide another, more common sense approach. I left that thought to percolate and didn't mention anything to the professor. Anyway, he was ready to move onto a more pleasant, casual topic. "How are things coming along with your pretty, little, fair dinkum?"

If we hadn't developed kind of a father-son friendship, one could have taken my expression as disrespectful but I was really just mugging for effect, "What's gotten into you today Doc? Was it something I said about evolution that threw you for a loop?

Normally, you have pretty good command of the English language but apparently I've set you back ... all the way to Canberra."

He laughed, "Sorry lad, I meant to ask you about your new Shelia." I made another face. "Oops, there I go again. How are you and Miss Harper getting along?"

"You tell me, Doc. I mean it seems like you know more than me."

He smiled knowing that I was onto his meddlesome match making, "Don't be cross now Seth. I'm only trying to give you a boost."

"I know that Doc. I think we're getting along just fine. I really like her. And you were right about Greene."

He gave me a good tug on my shoulders, "Let that be a reminder to you. You should always listen to the doctor."

His gentle prodding gave me the impetus I needed to get off my duff and reach out to my fair Sheila. I grabbed my phone in a rush of enthusiastic optimism, "Hey Faith, what's going on?"

"Oh, not much ... I'm busy with school and all ... like usual. How are things with you?"

I cut to the chase, "Oh, they're pretty good. Hey, I've been thinking. With the end of the summer session, I'm really going to miss our time together in class and our regular jaunts to our favorite hangouts around campus. But, you know, just because I'm at Wash U and you're at Lindenwood doesn't mean that we can't keep this hallowed tradition alive. We just might have to spend a little more time and gas money but we can do it. What do you say Faith? How about us making it a regular date every Thursday afternoon alternating down here and in St. Charles? And what do you think about kicking things off today?"

There was an uncomfortable pause, "Seth, I love the idea but I can't make it today." I immediately assumed the worst and was ready to drop the ill-conceived plan altogether. Faith rescued it, "I'm really sorry about today. I wish I could change my plans. But I do love the idea. Let's start next week at Hannigan's."

I was so happy with her response that I didn't bother to dig into what she had planned that day. It was a good thing because it would really have put her on the spot. The last thing she would have wanted to tell me is that Dr. Greene was back in the picture, at least temporarily. As Mosely had warned me, Greene's intentions were far from altruistic. In spite of Faith's proclamation that they should just be friends, Zeb Greene held out for something more. She had rebuffed him gently on several occasions but he was patient and persistent. Rather than giving up, he tried a new tactic to play upon her sympathies. He knew faithful Faith would not be able to turn down a friend in need.

In hatching his scheme, Greene stooped so low as to shamelessly use his mother in cornering Faith. She was hosting a formal reception for the Philosophy Department and Zeb was expected to attend. He told Faith a pitiful tale of how he had disappointed his mother by failing to develop a close relationship with a prospective soul mate in accordance with her more aggressive timetable. In a play for pity, he poured it on thick about how he had been unable to find the right girl … his job and work outside of school consumed his time, passion and interest. Although he wasn't ready for anything so serious, the pressure he felt from his mother was stressing him out to the point where he dreaded going to the reception unescorted. What he needed was a female companion … an understanding friend … who could help him get through the night by pulling off a bit of an innocent charade. All kinds of warning signs must have popped up in Faith's head but how could she deny him? After he had been so nice in helping her to feel welcome and fit in at Wash U, how could she not return the favor in this one small way? I could imagine Faith putting aside her reservations by telling herself that she would make it clear that this was nothing more than a favor among friends.

The satisfaction of helping a pal in a tight pinch waned almost instantly as Faith ran headlong into reality. She was incredibly out of place at the stuffy reception. Faith was, by far, the youngest person in attendance and philosophically a square peg in a round hole. Although it was mostly small talk and chit chat, the tone of conversation surely made her feel uncomfortable. It was foreign to her and in some instances almost hostile with an undercurrent of anti-Christian secular sentiment. Faith was like a peasant among the elites, a commoner among the royals. Gloria Greene, her royal majesty of the ball, was the most arrogant, self-absorbed one of all. It was as if she saw right through Zeb's pretense and had no qualms about unleashing her chastisement upon him in front of Faith who had to be as uncomfortable as Zeb was embarrassed. It turned rather ugly between Zeb and his mother and made for a short evening. He apologized profusely but the damage was done.

The next week at Hannigan's I had the presence of mind to casually inquire about the prior week's scheduling conflict. Faith shrugged it off and stretched the truth a bit by saying it was just a school thing. In her mind, it was not worth the risk of spilling the beans. She was certainly attuned to the envy and insecurity I had exhibited when I thought she and Dr. Greene were romantically involved and must have wanted to spare me from reopening those old wounds. Plus, she knew there was absolutely nothing between her and Greene, no reason to make any mention of it. No, she kept it to herself and buried her last, unfortunate social encounter with Greene deep down where it belonged. Unfortunately, he was like a zombie or cursed mummy that the tomb could not hold.

Greene would not take no for an answer. Every time Faith rejected his advances, he would wait a bit and return with some new excuse for a *friendly* rendezvous. It was not her nature to be impolite but Faith had to become uncharacteristically stern in her refusals. It must have bothered her to be harsh to anyone but he gave her little choice. Since her classes at Wash U were over, she didn't have to face him once a week any more. She stone walled him but when persistence failed him, Greene went back to the drawing board and dialed up dear old mom again. Greene begged and pleaded with his mother to apologize for her rude, obnoxious behavior at the reception. She grudgingly agreed to appease her baby boy who was on the verge of a tantrum. Of course, Faith really didn't want any part of the wicked, old witch again but how could she turn Greene down under the circumstances? As a Christian, she couldn't deny someone the chance to seek forgiveness and a peaceful resolution.

The setting was less imposing this time around in a comfortable booth at a trendy coffee house near campus but the *queen* was no less regal. Even though she was trying her best to be cordial, there was something about her *imperial majesty* that set her apart from the rest of us mere mortals. She did apologize and tried to explain that the pressure of the big evening had gotten to her. Unlike that night, she went overboard in playing the part of the doting mother and fawned over Zeb in such an exaggerated fashion that it had the opposite effect on Faith from the one intended. It was kind of creepy seeing someone so staid and proper babying a grown man that way. Things were so syrupy sweet between the formerly domineering mother and petulant child that Faith had the urge to shower when she returned home. Something about their farce made her skin crawl.

The more Faith reflected upon her two encounters with Chairwoman Greene, the more she developed an odd notion. As she would later recount to me, she didn't know why but Faith had the strangest feeling that Gloria Greene saw her as a rival. Was it because, in spite of her academic power and influence, she couldn't compete with Faith's youth and beauty? Had she somehow picked up on Faith's Christian background and loathed her traditional belief system as totally inappropriate for her little boy? Did she despise Faith's humble background and inferior education at *lowly* Lindenwood? All of those things would have made sense but Faith said she couldn't shake the feeling … call it women's intuition … that Gloria saw her as competing for the affections of her precious little boy. She tried to shrug it off but perhaps it was normal for a mother to feel that way about her son's love interest.

That was a sobering thought … love interest. She was anything but that no matter what Zeb Greene felt. Love is a two-way street and Faith was nothing but a dead end. She just waited for her rigorous rebuffs to sink in and have the desired effect. Faith could only hope to part as friends and let things fade into oblivion but Zeb could not be deterred with sober yet sympathetic and civil refusals. Even a cold shoulder was not enough. It seemed to make him try harder. Eventually, Faith had to figuratively douse him with cold water with a necessarily harsh, pointed brush-off that would leave no lingering doubts. Although I was not aware at the time, she flatly instructed him not to contact her any more under any circumstances. It must have been miserable for a caring person like Faith but the alternative had become unbearable. It was the only thing she could do given how our feelings for one another were blossoming. Still she kept the entire episode from me because she knew that I was working closely with Dr. Greene on the investigative team and would cross paths often at school given my major and didn't want to be a disruptive influence. I couldn't argue if she felt it was better to leave well enough alone now that he had presumably gotten the message and halted his unwanted advances. I guess I was pretty dense because on the rare occasions when we crossed paths with Greene at Hannigan's or elsewhere, I never noticed how she tensed up when he was around.

I was too caught up in the magic when I was with Faith to be bothered by much of anything. We started spending more time together after classes and on weekends. I didn't mind that Faith Harper was giving my park internship, studies and police work a run for their money in competing for my time and attention. The love bug had bitten me hard. For the first time in my life, I had someone I considered a steady girl. It wasn't so bad … in fact, it was absolutely wonderful. I had never been happier. I was so caught up in my feelings for Faith that I almost considered calling Walt and Gretchen to share the good news. Luckily I stopped short since I knew they'd pepper me with endless questions I preferred to avoid. That would come in time, I figured, because this was the real deal. But, for the time being, I just wanted to enjoy the ride without adding unnecessary complications. Love is a funny thing. We had only known each other for a few months but somehow I knew she was the one. That's why I didn't object when she invited me to attend one of Mosely's lectures at her church. I even agreed to attend their Sunday worship service beforehand. I was a whipped puppy and enjoyed every minute of it.

I was attracted to Faith by more than my amorous longings. I'm not a wimp, mind you, but I really enjoyed her companionship even in those rare moments when I wasn't fixated by her comely form. Yes, she was smoking hot but I was driven by more than hormones. There was something deeper to our relationship. It's hard to explain but I stopped having nightmares about the killings and the bodies I had discovered. When something about the investigation was troubling me, she could make it all go away … help me to make some sense out of it. It was that closeness that allowed me to put away my apprehensions about going to church with all of those *crazy* evangelicals. Faith had proven to be normal so maybe they weren't all a bunch of wild eyed lunatics like I had envisioned.

I was at ease entering her church that Sunday morning walking hand in hand but there was still a period of adjustment. Things seemed so much more formal than at my home church. The dress code was not nearly as casual and the liturgy seemed a little regimented to me. I had to pay close attention to the order of service in the hymnal to keep up. The old organ literally provided a blast from the past. There were no guitars, drums, contemporary music or video screens. Everything seemed to focus on the pastor and his message. On the positive side, the members were genuinely friendly and made me feel right at home. I joked to Faith that I was pleasantly surprised to find that they weren't dressed up in Puritan garb with blank, glassy eyes while reciting Gregorian chants in unison.

The pastor's sermon, the centerpiece of the service, was unlike anything I had ever heard before. First of all, he must have quoted the Bible at least a dozen times … something rare back home. In our congregation in Portland we'd get snippets that were mostly disconnected … sound bites that were invariably amplified to encourage us to tackle society's ills from poverty, famine and homelessness to all manner of injustice within our own shores to distant lands around the globe. Jesus was pictured not so much a savior as a great teacher, philosopher and example. WWJD was a popular slogan used to motivate us and guide our behavior. It was almost always about what we needed to do rather than what

Jesus had done for us. Faith's pastor, Pastor Moehlen, took what to me was a radically different approach. He talked about sin … our sin … and the consequences of sin, death and hell. In my church, hell was mentioned so infrequently that we assumed it didn't really exist.

Pastor Moehlen not only talked about sin but got very specific to the point that I felt uneasy. It seemed he was talking directly to me. He didn't whitewash it either … if you looked at a woman and lusted you were guilty of adultery … if you got angry at someone and felt like punching them in the face you were guilty of murder. But before I could despair under his legalistic barrage, I found myself uplifted. He didn't talk about what we should do or could do to make up for all of our sins. In fact, he said the opposite … that we were dead in our trespasses and sins and incapable of helping ourselves out of such a fix. Then he pointed to Jesus in a way that I had never seen him. Pastor Moehlen laid out God's plan of salvation in a very practical, businesslike manner showing how Jesus paid the price for all of our sins and credited his righteousness to our account. After having my guilt laid directly upon my shoulders in such a convincing fashion, I was incredibly relieved to hear what God had done to get me out of such a monumental mess with its horrific consequences. He even explained why God would do such a seemingly crazy, completely backward thing in punishing his perfect, innocent son to show mercy to a bunch of miserable, undeserving lowlifes like us. For the first time, I understood the true meaning of agape love.

The other thing about Pastor Moehlen's message that blew me away was the type of Bible references he used. Instead of snippets he related entire stories. In my church we rarely heard such tales because they were considered myths or fables used only to convey a higher spiritual meaning. Of course, that higher meaning almost always turned out to be what Pastor Moehlen might deem the social gospel. Given my background, I vaguely knew about the prophet Elijah but had never heard the story of his encounter with the prophets of Baal. Pastor Moehlen weaved the story masterfully into what he referred to as his law and gospel message. According to his sermon, Elijah had run afoul of King Ahab and his wicked Queen Jezebel who had a reputation for cutting off the heads of God's prophets. Elijah had the nerve, under God's inspiration, to challenge the prophets of the false god, Baal, to a showdown on Mount Carmel. He was outnumbered four hundred fifty-to-one … nine hundred fifty-to-one counting Jezebel's prophets of the grove but still had the confidence and faith to call out the people of Israel to witness the spectacle.

Here's the way it went down. The contest would involve two animal sacrifices, Elijah's and that of the false prophets. They'd both call on their gods to show his power and might by sending fire from heaven to burn the offerings. Baal's boys had first crack at it and failed miserably in spite of all kinds of chanting, wailing and slashing of their own flesh. Elijah went so far as to mock them … basically Old Testament trash talk. After their miserable, shameful failure, he upped the ante by dousing his sacrifice with barrels and barrels of water, not once or twice but three times. Then the one, true God came through for Elijah and consumed the dead animal, wood and even the stone alter with intense, unquenchable fire. After the magnificent triumph, Elijah and the people slew all of the prophets of Baal. But wait, that was only the beginning. Evil Queen Jezebel put out a contract on Elijah and his faith dried up to a wisp of dust. He ran for the hills and hid in a cave. As Pastor Moehlen explained it, in spite of the mighty miracle God had performed through Elijah, he was powerless when left to his own devices. But God didn't let it end there.

He came to the rescue again, this time in a still small voice and encouraged Elijah through his word, assuring him that he was not alone ... that there were still seven thousand faithful believers in Israel. The most amazing thing to me was the way that Pastor Moehlen relayed the story not as some fable but the absolute truth with a message from God about his love, promises, power and faithfulness.

After the service, we milled about for a while waiting for the Bible class to begin. The sermon had been a real eye opener and I felt pretty fired up. I expected Faith and the other members to be similarly charged and waited for the evangelical onslaught but, like Faith, everyone was very laid back. I asked Faith about it, "I'm surprised that no one has tried to *convert* me." She just laughed and let my remark go. I still needed to satisfy my curiosity, "No, I'm being serious. I've never known anyone more committed to their faith than you but I've never seen you give someone the hard sell. How can this be for someone who firmly believes ... what was that passage you brought up ... about people who believe and are baptized are going to heaven but those that don't believe are bound for hell?"

She only offered a clarification, "That's Mark 16:16."

I pressed on, "But if you believe that, how can you be so casual in, as you call it, sharing the good news? If it's a matter of eternal life and death, shouldn't you pound it into people that they're in danger of hell fire?"

Faith remained patient and calm, "You're right Seth that eternal life, heaven and hell hang in the balance. And God instructs us to share the good news about his plan of salvation. But that's as far as it goes. We can't save anyone by our own power of persuasion and certainly not through intimidation or coercion. People can only believe in Christ by the power of the Holy Ghost. Our job is to share the word and then leave it up to God to perform the miracle of creating faith in a human heart. We don't have any power apart from God. The power is in the word of God. And you can't scare people into believing. Yes, we need to speak the truth about sin and its consequences … death and hell. That's especially true today where so many people deny God's moral law and their own sin. But the law can't save anyone. If that were the case, we could save ourselves by keeping the law perfectly. Since that's impossible, we need to tell people that God has provided the only solution, Jesus Christ."

I didn't get a chance to ask follow up questions because Dr. Mosely was starting his presentation. He proved to be just as unpredictable as Pastor Moehlen and, to me, his message was similarly astonishing. It was fascinating to see him operate with the fetters of the educational establishment unloosed. His message was unabashed and clear. He started by questioning the foundations of the environmentalists. Who caused the Big Bang to occur? Where are the millions of transitional fossils that should be buried in the Precambrian and Cambrian layers of sediment? Who programmed our DNA which is millions of times more dense and complex than our most sophisticated computer programs? Where did we get the laws of logic and morality if we evolved by chance from animals? As he went on, the questions he posed seemed natural, logical and in keeping with common sense. The setting was so different. People asked questions and challenged things that they didn't understand but were courteous and thoughtful. There was no name calling, no outright rejection on the basis of settled science. Viewing evidence in light of the literal six-day creation account of Genesis seemed perfectly normal.

Next Mosely launched into a discussion of a young earth. He referred to Mount St. Helens again but this time had some incredible pictures he displayed on a screen. He made one point that we hadn't covered before. The professor took another swipe at uniformitarianism by showing how catastrophic geologic events have been observed to demonstrate rapid erosion like the canyon formed by Mount St. Helens volcanic flows that deposited incredible amounts of materials at the base and two years later were carved out by mud flows resulting from another minor eruption. From there it was a hop, skip and a jump to go from that relatively small scale to show how a global flood could cut the Grand Canyon. He went on to discuss other evidence of the great flood … universal examples of the rapid burial of plants and animals, rapid formation of the earth's strata with no evidence of erosion between them, fossilized sea creatures deposited high above sea level and rapidly deposited sediments transported over long distances. The latter included the Grand Canyon but also many other examples worldwide.

Doctor Mosely didn't shy away from difficult topics like Noah's Ark which, for secularists and non-evangelical Christians like me, often proved to be the most troublesome and controversial. He used history this time to rattle off an amazing assortment of flood traditions from just about every culture imaginable … from the Polynesian Islands to China, Africa and South America. There was a stunning consistency to the legends that had been handed down from generation to generation paralleling the story of Noah in many ways. One that caught my ear and made me think of Michael Muraco involved the Native American tradition which was very similar to the Chinese tradition which, according to Mosely, made sense because Native Americans are thought to be of Mongolian or Asiatic origin. Their story is one of a man who floated his family on a raft of logs while picking up swimming animals of every kind until he had two of each. After many days, the waters receded and he landed on a high mountain and his family provided the rescued remnant from which the world was repopulated. There are some minor variations from tribe to tribe but all-in-all there is great consistency across the Native American peoples.

As if we weren't far enough out on the proverbial limb, Dr. Mosely finished by taking things to a whole new level. Instead of sweeping what many people believed were the most far-fetched tales of the Bible under the rug, the professor brought them out front and center not to debunk them but actually to demonstrate the harmony of scripture with the hard sciences. Even though he had told me several times that it all depends on your frame of reference, I had a tough time swallowing what he served up next. Two stories in particular seemed like pure fantasy to me. First, he used a biological and zoological approach to validate the saga of Jonah to propose he was actually swallowed up, transported in the belly of a great fish and then spat out on the shores of ancient Assyria to reluctantly deliver God's message of forgiveness and salvation to the dreaded enemies he and the people of Israel loathed and feared.

Although I was not on my home turf, I couldn't help but ask a probing question, "Dr. Mosely, how could it be possible for a man to fit through the narrow throat of a whale?"

He could have made an example out of me with ridicule but responded in his typically patient, understanding fashion, "I guess the first thing to clear up is whether it was a whale or a great fish. In spite of the KJV translation, if you go to the original Hebrew, dag means fish and the New Testament Greek word ketos refers to a monster rather than a whale. Nevertheless, you are correct that most species of whales have an esophagus that is too small to accommodate a whole man. However there is at least one type known as the mysticete whales that could get the job done. More specifically, the Megaptera Medosa or humpbacked whale family has no teeth and swallows its food whole. The largest variety known as the Balaenoptera Musculus or more commonly the sulfur bottom whale has been measured at ninety-five feet and six inches. This largest recorded specimen was caught off the west coast of North America by the crew of the Norwegian whaler N. T. Nielson Alonso some years before it was sunk by a German U-boat in 1943. The air storage chamber in the whale's massive head measured fourteen feet long by seven feet wide by seven feet across. These whales have been known to take objects too big to swallow and thrust them up into the air chamber. There are recorded cases of such whales swimming toward land into shallow water and ejecting the *passenger*."

He continued, "In any case, let's suppose that, as the original language suggests, God prepared a great fish or sea monster to transport Jonah. The question we have to ask is whether there is such a beast alive today that might fit the bill. The most likely candidate by all accounts is the Rhinodon Typicus sometimes called the whale-shark. This giant shark which can reach seventy feet in length has no teeth and eats its food whole like a whale. It is a fish rather than a mammal and has a capacious maw that can easily swallow a man whole. While many reports have been confirmed the most compelling is the story of the English sailor who was swallowed by a Rhinodon in the English Channel in 1926 and recovered by his mates forty-eight hours later. When they killed the great fish and cut it open, he was unconscious but alive. He survived to become billed as the Twentieth Century Jonah by the London Museum where he was put on exhibit for a shilling admittance."

"Was Rhinodon the great fish that God prepared? I don't know for sure but we see that it can and does happen. What is most important is that we trust the veracity of scripture. Christ himself made reference to Jonah in confronting the Pharisees who demanded a sign from him … 'But he answered and said unto them, an evil and adulterous generation seeks after a sign; and there shall no sign be given to it, but the sign of the prophet Jonas: For as Jonas was three days and three nights in the whale's [that is ketos or sea monster's] belly; so shall the Son of man be three days and three nights in the heart of the earth. The men of Nineveh shall rise in judgment with this generation, and shall condemn it: because they repented at the preaching of Jonas; and, behold, a greater than Jonas is here.' (Matthew 12:39-41). If we cannot trust our Lord and Savior Jesus Christ in this matter, our faith is foundationless."

He finished with the use of physics and astronomy to demonstrate how God actually slowed the rotation of the earth to produce Joshua's long day. This time I did not give into curiosity but listened intently as he dug into the details on this topic too. First he established the historicity of the day by chronicling the lead-up to the great battle on the plains of Beth-horon. I learned how the great statesman, Adoni-zedec, formed an Old Testament *League of Nations* among the Hittites, Amorites, Canaanites, Jebusites, Perizzites and Hivites to stop the advance of the Israelites into the Promised Land after their conquest of Jericho. When Adoni-zedec attempted to offer up the Hivites as a sacrificial lamb to buy time for the rest of the alliance, it backfired when they appealed to Joshua and formed an alliance of their own. Dr. Mosely seemed more intent on establishing the significance of this great, world-changing battle than anything else.

Then he took a matter-of-fact approach in demonstrating, once again, the inerrancy of the Bible. I had a tough time following the fascinating facts he laid out so meticulously. As with the flood, there were traditions abounding in many cultures about the long day that he shared. He then recounted how astronomers have been able to pinpoint the exact date and time of the battle by an unmistakable marker left in Joshua's inspired account. When Joshua appealed to God for help, the sun was directly above Gibeon and the moon was setting in the valley of Ajalon directly in between the canyon walls just above the edge of the horizon. Using calculations of longitude, latitude and altitude and ancient astrological charts, the date was fixed as the twenty-first day of the fourth month, Tammuz, of the Hebrew calendar. By our calendar this would be July twenty-second. According to ciphering of the ancient astrological records it was a Tuesday. On this day God slowed the earth's rotation to extend the battle and assisted Joshua in claiming a resounding victory that changed earth's history forever.

Dr. Mosely then shared an account from one of the early *creationists*, Dr. Harry Rimmer, who explained how astronomers have been able to calculate that our modern calendar is missing a day. Rimmer liked to regale his readers with the discourse of Professor C. A. Totten of Yale who wrote in 1890 about a gentleman's wager between him and a fellow professor who was an accomplished astronomer. The point of contention was whether astronomy validated or disproved the inerrancy of the Bible. The skeptical astronomer cheerfully announced to Totten after painstaking calculations that the Bible was in error because only twenty-three hours and twenty minutes had been lost from our modern calendar. He declared that the Bible could not be the word of God if it contained an error of forty minutes. Totten got the last laugh though. He pointed out that the original text of Joshua said the lost time was "about" the space of a whole day. Totten then referred his colleague to Isaiah 38 where God rescued King Hezekiah from a deadly sickness and answered his prayer by promising to add fifteen more years of life. To confirm his promise, God told the King to look at the sun dial of Ahaz where he would make the shadow go back ten degrees. Ten degrees on a sundial is equal to forty minutes on the face of the clock! Upon hearing this, the astonished astronomer was moved to believe in God and the inerrancy of his word.

Mosely was so matter of fact in speaking these things he made the miracles seem almost passé. He declared nonchalantly, "So often we try to make God too small. He created the universe and everything in it just by speaking the word. Of course he can slow the earth's rotation. Certainly he can preserve a man in the belly of a great fish for three days. And most importantly, he can undoubtedly preserve the truth in written form through his prophets and servants." I was flabbergasted but again had to agree it made logical sense if you believed in an omnipotent God. To Dr. Mosely the spiritual blessings imparted by the love and grace of God were much more astounding than the miraculous physical feats he performed.

It was all so difficult to absorb because, like with Pastor Moehlen's sermon, I heard many things that no one had ever shared with me before. There was something else new that I experienced that day. Dr. Mosely had not been shy about his faith but I'd never seen him express it so plainly on the basis of scripture. He had a surprising command of the Bible and interjected it liberally here and there with the aplomb of a theologian or biblical scholar. He referred to Proverbs 3:19 as proof that God is our one and only intelligent designer ... "The Lord by wisdom hath founded the earth; by understanding hath he established the heavens." He countered the secularist scoffers who heap disdain on believers and creationists with I Corinthians 3:19 ... "For the wisdom of the world is foolishness with God. For it is written, he takes the wise in their own craftiness." He turned to eyewitness testimony … the only person, that is God, who observed the creation … to support the Genesis account of our origins along with the culmination of God's plan of salvation in II Peter 1:16 … "For we have not followed cunningly devised fables, when we made known unto you the power and coming of our Lord Jesus Christ, but were eyewitnesses of his majesty."

The reference that hit me the hardest was a bit of prophecy he used to show why, he said, the world was now given over to faith in evolution. He opened the book and read from II Peter 3: 4-7 … "And saying, where is the promise of his coming? For since the fathers fell asleep, all things continue as they were from the beginning of the creation [uniformitarianism]. For this they willingly are ignorant of, that by the word of God the heavens were of old, and the earth standing out of the water and in the water: Whereby the world that then was, being overflowed with water, perished: But the heavens and the earth, which are now, by the same word are kept in store, reserved unto fire against the day of judgment and perdition of ungodly men." He drove this home further with II Timothy 4:3-4, "For the time will come when they will not endure sound doctrine; but after their own lusts shall they heap to themselves teachers, having itching ears; and they shall turn away their ears from the truth, and shall be turned unto fables."

I wasn't ready to agree but I was struck by how the Bible precisely predicted that there would come a time when the world would ignore the evidence in nature and deny the Genesis accounts of creation and Noah's flood. Although I couldn't yet accept these biblical stories literally, their inference made sense to me logically … that denying the veracity of parts of the Bible would necessarily call into question God's promise of the second coming of a resurrected savior. This and the chilling warning at the end in II Peter 3:7 stuck with me.

I was so keyed up after my Sunday morning epiphany at Faith's church that it took me a long time to settle down. When I finally had my head back on straight I began to wonder what in the world had happened to me. Why did I come to this crazy town? First I got wrapped up in a murder investigation where a good portion of the population believed a werewolf was on a killing spree … a werewolf! And now I had visited a church where the Bible was preached as literal truth and sat through a lecture where science was set back by at least three hundred years. I momentarily wondered if I should get the hell out of there and transfer to Eugene or Portland State. Eventually, I calmed down and realized I was in no danger, there was nothing to fear. I wasn't being brainwashed or deprogrammed. My freedom, intellectual and otherwise, was not under attack. There was nothing threatening about kindly, comical Professor Mosely. Then I turned to Faith. She was the best thing that ever happened to me. If it meant opening up to some weird, sometimes uncomfortable new vistas, it was more than worth it. On second thought, all I could think was thank you St. Louis!

I couldn't be preoccupied with matters of church and religion for long. There was school and work and, most prominently, an ominous reminder looming overhead. When I looked into the night sky and saw the moon gradually coming to full circle, I imagined the face of a gigantic clock hovering overhead. It carried the expression of a celestial spook whispering a warning … beware the full moon, the full sturgeon moon. As the day approached, fear and panic gripped the area. It was unavoidable. All of us involved in the investigation were no different. The worst thing was the feeling of inevitability and helplessness. How do you take precautions when you have no idea of when and where the monster will strike? There was no discernible pattern to follow. As Dr. Mosely had pointed out, we had no motive to analyze. Still we did our best to try to protect the community from the ubiquitous threat of the man-wolf.

We met as a team the day of the full moon to ready our plans as much as possible. Surveillance teams were fully deployed but spread woefully thin across such a wide expanse of territory. Public service announcements offered cautions that had everyone on high alert. In a bold move showing solidarity across geographic, political and administrative jurisdictions, the various authorities collaborated in shutting down all state, county and local parks in the area. Police patrols were stepped up in neighborhoods surrounded by large wooded areas. As for our team, we brainstormed but didn't really come up with much. It seemed as if every possible precaution including helicopter patrols with floodlights had been deployed. Michael warned in his spookiest voice that there was only one way to stop the Loup Garou and that would be to kill him. I could tell that Sloan was about to blow a gasket as Michael reminded us how difficult it is to stop the Loup Garou with its supernatural powers. I stepped in to ward off another conflict and asked Michael about the legend of the great Indian chief who saved mankind from the terrible flood. He confirmed the story in a casual manner that assumed the tale was common knowledge.

Of course, Flip Flannigan and the rest of the local media were all over the story. They trumpeted the sturgeon moon and battered us with the stories of the past victims over and over. It had to be excruciatingly difficult for the families of the six people who had been slaughtered. I imagine they kept their TVs turned off or perhaps even left town. For once, Sloan didn't mind all the sensationalism and werewolf hype. He considered it a benefit in that no one in their right mind would be out and about late at night ... not in the woods, not on abandoned properties, not in any remote areas. No, after their alarming 24/7 coverage, Sloan doubted than anyone would venture into their own back yard that night. He was wrong.

Ray Slaten was a nonconformist of the highest order. He had a small plot of land in the area near where the airport had expanded for its new runway. Most people had long since abandoned this section of Bridgeton even though there was no threat of air traffic noise since the city of St. Louis had badly miscalculated Lambert's growth potential. St. Louis was no longer a hub thanks in no small part to 9/11. It was difficult to find a direct flight to anywhere other than perhaps Chicago. It was a monumental waste of tax payer money and laid bare many desirable neighborhoods that once helped to make Bridgeton a thriving suburb. Now these former bee hives of activity were leveled flat and resembled the barren landscape of the moon and had no use beyond serving as dumping grounds for uprooted trees and other debris left behind during the big tornado of 2011. This suited Ray just fine because he didn't like neighbors. While others fled to avoid dropping property values, he preferred to live in an area adjacent to the airport expansion where he wouldn't be looked down upon for the ramshackle trailer he called home or bothered by nosy neighbors who might take exception to his rustic lifestyle.

Ray worked odd jobs but only so often as it took to earn enough money on which to get by. He supplemented his currency with the old fashioned sweat of his brow and every imaginable craft he could perform by hand. He was not a Jiffy Lube kind of guy. He maintained his old truck himself and personally changed the oil which he dumped out back or down a nearby sewer when no one was looking. He was both libertarian and libertine. Ray shunned polite society, was morally bankrupt and lived according to his own rules. He resented even the smallest form of government intrusion into his life and was only subject to the curb of the law in so far as it allowed him to keep them off his back. He kept to himself for the most part as if he were a mountain man living in the isolated thin altitudes of the Rockies.

Ray was a real throw back. He didn't have a working toilet in his trailer which was no problem for him given the privacy afforded by the nearby woods. Toilet paper was a luxury to be supplemented by leaves or corn cobs as necessary. Anything homemade was preferred over store bought goods including a little bath tub hooch. When it was necessary to get something outside the home, Ray wouldn't hesitate to practice a little five finger discount whenever possible. If he was driving by a farmer's field ripe with corn or an unattended produce stand, he'd help himself. Ray even fashioned a few of his clothes and blankets out of animal skins. Anything that moved was fair game for Ray. This included squirrels, rabbits, deer and even a stray cat or dog. He'd use the hides, meat, bones … everything. Ray was fond of fishing … not for sport but meat alone.

You'd think Ray would be simpatico with the environmentalists who advocated his back to nature lifestyle. However, he despised them for all their rules and regulations and what he considered phony baloney attitudes and pampered lifestyles. They talked a good game but, in his opinion, didn't walk the walk. The feeling would have been mutual especially from the PETA types due to his abuse and misuse of animals and *greens* who would have been appalled by his littering and dumping. Ray was an ally to no one including mother earth and our furry little friends. He was an opportunist who lived off the land with no regard for conservation, renewal of resources or any other such nonsense. The environment was there to serve him and not vice versa.

Ray didn't have a TV but he had enough contact with the world to be aware of the werewolf story which he considered a hoax. He paid no attention to the warnings of potential danger. In his mind, it was the wolf or any other beast of the forest that should be worried about him. He'd have the damn thing for dinner if he ever got the chance. Ray carried a huge buck knife and Colt 45 replica on his excursions into the wild ... more than enough firepower to handle anything that might come his way. To Ray's way of thinking, that night in late August was the perfect time for one of his clandestine forays into the forest. The full moon would light his way and, with all the warnings, he wouldn't have to worry about crossing paths with John Q. Public.

The park closings helped pave the way to one of his favorite fishing spots. Well it wasn't really fishing since Ray didn't like to play by the rules. Let's call it poaching. He headed down to the Missouri River along the bank inside the Bridgeton Riverwoods Trail Park, not more than a couple miles from where Merle Polk's body was discovered. According to the Missouri Department of Conservation trot lines were illegal. Nevertheless, Ray liked to set a trot line here because he could easily walk way out on a rock levee and stretch the main line almost two hundred yards ... more than enough length to drop plenty of snoods with hooks loaded with stink bait, worms, raw shrimp or dough balls ... just the thing to catch a large mud cat, blue channel cat or perhaps even a spoon bill or sturgeon. He'd anchor the main line to the bank on one end and the levee on the other and weigh it down enough in the middle to drop it below the water level to hide it from any nosy conservation agents. It didn't have to be attended like pole fishing so he could head back home after making sure the line was secure. PETA thought this was a particularly cruel practice since any fish that was hooked might languish for hours or days before being hauled in.

Ray surveyed the situation and admired his work under the moon's shimmering glow that reflected off the river's swirling ripples like an elaborate laser light show. He plucked the line as if he was tuning a bass fiddle and was pleased at how the taut cord hummed with the vibration. With his mission accomplished, Ray started down the trail back to where his truck was parked inconspicuously among some of the junk heaps at Art's Auto Salvage. Suddenly, he slid to his left off the asphalt walkway and dropped down low. He had heard something behind him. Ray was no neophyte like the Armadillo. He knew someone or something was tracking him ... probably a park ranger or perhaps some claim jumper looking to rob his trot line. He automatically eased his buck knife out of its sheath with one hand and extended his other hand down to his waist band to clasp the Colt. Ray wasn't about to get caught unawares and had no compunction about killing anyone that was a threat to him. There was enough moonlight that he could make out the shapes of two figures that stepped out from the trees just ahead of him. He carefully raised his pistol and took aim. The last thing he remembered was some kind of bug or spider biting his neck with the ferocity of a hornet's sting.

The good folks at the Bridgeton Parks & Recreation Department and local police were familiar with Sloan and our team from our earlier encounter after the death of Merle Polk. Thus, they contacted us immediately when they discovered Ray Slaten's dead body the next morning. Everything at the murder scene was regrettably familiar with one major exception. There was an envelope near the body marked to the attention of Detective Sloan. Following proper protocol, nothing was touched and the envelope was unopened. Sloan knew better than to make the contents public so he waited until the scene was processed and we reconvened at his office to open it. There was a disturbing letter inside that Sloan read to us.

> "Detective Sloan,
>
> If you're reading this letter, then you've already seen my latest handiwork. You must think I'm a vicious killer who takes perverse pleasure in mutilating my helpless victims. Please let me assure you this is not the case.
>
> I am deeply troubled by what I have done and wish I had the fortitude to turn myself in. Unfortunately, I am no better than a worm and cannot bring myself to do what is necessary to end the senseless slaughter.
>
> I don't expect your forgiveness but beg your understanding. I am driven by forces outside of my control … powerless to resist the moon's invisible hand. It transforms me into something unspeakable, savage and bloodthirsty. Please do not dismiss this as myth, legend or a figment of my imagination. The monster in me is all too real.
>
> I implore you to find a way to help me escape this curse. The killing must stop but I am helpless on my own. Danger lurks in the shadows. Please make haste before the next full moon when I will be driven to strike again and satisfy the prurient desires of my wicked fangs with human flesh and blood. May my tortured soul escape Satan's grasp.
>
> Lew Carew

Sloan didn't know what to make of the letter. Unfortunately, the author had taken care to leave no fingerprints or trace DNA. Could it be the work of a sick copycat killer yearning for attention? Or was our perpetrator getting bored with the same old same old and looking for a way to spice things up? It was a new twist but didn't bring us any closer to solving the crime spree. Perhaps it was just a sick joke but if the killer thought he could convince Sloan the werewolf was real, he was mistaken. He remained as skeptical as ever. There was only one incontrovertible fact that Sloan took from the letter, "Gentlemen, we have a leak somewhere inside the investigation. The only people who heard me refer to the killer as Lew Carew are insiders. Someone has spilled the beans and I intend to find out who it was!"

CHAPTER 8

HARVEST MOON

I COULDN'T IMAGINE ANYONE ON OUR team or Sloan's staff leaking information about the case. It was such an infrequent reference only used a few times when the detective was frustrated by our lack of progress. There was nothing particularly noteworthy about the sarcastic moniker. Perhaps someone might have slipped and shared it in jest but that wouldn't make sense since it was an inside joke. Unless you were familiar with the legend of the Loup Garou, the silly play on words wouldn't register on anyone's funny bone. Yet there was no denying that it had somehow leaked out and spread enough to reach the itching ears of our murderous perp. Maybe the killer was one of those hangers on who had found a way to stay close to the investigation … a classic case of returning to the scene of the crime. Perhaps he was a member of the media or an employee of one of the many service industries that supported the police and forensic teams. In any case, I knew I was not the source of the leak but still felt guilty as though I was the object of Sloan's *inquisition*.

With that in mind, I hesitated to reveal my conversation with Dr. Mosely but felt compelled to share the idea that kept creeping forward from the back of my mind. I eased my way into it during our next team meeting, "I want to make sure you understand that I would never share any of the details of this case with anyone outside the team." Sloan immediately locked his gaze on me as though a confession were forthcoming. "I know better than to share anything remotely confidential that might compromise our investigation … including something as seemingly trivial as the name Lew Carew. But I had a conversation recently with one of my instructors, Dr. Mosely, whom you met at Hannigan's during our dinner meeting. All I did was ask his opinion based on what he had heard on the news and read in the papers. What he said got me to thinking … thinking that perhaps we could use someone like him on our team … a fresh mind with a new way of seeing things."

Greene frowned demonstratively and Michael crossed his arms defensively but Sloan was clearly intrigued, "What did he say? What is this new way of thinking you mentioned?"

I tried to ignore the daggers coming from Greene's and Michael's eyes, "Basically, he said we're being misled by our own preconceived notions in interpreting the evidence. He said that, from his point of view, it's rather simple … we don't have a wolf-man … we should be looking for a man and a wolf."

Sloan perked up and smiled broadly, "Okay, tell me more."

"He said we should focus on the motive in order to figure out who is responsible."

Sloan persisted, "Go on Seth." I squirmed a bit, "That's it in a nutshell. I don't want to put words in his mouth. Maybe you should talk to him directly."

Sloan pulled at his chin, "Hmmm, you know, you may be right."

Before this thought could take hold Greene jumped in, "You know what they say. Too many cooks can spoil the broth. Will adding another team member at this point help us home in on the killer or could it get us off on an unproductive tangent? We'd all welcome additional resources but I'm concerned this would just put us on a wild goose chase. I know Dr. Mosely as a colleague from the University. He's a wonderful fellow … he lied through his teeth … but, in academic circles, is known as somewhat of a crackpot. Can we really afford such distractions?"

Before Sloan could respond, Michael Muraco added his two cents worth, "We have finally made some good progress in opening our minds to all the possibilities. We've been able to see the evidence in a new light for what it is. If we discount the Loup Garou, we will live to regret it … we will only open the door to more killing and prolong the terror."

Wes and Tracker Joe didn't have a horse in this race and remained silent. I didn't want to get sideways with Professor Greene or Michael but felt they were not being objective. Even though I was personally more comfortable with his world view, it seemed to me that Dr. Greene was more the ideologue than Mosely. Whenever I asked him a probing question regarding the environment or origins based on information I'd gleaned from Mosely, he responded with invectives instead of facts, casting dispersions and belittling my inquiries. Maybe I was being swayed by my feelings for Faith and fondness for Dr. Mosely but the more I had been exposed to their ideas and beliefs the less radical they seemed. I refused to believe that I was being brain washed. The things they said just appealed to my common sense in so many ways. I had to come to Dr. Mosely's defense, "Professor Mosely is definitely unconventional … but if you listen to him and hear him out he has some very good ideas … he just makes a lot of sense. What would it hurt to give it a try? If it turns out that he's counter-productive, we can always drop him later." I was starting to sound like Mosely by employing simple logic rather than emotion. I figured it's hard to argue with common sense.

Sloan settled it, "You're absolutely right. This investigation is stalled and we need a jump start. Let's give Mosely a shot. If it doesn't work out, we can drop him like a bad habit. What's his phone number?"

He was very reluctant to get involved but Sloan was able to twist Mosely's arm. Unlike some of the others, Mosely turned down any offers of remuneration. Our next meeting started out tense with an electrical charge in the air. I'm sorry for another Jaws reference but I love that classic, old movie. If Michael Muraco was our Matt Hooper, then Mosely was our Captain Quint. His entrance wasn't quite as dramatic but, for Professor Greene and Michael, it had the same effect as Quint dragging his nails across the chalk board. Sloan gave him the floor, "Welcome aboard Dr. Mosely. First let me caution you and offer a fresh reminder to everyone that everything we share must not leave this room. We need to maintain the strictest level of confidence. With that said, would you mind offering your first impression of the case as a new member of the team?"

The old Aussie, never one to be bashful, came out swinging, "I don't mean to offend anyone but I think you're woefully off track."

Sloan was eager to head in a different direction but still taken aback by his bluntness, "How so, Doc?"

Sloan's reaction was a good reminder to Mosely to temper his brashness and catch his breath lest he launch into an unintelligible Aussie-speak diatribe. "I'm sorry for being so direct. Again I don't want anyone to get their nose out of joint. You must understand that I'm operating at a disadvantage. Everything I know at this point comes from the media. They've given me the impression that you've bought into this werewolf poppycock." Greene winced and Michael's mouth bowed downward forming a most stern, stone-faced expression. "I'm sure there's much more to it than that so please forgive me if I sound judgmental. It's just that again, based on what I've been able to gather, we may be missing our best opportunity to track down the killer. In my humble opinion, we need to focus on the man and the motive." Greene could barely contain his personal animosity toward Mosely and Michael struggled to remain still. They both held their peace not wanting to appear biased.

Sloan broke the silence, "So what do you suggest?"

"Again, I'm really at a disadvantage. I've got a lot of catching up to do before I can think of contributing anything of value to this team. I'd like to have access to all of the case files and evidence if you don't mind. Then could you extend me the courtesy of the remainder of the week for me to study everything thoroughly?"

Sloan didn't waste any time, "Okay boys, meeting adjourned. We'll get together one week from today to see what the Doc comes up with."

I was excited to tell Faith about Dr. Mosely joining the team. She was very fond of him too. Instead of our normal routine, I reluctantly agreed to have dinner at her parents' house. It wasn't as awkward as it could have been since I had already been introduced to them at church and they both seemed very nice and down to earth … just like their beautiful daughter. They were a handsome couple and I could see where Faith got her good looks. Her mom was still sizzling at forty-something. Her dad reminded me of Walt with his practical side, "So what do you plan on doing with an environmental sciences degree?"

"Well, I haven't made up my mind for sure but I'm minoring in business in case I need something to fall back on." They were both very interested in hearing about the police investigation and it provided a nice boost to our conversation but I was careful not to get into anything outside of what was in the public domain. They didn't pepper me with too many prying questions about me and Faith and made me feel comfortable and welcome in their home.

Deborah and Dan exercised great diplomacy and understanding when they shooed us off to the basement, "We don't mean to be rude but we have some errands to run. Why don't you guys make yourselves comfortable downstairs and watch a movie or something."

As soon as we settled in on the couch, I began to relay more tidbits about the investigation and our strange new team dynamics. I thought Faith would get a kick out of the way Professor Mosely and Dr. Greene were sparring. Oddly, she avoided the subject. I had no way of knowing that she wasn't bored with the investigation but rather wanted to shy away from any discussion regarding Zeb Greene. In any case, I didn't really care because she used a most effective means to divert my attention. Faith scooted close to me and laid her head on my shoulder then snuggled upward like a tulip blooming and planted a long, luxurious, velvety kiss smack dab on my accommodating lips. She finally let me come up for air, "Wow, what brought that on?"

"Oh, I don't know. You were just so cute with my mom and dad. It made you even more kissable than normal which is a lot." I wasn't about to argue. It was a good thing because she pushed me over and pinned my back to the couch as she eased her way on top of me like a warm wave sliding up a sandy beach.

I protested weakly, "What if your parents come back unexpectedly?"

It was too late. She barely had time to issue her breathy reply, "Never you mind," before burying me under another avalanche of her luscious lips.

Deborah and Dan were accommodating but not dumb. They trusted that Faith wouldn't go too far but naturally didn't afford me the same confidence no matter how well I'd done in making a good first impression. With impeccable timing, they came back home and made just enough noise in closing the door to announce their arrival. I reflexively moved to sit up but Faith didn't want to let me off the hook so easily. She kept her full weight on me and continued to pepper me playfully about the mouth, cheeks and neck while pretending to be oblivious to the panicked protestations I urgently whispered. It wasn't until the basement door opened and Deborah coyly announced, "I hope you two don't mind but I've got to put a load in the laundry." Even then, Faith timed her reluctant retreat so as to not be sitting up straight until a split second before her mom reached the bottom of the staircase. I was the only one uncomfortable with the little charade as my face flushed red. Deborah and Faith exchanged coquettish grins while barely pretending to ignore the obvious.

On my way home, I couldn't get Faith off my mind. I wondered if I had been the victim of a conspiracy at the hands of Faith and her mom because I was more attracted to her than ever, if that's even possible. I had just spent the evening with her but couldn't wait to see her again. Maybe she was slipping something into my soda because I was becoming addicted to Faith Harper. Nah, it was just that old drug called love. Tomorrow was not soon enough. I called Faith from the car before I hit highway 40, "Hey doll, miss me yet?"

"You bet I do."

"I just wanted to tell you I really enjoyed getting to know your mom and dad better."

"I see … then I'm sorry I took you away from them while we were down in the basement. I hope I didn't bore you too much."

"Oh that's very funny! What got into you anyway?" What a stupid question! I recovered before she could answer, "Never mind that! Whatever it was I can't wait for a second helping."

It was time to shift gears, "I wish I could reciprocate and introduce you to my parents but that will have to wait until they come to St. Louis or we head out to Portland."

"That sounds good; I'm game."

"Ah, if only we could but I don't think we'll be getting together until Christmas at the earliest. In the interim, the next best thing is my boss Wes. I'd be happy to introduce you to him."

"That would be great, Seth."

"Are you free tomorrow afternoon? We'll be out at Creve Coeur Park. After you meet Wes, we could take a stroll around the Lake." Wes got a real kick out of meeting Faith. A near smile creased his face at least three times which, for him, was a wild display of emotion. Faith was a good judge of character and immediately understood why I was close to Wes and considered him to be more than just a boss. After parting ways with Wes, we took a long, slow stroll around the Lake hand-in-hand. Along the way, I stole many a kiss and Faith paused more than once to energize me with her generous hugs.

I was losing my mind or better judgment because I betrayed my instincts and called Walt and Gretchen that night. Walt was always the comedian, "To what do we owe this pleasure? Let me guess, you want some money or need us to bail you out of jail. Am I right?"

"Oh, you're a barrel of laughs … you're killing me Dad." I had to pause to gather my courage.

"Are you okay, son? Is there something wrong?"

"No, no, everything is great. I just want to share some good news with you and mom."

"Okay, hold on and let me put this on speaker."

Gretchen was her old, cheerful self, "How's my baby boy doing?"

I cleared my throat and tried not to sound melodramatic, "I just wanted to let you guys know that I met a girl here in St. Louis."

"And …" Walt waited for the other shoe to drop.

"Her name is Faith Harper and I really like her. Um, I guess what I'm trying to say is that I have a girlfriend."

Gretchen squealed with delight but Walt got right down to business, "So what does she look like? Got any pictures you can email?"

"Dad, you won't believe it. I'm not going to send you a picture because you might get the wrong impression … that I'm only interested in her body!"

Walt cracked me up. All he could say was "Hubba, hubba," whatever that meant.

"I'll tell you want I can do though. Faith and I will get on the webcam together sometime soon so you can see her and have a chat."

Gretchen could hardly contain herself, "I'm so excited … I can't wait."

Walt dead panned, "I can't wait either. See if you can get her to wear a bikini."

The week passed incredibly fast. Everything seemed to speed up under the pressure of the advancing moon. I was anxious to see what Dr. Mosely thought after churning through the evidence. I'm sure Professor Greene was dreading it. Sloan was the last one to enter the room and I expected him to be eager to get Mosely's take on things too. He was in an oddly subdued mood which soon became apparent when he revealed that he had received another letter from Lew Carew. He read it to us verbatim.

> Detective Sloan,
>
> While it is yet over two weeks away, my apprehension is mounting again as we advance toward the full moon, the harvest moon of September. In the distant past, this moon afforded bright nights for gathering ripe, abundant crops but now, for me, it portends a bloody harvest of more unfortunate victims.
>
> I implore you once again to not discount the monster that I shall become under the sorcerous moon's implacable power. My heart trembles at the dreaded thought of undergoing another diabolical transformation of sinew, fang and claw. The only thing more excruciating than the physical pain it brings is the emotional trauma that besets me when I realize the mayhem I've left in my murderous wake.

> You must cut me off from every deadly feast
> of the harvest. You should cancel every activity
> that might put people in harm's way under the
> full moon's glimmer. Fall festivals and late night
> hayrides will only sound a death knell in my evil,
> ravenous ears.
>
> I beg you sir to take every precaution possible
> to thwart me until the harvest moon is past.
>
> Lew Carew

This gave Michael the perfect segue to launch into another plea. "Listen, my friends, to what he has to say. As I told you, the man does not sleep when Loup Garou comes. He is one with the beast and aware of everything. This one, he has a conscience but Dr. Jekyll is no match for Mr. Hyde. With the physical transformation there is also a spiritual one, a tidal wave of evil that cannot be denied. When the beast stalks his prey the man is powerless to deny his bloodlust. It is only afterward that he comes face to face with his regret but then it is too late. This Loup Garou is tortured by the memories of his demonic deeds. We can be thankful that there is at least a partial struggle between good and evil. I have heard of others completely possessed that wreak havoc much worse than what we have seen here. The spark of good that inhabits the man is the only thing that keeps him from using his full power. That is why, I believe, this Loup Garou is only transformed by the irresistible force of the moon and not at other times of his own volition. If we can catch him at just the right moment, in his remorse and not under the moon's influence, we may just be able to play upon his conscience and bring this bloody saga to an end. But to do so there is only one way … we must seek Loup Garou on his terms … we must believe in order to triumph."

The Chief had spun quite a yarn or, perhaps better put, a web of influence that had us spellbound ... that is to say everyone but Noah Mosely. He struck without tact, diplomacy or any remorse with the deadly swiftness of a cobra. "What a bunch of rubbish! We might as well just fill our pouches with koala crap, mates!" He made sure the trance was broken ... that we'd be under no misconception. "Now that I've had a chance to mull over the evidence for a good while, I can tell you there's no werewolf on the prowl. We have an old fashioned, two-legged killer in our midst. And I think I have a good idea of what he's up to. Now if you'll bear with me, I'd like to go over my findings."

Zeb Greene did not want to waste the opening Michael had created so he interrupted to take a slightly different tact. "My good Doctor, I can understand your aversion to myths and legends. I too have difficulty with the notion of a werewolf on the prowl ... at least what we've come to recognize through Hollywood's eyes. As scientists, we have no choice but to reject such superstitions and the conjuring of pure imagination apart from the facts. However, I submit to the group that there is another explanation that can bridge the gap between empirical science and the fantastical circumstances with which we're confronted. Have you heard of the malady called lycanthropy?"

Greene momentarily thwarted his philosophical nemesis, Dr. Mosely, and drew our attention away. "Lycanthropy is a mixed bag and we must be careful to separate fact from fiction. Going way back in time, in many circles lycanthropy was part and parcel to werewolf mythology. In the original Greek it literally referred to wolf and man and gave birth to the monstrous transformations of legend. In classical Greek mythology, King Lycaon of Arcadia tried to put Zeus to a test and incurred the Greek god's wrath after failing to disprove his divinity. He sacrificed his infant son and mixed the bloody entrails in with some food for Zeus who was visiting Lycaon in the guise of a mortal. After the foolish plot came to light, Lycaon paid a terrible price when Zeus transformed the King into a wolf. The Roman poet, Ovid, later captured a version of the story in his first book of the Metamorphoses which popularized the notion of human transformations into animals."

Greene continued before an objection could be raised. "In more modern times, we've been better able to reconcile science and mythology through the diagnosis of clinical lycanthropy. It refers to a rare but well documented mental illness where the sufferer believes they have the power to transform and take on wolf-like characteristics. Although a physical transformation does not really occur, a psychological metamorphosis takes place that makes the subject absolutely believe that a physical change has occurred. The delusion can be so powerful that the subject's behavior is changed accordingly. They feel and act like they are part man and part wolf. Under such circumstances, it is not unusual for the lycanthrope to act upon irrational fears and anger that might otherwise stay buried deep within their psyche. There have been cases where lycanthropes go so far as to dress the part with hair, fangs, claws and make-up. It can be frighteningly realistic and no doubt has helped to feed and perpetuate werewolf legends right up to the present time. Our case may or may not involve clinical lycanthropy but it's something we should consider."

For the first time, a rift occurred between the two kindred spirits, Greene and the Chief. Michael stood, towering over the rest of us, "Loup Garou is real my friends. My grandfather, father and … yes … I through them have seen Loup Garou. They told me how they encountered Loup Garou with their own eyes many years ago. It is not the figment of someone's imagination or the product of costumed trickery. The sooner you accept this, the quicker we will catch the killer. Look at the facts. Listen to what Loup Garou is trying to tell us in the letters. Can't you see that Loup Garou provides the only reasonable explanation? Why are only the throats torn out and the bodies resting peacefully with no other marks or wounds? Only Loup Garou walks on two feet and possesses the lightning fast reflexes to strike at the victims' throats without first knocking them to the ground. They are paralyzed at the sight of the fearsome creature that appears with mercurial speed. He pounces so quickly that his vice-like jaws suffocate the life out of them before they can muster any resistance. He tears through their windpipes and severs their jugulars in one stunningly swift, vicious motion that robs them of their breath and life's blood. And why are they found in such peaceful repose? Look at the letters again. After the evil ebbs and his once dormant conscience is restored, he places the bodies at rest. He is driven by remorse ... tortured by unrequited repentance. That is why the bodies of the two teenagers were found side-by-side as if in a slumber."

Mosely had been more than patient but felt it was time to replace the rug that had been pulled out from under him. The interruption had given him time to cool his heels and adopt a more diplomatic approach. "Michael my friend, I can respect the culture from which you hail and the rich traditions you've been taught. You strike me as most sincere and not a charlatan. I do not see anything you might seek to gain from deception anyway. I must add that your analysis is compelling. While I personally cannot accept the existence of a werewolf or whatever we might call such a transformational creature, it does seem to offer some reasonable explanations for the odd circumstances surrounding these murders. The question is ... are there any other reasonable theories that can offer a better explanation? I think perhaps there are and I only ask that you would give me a chance to submit them for your consideration."

Dr. Mosely then turned to Greene while doing his best to put aside any personal animosity between the two polar opposites. "To you Dr. Green, my esteemed, young colleague, I respect and appreciate the way you've attempted to address the conundrum the evidence of this case presents. Your theory of clinical lycanthropy lends itself to a rational, scientific approach to the bizarre circumstances that seem steeped in myths and legends. It certainly deserves our consideration and further study." Having appeased the competition and restored the peace, Dr. Mosely turned to Sloan. "Detective, it appears we have several good alternatives to place under the microscope. As I said before, I think there is another one to throw into the mix if I may have your permission to share the findings from my review of the evidence."

Sloan was typically brusque, "Have at it Doc."

"If you believe all the crime shows on TV today, most investigations into serial murders focus first and foremost on developing a psychological profile of the killer. While that is important and can be helpful, I've taken a different approach. Remember that the key to solving these crimes, in my opinion, is motive. Frankly, this area has been somewhat neglected since what kind of motive can you ascribe to a wolf or for that matter a werewolf? Since I'm coming in fresh as the new kid on the block, I feel I have an open mind. With that, my first step was to delve into the victim-ology. That is to say, what do we know about the victims besides their whereabouts; time, place and cause of death? I studied the background of each to see if there were any similarities that might attract a particular type of killer. At first glance they seem to be quite a disparate group on the basis of age, sex, occupation, socio-economic standing and just about any other demographic you can imagine. But as I dug deeper, there's one thing that stood out in my mind."

Dr. Mosely paused to quench his thirst. There was no threat of him being pre-empted again because we were putty in his hands, dying to hear what new twist he had come up with. "There is only one thing that seems to link all of the victims together. They were all enemies of Mother Nature … at least in the mind of the killer. From an environmental standpoint, they all had some serious black marks against them. Take for instance the first victim, Merle Polk. He was a reprobate dumper … a serial litterer. The only thing worse to an environmentalist than literally trashing mother earth is to do so for profit like Merle did. Now look at Hanley Wilson. The parallel to Polk couldn't be any clearer. He was up to his neck in dirty dealings with corporate scofflaws willing to rape the environment to save a few extra bucks. Wilson turned good farmland into a hazardous waste dump for the love of filthy lucre. Then there's Brantley Earl, an environmentalist's worst nightmare. You and I might applaud his efforts to help increase agricultural productivity and fight famine but, to the *greens*, he was a hated man. Monsanto has a big bull's eye on their back to this day because of their leading position on GMO technology. Earl was one of the founding fathers who helped them advance from laboratory research to commercial production. That's a definite no-no in the *green* community."

I felt the urge to jump in, "But what about Mike, Carol Sue and Billy? They were just kids."

Professor Mosely shook his head sadly, "Yes, to you and me they're just kids and we can overlook all the wild, silly and impetuous things teens do. But to a true ideologue, there can be no exceptions. Even the smallest perceived infractions against Mother Nature must be met with severe punishment and the perpetrators stamped out for the collective benefit of the common good. To you and me they were young innocents but to a truly devoted, fanatic defender of the earth, they committed unforgivable sins. Mike and Carol Sue, along with their friends, turned a wildlife habitat into their own personal playground. They littered, disturbed and burned in order to satisfy their destructive, hedonistic desires. Billy and his pals had the unmitigated gall to defy the conservation department and invade a protected wildlife sanctuary like so many marauding barbarians. They were guilty of looting ... they did cut down some small trees ... littering, burning and trespassing in the eyes of the killer. To you and me this sounds crazy and it is ... sheer lunacy ... but to the killer it was pure justice rightly served."

That helped explain the teens but I was still puzzled, "What about our last victim? All he was doing was fishing. What could possibly be wrong with that?"

Dr. Mosely offered a forlorn smile, "You must remember what kind of person we're dealing with. He doesn't think like you and me. Mr. Slaten was fishing illegally, using a trot line which is outlawed by the conservation department. But that wasn't his great sin. The way he caught the fish, legal or illegal, was considered cruel and torturous. Ray Slaten was a litterer and dumper although on a much smaller scale but that wasn't his big crime. He was an animal killer. Ray killed for food, clothing and other provisions which to some might seem laudable with him living off the land. But, to an extreme environmentalist, what he did to animals was tantamount to murder ... he was an animal serial killer."

Greene wanted to regain the spotlight but did so politely responding to Mosely's courtesy in kind, "Well done, Dr. Mosely. That is a very interesting theory. It would explain a lot of what we've seen but there seems to be a rather large hole remaining.

Where does a wolf come into play in this scenario? How do we explain the method of death, DNA, hair and prints?"

Mosely nodded in friendly affirmation, "That is an excellent observation Dr. Greene. It's one I've been pondering. I'm not sure how he's accomplished it but there must be a clever ruse in play. All I know for sure is that the killer is diabolical and very, very intelligent. However he's doing it, I believe this werewolf mania is something he's created intentionally to cover his tracks and distract us all."

Michael was not finished stating his case but was not compelled to maintain the polite decorum that Mosely and Greene established, "Now who is turning to faith and fantasy over plain facts? You disparage my heritage as spiritual nonsense and mythology then turn around and cast a blind eye to indisputable forensic evidence. Oh, there must be an explanation you say ... I just don't know what it is. How should we account for the hair, blood and prints? A clever ruse you say ... isn't that another way of saying it must be magic, a slight of hand trick?" Then in a move that startled me he turned on his erstwhile, naturalist ally, "And you ... you want us to believe that it's nothing more than mind games. Yet you offer no explanation of how this supposedly mentally ill person is able to carry off his charade so convincingly. It takes much more than costumes and make-up to account for the hair, blood and prints of the Loup Garou not to mention killing a man by ripping out his throat without a knife ... with the fangs of a wolf."

Michael Muraco stood up but this time it was not to intimidate anyone. He started to walk to the exit then stopped and turned to address us once more, "You are hypocrites and fools. The only explanation that makes any sense in light of the evidence is the Loup Garou. However, your minds are all too small and tightly shut to accept anything you don't fully understand. I cannot help you. I must leave this team … leave you to suffer the consequences of your own folly."

Before he could make his way out the door Sloan spoke up, "Chief, please wait! Look, we have strong personalities on this team and clear differences of opinion but you're still a valued member of the team. Won't you please reconsider?"

Michael scoffed, "That's something coming from you. Of all the people on this team, you are the most skeptical. You have been the most rude and obnoxious with your sarcasm and infantile mocking with Lew Carew."

Sloan tried to be uncharacteristically gracious, "You're right. I can be a real jerk sometimes. Diplomacy is definitely not my long suit. But that doesn't mean I'm not taking you seriously. Yeah, I have real trouble believing in a werewolf or the Loup Garou as you call it but still I can't discount the way your theory fits perhaps the best in many instances. We've come too far to give up. Come on back and sit down, Chief, please."

Michael was swayed by this honest appeal but needed something to sooth his wounded pride. Surprisingly, it was quiet, unobtrusive Wes who offered a face saving idea. "I don't know about the rest of you but I'm lost. We have several theories that all seem to make sense in one fashion or another but no clear winner. There are some big holes in all of them. I might have a way to sort this out though."

Sloan welcomed anything that would keep the team from splintering, "Okay Wes, what have you got?" Wes cracked me up with his relaxed manner. Most people would seize such an opportunity by standing and launching into their most polished, professional, persuasive presentation mode. Not Wes, he folded his hands behind his head, leaned back in his chair and actually put a foot up on the conference room table. "What we really need is to catch this son of a gun in action."

Wes' plan was very well thought out considering it was pretty much off the cuff. Still waters run deep and tight-lipped Wes had obviously been listening carefully with the wheels churning busily in his head. "From his latest letter, we know the killer is aware of all the activities planned for the end of the month under the full moon. Let's take his advice and shut down all the hayrides and festivals across all the Parks and local communities ... except for one. Let's see if we can draw the bastard out to one location where we can get a look at him."

Sloan liked what he was hearing. It was kind of like a police stake out maneuver, "Where do you suggest?"

"How about if we pick a spot where he's comfortable, someplace where he's killed before?"

Sloan agreed enthusiastically, "Yeah, I like the way you're thinking."

Wes suggested, "Let's set it up for Creve Coeur Park. I know just the right spot."

Wes had struck a cord and gave the embattled team something to rally around. Sloan took the ball and ran with it, "You know, I think we could sucker the dip thongs in the media into helping us. Normally, I don't like to dump fuel on the fire but can you imagine the press we'd get if we provided a copy of the letters from Lew Carew to the local news? Then we could follow up with public service announcements about the cancellations ... that is, everywhere except Creve Coeur Park. We'd promote it as the one remaining site where we can guarantee proper security. The public will certainly understand the need for us to shut down everything and the people crazy enough to venture out under the full moon will flock to Creve Coeur."

Leave it to me to throw a monkey wrench into the works. "If this works and we draw the killer to Creve Coeur Park, won't we be putting people's lives at stake?"

Sloan sneered at me as though I intended my question as a personal insult to his intelligence and integrity. "Do you really think I'd use innocent people as bait? Look, we will have plain clothes cops on every hay wagon. And with Wes' help, we'll have surveillance cameras installed throughout the park so we can catch this devil before he has a chance to claim another victim. Can you do that Wes?"

"If you can provide the hardware, I can install them strategically so no one will be able to slip through our fingers this time."

This sounded reasonable but I still had my worries, "This person, this thing has duped us before. Do you remember the traps we set up around the goat? Also, Mike and Carol Sue were safe within a large group but then wandered off by themselves."

Sloan pooh-poohed my paranoia, "Those traps were clearly marked with warning signs. Wes will put these cameras where no one will notice them. This time we'll have armed undercover cops all around to make sure someone doesn't wander off from the herd." I nodded but still had an uneasy feeling.

Wes had one week to survey the Park and develop his strategy for setting the high-tech trap before the harvest moon festival and hayride around Creve Coeur Lake. After leaving the meeting, I had a chance to chat with Dr. Mosely who had given me a ride from Wash U. "Doc, why do I still have an uneasy feeling about this plan? Are you okay with it?"

"Seth, I think your instincts are good and you're wise to remain very cautious. Regardless of the professional courtesies you just witnessed, mark my word. We are dealing with a man and not just any man. There is a vicious killer on the loose who is on a mission. He selects his victims with malice aforethought. He is driven by ideology and madness but he is not crazy in the sense of being careless, clumsy or reckless. We are dealing with a highly intelligent, cold, calculating, resourceful and completely remorseless killer."

I reacted to the chilling picture Dr. Mosely painted with tense curiosity, "Do you have any idea of who could be doing this?"

"No Seth, unfortunately I do not. I've yet to develop a full profile of the killer beyond his radical environmental beliefs. I fear there is something deeper and much more sinister that is driving him."

"Do you mean there is a different motive?"

He mused, "Well I don't mean to sound vague but I have to say yes and no. There is something more than perceived environmental transgressions that drive the killer. He is deeply disturbed on another level and is possessed with an uncontrollable anger that I believe is being redirected and channeled into what he sees as a just and righteous crusade … nature punishing evil mankind."

The Doc was giving me the willies so I changed the subject, "So do you really think Dr. Greene has a point with his theory on clinical lycanthropy or were you just being polite?"

He chuckled, "Aren't you the perceptive one? Actually, it's not a bad idea except that our killer seems too much in control of his faculties to be suffering from such a debilitating mental illness. The letters from Lew Carew don't make sense to me in the context of a lycanthrope. I have a sneaking suspicion they are not a cry for help but rather are intended to manipulate us. Still there are elements of the theory that are worthy of our consideration."

"So you and Dr. Greene kind of see things eye to eye?"

"I wouldn't go that far. Don't be confused by our exchange of pleasantries. That man cannot stand me. We're as far apart as the east is from the west." I had a puzzled look on my face that drew a deeper explanation from the professor, "In spite of what you see on the surface, this has nothing to do with our scientific outlooks. Our differences are not a matter of debating origins or the fossil record. To Dr. Greene, I am the most dangerous threat imaginable ... I am the personification of evil in his mind."

This set me back in my seat, "Doc, that seems awfully strong, don't you think?"

He shook his head slowly, "Seth, you'll never understand unless you focus on the root cause. God is at the heart of the matter, plain and simple. I'm a grave threat because, if I'm right, it destroys the very foundation of life for people like Dr. Greene. If God exists, if God is our creator, then we must answer to him. We are subject to his authority, his law, his morality. The secularist must take God out of the equation in order to be the master of his own destiny. At the bottom line, it's man's way of escaping the sin problem on his own. If man is the highest authority subject to only his own, ever-changing, relative sense of morality then there is no sin and certainly no need of a divine savior. It all boils down to two different views of freedom ... the temporal freedom to do as we please in this life versus the spiritual freedom spoken of in John 8:31-32 ... the freedom from sin, the second death and the devil."

Now my head was spinning. I thought I was catching on by being around Faith, going to her church and hearing some of Dr. Mosely's lectures there but this was a little too deep. "What do you mean by the freedom from sin ... that it's okay to sin since our sins are forgiven? And what in the world is the second death?"

He patiently explained, "Yes our sins have all been paid for but it's not okay to sin. That's an old fallacy that cropped up among the early Christians in Corinth ... our sins have all been paid for by

Christ so while we're on this earth we can live it up. No sir, read through Paul's letters to the Church at Corinth sometime and you'll see how he laid that foolish notion to rest. When Christ tells us in John 8:31-32 that we'll be free if we continue in his word, he means we'll be free from the consequences of sin. That is not to say that we won't suffer earthly consequences of our sins including temporal death but, by faith and the power of the Holy Spirit working through the word, we'll be reconciled unto God and avoid the eternal consequence of the second death ... the death of the spirit in hell ... eternal separation from God."

He went on to stress that such things could not be understood apart from God. Dr. Mosely often talked about seeing things through God's eyes rather than our own. He called it spiritual glasses rather than worldly lenses. He compared and contrasted God's economy versus ours. In our world you have to earn your way and you get what you pay for. That's why it seems so appealing when churches teach that we must work our way into heaven through our own good deeds. My church in Portland was a prime example with its focus on the social gospel and our endless efforts to feed the poor. It's not that there's anything wrong with such aid but, as Dr. Mosely liked to point out, God loves a cheerful giver and not one that expects to get something in return and certainly not salvation. He helped me to understand that such charity is actually an affront to God if it brings with it a rejection of the truth that Christ accomplished everything necessary for the forgiveness of our sins and full salvation.

Maybe I was being brainwashed because I was starting to understand Faith and the Professor more and more when it came to the Christianity I claimed. Somehow it started with Dr. Mosely poking holes in evolution and the *settled science* being espoused by so many people like Dr. Greene. Speaking of him, it raised another question in my mind, "So, I guess down deep you and Dr. Greene hate each other?"

"No Seth; that is where you are mistaken. I know he's not fond of me to put it mildly. To the contrary, I'm sure he sees me as a mortal enemy of sorts. But Christ has set a clear example for us ... that we are to love our enemies. I may despise what people like Dr. Greene stand for and am duty bound to take them to task for the false, anti-Christian doctrine they endlessly weave but must still speak the truth in love. You see, Dr. Greene is no more deserving of God's wrath than you or me. Christ died for him as well as for you and me. Jesus paid such a terrible price for his salvation as well as ours that we must see him through Christ's eyes and reach out to him in our prayers, thoughts, words and deeds with an earnest longing for his eternal good."

Just when I thought I had Dr. Mosely figured out he would throw me for another loop. I think he could see that my brain was starting to hurt so he graciously changed the subject, "So, when will I be getting a wedding invitation?" All I could offer was an incredulous double take. "Come now Seth, don't act so bewildered. I can see the way your face lights up whenever you're around her. And you must admit that you've overcome your fear of her being some kind of fanatical Bible thumper." He was right on target and, if I was completely honest, I would have to admitted that I'd given some thought to it. In my mind, I was reconciled to the fact that she was the one. But he was getting the cart way too far out in front of the horse to suit me.

"Oh, I really like Faith a lot but let's not start ringing the wedding bells just yet."

He snickered at my apprehension and continued to rib me, "I understand that you'll want to graduate and get a job first ... but it takes an awfully long time to make all the arrangements so I wouldn't procrastinate."

"Very funny Doc but I'd say we have plenty of time to spare."

He was relentless, "I see; then you must believe in long engagements."

"Oh yeah, do you think Faith would accept one of those lollipop rings because that's about all I could afford at this point."

Like a dog with a bone he wouldn't let go and hit me with one final zinger that made me pause and think, "Well don't stall too long, mate. There are a lot of other fishermen near the sea and Faith is quite a catch."

Although he said it in jest, Doc's last remark left me wondering nervously as he dropped me off in front of my apartment. It stirred up old, unwelcome feelings of jealously and inadequacy and reminded me of the time I thought Faith and Dr. Greene were romantically inclined. I knew such thoughts were silly but nevertheless decided to phone Faith as soon as I got inside. Money and time were both tight and I knew I should stay home and study but I had the urge to see her. Maybe all I needed was to hear her reassuring voice but unfortunately the phone was busy and before I could leave a message there was a knock at the door. My heart leapt thinking maybe it was Faith and she'd been waiting nearby for me to come home from the meeting. To my surprise, Dr. Greene was at the door.

At about the same time, Wes Woodson was on the phone with Detective Sloan. He was ready to finalize the arrangements for our big stake out. The Police Department had appropriated enough wireless, battery powered cameras to cover Wes' plan. The official full harvest moon and night-time festivities at Creve Coeur Park were only two days away. The media had been alerted and good, old Flip Flanagan had taken the bait and made enough hay with the Lew Carew letters to supply our entire hayride and then some. The people of St. Louis and the surrounding area were on high alert and only the most hearty, adventurous, fun-seeking souls would be coming to Creve Coeur Park. Two dozen plainclothes officers had been briefed and would be on hand to serve and protect. All that was left was for Wes to install fifteen surveillance cameras in carefully chosen, well hidden, strategic locations. Wes refused any assistance in order to maintain as much confidentiality as possible and planned on getting the job done in the wee hours the night before the hayride so as to not alert anyone to the cameras' whereabouts. The cameras were small with easy to install brackets ready to be affixed to trees with sharp stakes at almost any angle. He figured it would only take an hour or two to set them all in place.

That night when Wes entered the Park through the back gate, the nearly full moon was high in the sky. He still needed a flashlight because the low cloud cover that swept across the sky like a misty river flowing beneath the silvery orb obscured the moon's glow and cast eerie shadows everywhere. I had offered to help but Wes assured me it was a one man job. He said he wanted me to be bright eyed and bushy tailed for the next night during the hayride. I wasn't about to question his judgment or capabilities and followed the boss' orders. True to form, Wes had the logistics all worked out to start at the location nearest the back gate, work his way around a wooded section of the Lake and finish up back near his truck.

Sloan arrived in Clayton very early the next morning to check on the feed from the cameras. Even though it was a Saturday morning he rousted one of his IT guys from a peaceful slumber and ordered him to get down to the office right away. There was some kind of technical issue on his end or out in the field because all of the monitors were blank. Perhaps Wes had forgotten to turn on the cameras but he felt it was more likely a glitch on his end. It didn't take long for the sleepy geek Sloan rousted to assess that everything was up and working fine in the Clayton HQ. Sloan next tried to dial Wes to have him check things out in the Park before it opened. He figured Wes was sleeping in since his phone was not turned on. As a fall back, he called me and, unfortunately, my phone was on ... another Saturday snooze-fest interrupted. "Seth, is that you?"

"Yeah, who's this?"

"It's me, Sloan."

"Oh yes, Detective Sloan, good morning."

"No, it's not a good morning. None of the cameras are working and I can't get a hold of Woodson. Can you get out to Creve Coeur Park right away and let my tech guy in and help him find the cameras?"

"Sure, it's no problem."

"What are you waiting for? Get your butt in gear and call me as soon as you've got it figured out. The clock is ticking and we've got to get ready for tonight." He hung up before I could say yes sir or ask the name of his techie.

I tried to call Wes on the way to the Park but it went directly to his voice mail. This was out of character for him. Maybe he was sick, sleeping off a bender or got lucky and was indisposed. Fortunately, Wes had trusted me enough to bounce his plan off of me so I had a good idea of where to look for the cameras and help Sloan's tech man. When I got to the back gate it was still open and Wes' truck was parked nearby. This was odd but I didn't worry. Wes was like Superman to me and I considered him invulnerable. I called out to no avail and thus headed toward the woods where the first camera should be. It wasn't far off the path where the hay wagons were supposed to follow their route later that night. I was keeping my eyes on the narrow dirt walkway and the clear trail left presumably by Wes. Consequently, I didn't notice anything odd up head until I was darn near right on top of it.

The first sign of trouble was a box sitting unattended that contained all but one of the cameras. This immediately put my jagged nerves on edge and my heart began to pound uncontrollably. The next thing that caught my eye in the early morning light of an overcast sky was a drop of moisture that came to rest in a shimmering black pool several yards ahead. I stopped and looked down until another drop splatted into the viscous puddle and then traced its path upward to the source. At first the odd shape didn't register but once it dawned on me, my knees turned to jelly and I collapsed on all fours and wretched uncontrollably. I didn't want to believe my eyes. Wes Woodson was suspended upside down from a branch like a deer that had been field dressed and left to bleed out. His throat was virtually nonexistent barring some bloody strands of flesh and a camera with its tree bracket stake was thrust into his heart.

Autumnal Equinox ...
Lunar-cy Unleashed

CHAPTER 9

○

BLOOD MOON

I WAS SO FILLED WITH ANGUISH over the death of my dear mentor and faithful friend, Wes Woodson, I temporarily forgot about the terribly distressing news Dr. Greene had shared with me the night before. Everything had happened so fast I hadn't even had a chance to discuss it with Faith. Apparently, beneath his cold exterior, Zeb Greene not only had a heart but a conscience as well and felt an obligation to me as a student but more so a comrade in arms on the investigative team. He came to me hat-in-hand to say that Faith had tried to rekindle their relationship behind my back. According to Greene, he did the only decent and honorable thing he could do considering our friendship. Greene had gently rebuffed her because of me and, as he further explained, he was in a new relationship with another female companion and it was turning rather serious. The only thing that didn't add up is why he felt the need to share his true confession with me. Did he think I needed protection from a faithless Faith? Was he trying to spare me from a broken heart somewhere down the road? Then he floored me with something so out of character for the Faith I thought I knew that it took a while to sink in. Greene claimed that Faith had not taken his polite but firm rejection well and tossed quite an angry fit. You know, love hath no fury like a woman scorned. He said she even went so far as to issue a threat that she planned on fabricating a story of how he had pressured her with unwanted advances. Greene didn't think she'd do it after having a chance to cool off and lick her wounds but wanted to be proactive in warning me, just in case.

I stewed all night trying to think of how to broach the subject with Faith. There are always two sides to every story but, based on what Dr. Greene had shared, I knew I had a real cause for concern. Where there's smoke there must be at least some fire, right? It was then that I really realized how much Faith meant to me and how close we had become … at least in my heart and mind. I tried to fight off the intensely bitter feelings of betrayal. It was more than a feeling of foolishness for having fallen head over heels in love with her. She and her *accomplice*, Dr. Mosely, had started to change my whole outlook on life. They had changed the way I looked at everything … the way I approached my studies … even the way I practiced my faith. They actually had me reading the Bible on my own in my spare time. I was even referring to devotional booklets and a ridiculously thick, four-volume, Kretzmann Bible Commentary set that Dr. Mosely had lent to me. It just didn't seem possible … unless I had been betrayed by my own emotions. How could I have been so dumb? Why didn't I see it coming? Was I that shallow to allow myself to be brainwashed solely on the basis of Faith's stunning good looks?

I tried to sleep but was really a mess as I tossed and turned in bed most of the night. My mind was still churning over what to do. I thought perhaps I should say nothing and wait for Faith to make the first move. If she came to me with slanderous accusations against Dr. Greene, that would be proof positive of her guilt. But what if she said nothing? I couldn't just let it go. How would I act around her? Would I be able to hide my feelings from her? No, in my tumultuous state of mind she would see right through me. There would be no way to avoid a confrontation. I didn't feel up to the task but knew I'd have to tackle this head on ... but how? Before I could resolve my dilemma, sleep finally overtook me and brought me some much needed rest. When I was jolted awake by the phone call from Sloan, I was still preoccupied with Greene's bombshell but then the discovery of Wes' poor, desecrated body pushed any thought of Faith's purported indiscretion completely into the far recesses of my mind.

Later that day, Faith called and I had to relay the shocking news of Wes' death. She said she was coming to see me right away and I tried to make up excuses to avoid her but she insisted. She had no way of knowing that she was in no position to console me at that time. Faith could tell that something was amiss but didn't question my strange behavior. I'm sure she figured I was just out of sorts over the loss of my cherished cohort, Wes. Seeing Faith left me with mixed emotions. In spite of the suspicions that wormed through my brain, it was still oddly comforting to be in her presence. I fought the urge to let my guard down but she was just so ... I guess the right word would be enchanting. Yeah, Faith was an enchantress or a darned good actress. There wasn't a hint of betrayal or deception behind her guise of care and concern. My indignation rose up to challenge my longings and weaknesses. Faith noticed how troubled I was and reached out to place her hands caressingly on my cheeks. I noticed a bruise on her wrist when her long sleeves receded as she stretched out her arms. When I asked her about it, she made some lame excuse about being clumsy. I let it pass.

Thankfully, I was rescued from that awkward situation by Detective Sloan who wanted to set up a briefing right away. For the first time, we had not been asked to stick around the crime scene as it was fully processed. Initially, I thought it was just Sloan's way of sparing us from the pain of examining the horrific circumstances surrounding one of our own fallen comrades. I learned otherwise when I arrived for the briefing to find that it was a private meeting between me and the detective. "Where's the rest of the team, Detective Sloan?"

"I'm disbanding the team; at least as a collective unit."

"Do you mind if I ask why?"

"No, not at all … I'll tell you why. There's something rotten in Denmark." My puzzled look revealed that his archaic slang hadn't registered. "We've got a rat in our midst … a traitor."

I was shocked, "Do you think I had something to do with Wes' murder?"

This didn't get a hint of a rise out of the old, homicide veteran, "I'm not ruling out anything at this point. All I know is that first we had the Lew Carew thing leak out and now this. Only someone on the inside could have known when and where Woodson was setting up those cameras."

I was appalled at the thought of being a suspect in Wes' murder, "What makes you think it couldn't be a horrible coincidence? The murderer struck Creve Coeur Lake once before."

He sneered, "I don't believe in coincidences when it comes to premeditated murder. Lew Carew didn't just stumble upon Wes Woodson by chance."

I offered another challenge, "But how do you know that for a fact?"

"Okay smart guy, riddle me this. How did the killer get to Woodson before he could get any cameras up and running? He laid in wait at the first site. Then look at the body. You saw it! This was personal for someone. He was made an example. Woodson was treated like an animal and put on display ... mounted like a trophy. No, this was no coincidence my young friend."

Sloan took a minute to fill his coffee cup and settle back down. "I don't know who would want to do this. But I do know this. It's someone with inside information who has access to what you and I know about the case." I cringed at the personal reference to me. He paused to let this sink in and then took a rational, thoughtful tone, "You know, I think your pal, Professor Mosely, hit the nail on the head. It's all about the motive. I can't for the life of me figure out why anyone on our team would want to kill Woodson and in such a gruesome fashion."

I lunged, "So you think it's someone on our civilian support team?"

He countered, "Don't put words in my mouth. I didn't say that. It could be anyone on my staff, anyone who has access to the case files."

I pondered, "If it could be anyone from among dozens of people, then why disband our team? Couldn't this alert the killer that you're onto something?"

Sloan was defiant, "I have my reasons. And I don't care if the killer gets wind of my suspicions. It's about time I put that bastard on the defensive."

I was still puzzled about the murders, "What about the whole werewolf thing? Was there anything different about the evidence this time?"

"Other than the weird position of the body and camera bracket spiked through his heart, it's the same old story. The forensic evidence tells us that we have a man and a wolf involved … or a wolf-man if you believe the Chief. This time though I'm really at a loss. How could this guy or animal get the drop on a tough as nails dude like Woodson? I mean, he was an experienced, alert outdoorsman carrying a side arm. There was no sign of a struggle, not one defensive wound. Something's not right here. I don't think Woodson would hit the bottle before such an important task but I've ordered a full blood toxicology report. " Sloan then drew near and lowered his voice to just above a whisper, "Just between you and me, I wonder about the Chief. There's something weird about the guy. This Loup Garou stuff is too much." I didn't necessarily agree but nodded anyway. When I left I wondered what he would say to the others about me. Sloan was a clever, sneaky son of a gun and I wouldn't put it past him to play each of us against the other.

When I left Sloan's office I was still disturbed by what he said about the killer having inside information. As far as I knew, I was the only one Wes had talked to about the layout with the camera locations. My mind was tied in knots until it dawned on me that Wes had to have at least shared the layout with Sloan. Perhaps the Detective shared the information with someone else on his staff. But I had trouble seeing why he would have brought anyone else on our team into the loop other than perhaps Tracker Joe. It didn't matter really because I knew I had nothing to do with Wes' demise. I had the uneasy feeling I was being manipulated like a puppet by Sloan so I reluctantly contacted Dr. Greene. It felt awkward talking to him even though he had taken me into his confidence. When I asked him about the team, he gave me a terrible jolt when he said Sloan had phoned to tell him the team was disbanded but offered no explanation and didn't call him in for a meeting. I thanked him, hung up and immediately made my way over to Dr. Mosely's office.

"Hi Doc, I'm sorry to barge in on you like this but I need to talk to you."

"It's no bother mate. What's on your mind?"

I paused to catch my breath, "Did you talk to Detective Sloan?"

He remained nonchalant, "Yes, he called me earlier to tell me he was disbanding the team."

"Did he say why?"

"Yes but you know how he is, rather tight lipped."

I grew impatient at the way I had to pull it out of him, "Well, what did he say?"

Dr. Mosely grew a little concerned over my insistent manner, "Is there something wrong, Seth? You seem agitated about something."

"Please, just tell me what he said to you."

"All right then but it wasn't much. He said he couldn't justify putting civilian resources at risk any longer after Wes was made a target by the killer."

I was still on edge, "Is that it? Didn't he ask to meet with you personally?"

"My word, what is the matter with you? Of course he didn't ask to meet with me. He was polite, short and sweet. He thanked me for my service and said he was grateful for everything he had learned from our team members. That was it."

My nervous behavior raised Doc Mosely's curiosity, "Something has obviously gotten under your skin. Tell me; what's the matter, Seth."

I was hesitant because my mind was jumbled up and I didn't know who I could trust anymore but I desperately needed to confide in someone. Under better circumstances it would have been Faith but that was out of the question so I opened up to the Professor, "I think Detective Sloan suspects me of having something to do with Wes' murder."

Doc laughed in disbelief, "That's ridiculous, Seth. What gave you that silly idea?"

I relayed the whole story to him and his countenance changed, "Now I see what you mean. Let's think about this for a minute. There has to be another explanation. You know Sloan … he's a wily bugger. There's no telling what he may be up to. Perhaps he's using you to smoke out another suspect or maybe it's some kind of test. Whatever the case may be, you have nothing to worry about. He's got to know that you're completely innocent … that you would never hurt Wes Woodson or anyone else."

This did nothing to calm my fears, "All he knows is that I knew the location of the cameras and I was the first person to show up at three of the crime scenes." When I left the Professor I was an inconsolable wreck.

October was a fitting month for the surreal terror that had such a firm grip on the community. Under the circumstances, you'd think that people would back away from the mock mayhem and macabre merriment surrounding Halloween but it had grown too big to contain. Other than Christmas, Halloween was the most widely observed holiday of all which translates to big business. What had been a festive occasion for kids now consumed the adults as well. Sales of candy, costumes, food, booze, decorations and advertising generated billions of dollars in revenue. It helped grease the wheels of commerce and was so pervasive you couldn't walk into a mall, supermarket, convenience store or just about any business or home that wasn't festooned with pumpkins, ghouls and goblins. St. Louis was no different than the rest of the nation and was swept up in a tide of orange and black in spite of the grisly string of murders that haunted us all.

As misfortune would have it, the full moon was set to bloom at the very end of the month on October 31st. This was not lost on the media that breathlessly awaited the next abomination to be committed by Lew Carew. Many of the news outlets referred to the Algonquin tradition of October as the full harvest moon. Only it was not depicted as a friendly, luminous aid in gathering the autumn crops but rather a misguided light sent to assist a madman or beast in reaping a fresh harvest of victims. You would think people had more than enough true fright to go around but still the haunted houses were jam packed, mainly with teens jacked up for holiday excitement. They seemed impervious to the real danger lurking in the shadows. Several of the spook houses and fright fests that sprang up locally adopted harvest themes in honor of the moon … harvests of ghouls and zombies … bloody harvests … one tasteless entrepreneur even set up what he called Lew Carew's Harvest House of Horrors.

Flip Flanagan, like usual, blazed his own trail. He eschewed the more tame Algonquin legends referred to by others and reverted back to pagan tradition and labeled it the month of the blood moon. His instincts proved reliable again in capturing the mood of the folks. The desecration of Wes Woodson and insane tone of Lew Carew's letters cast a demonic shadow that had many people convinced Satan was on the prowl in our fair city. He fed our worst fears with frequent forays into pagan and Wiccan beliefs and rituals. For example, we learned that October 31st is known to them as Samhain, the eve of All Hallows Day, which is the time to celebrate the cycle of death and rebirth and salute Samhain, the lord of death. It is thought to be the best time to reconnect with ancestors and honor the dead. Supposedly, it is a season of strange energy when the veil between our world and the spirit realm is so thin it provides a perfect opportunity to make contact with the dead. Flanagan was a master and had quite a knack for grabbing headlines and remaining in the spotlight.

He even created a myth of his own. In a flight of fanciful fright, Flanagan proposed that Lew Carew scoped out his victims and eluded the police with the aid of felonious feathered friends. He presumed that the wolf man had eyes in the sky in the form of a flock of devilish blackbirds which he noted to his delight are appropriately called a murder of crows. He leaned on his own Emerald Isle heritage to point out how crows, in Irish mythology, are associated with Morrigan, the goddess of war and death. Flanagan reveled in the spooky fact that the bloodthirsty birds were known to work in concert to kill a dying cow. It was all we needed. Every time someone walked by a telephone line or fence post occupied by a flock … excuse me, I mean a murder … of crows, they'd wonder what was going through their demented little minds and flash back to scenes of Hitchcock's Birds being unleashed to pluck out eyes and tear at human flesh.

He also coined a new term in order to whip us into further frenzy. Flanagan deemed Lew Carew to be a *lunar-tic* and labeled his relentless killing spree to be an act of *lunar-cy*. He milked this play on words to focus everyone on the moon's inexorable cycle as we marched toward the crescendo on October 31st, All Hallows Eve. Flanagan flipped the truth to concentrate solely on the notion that October 31st is a date steeped only in pagan lore.

It gave our modern Halloween celebrations a creepy, misguided, illegitimate feel. It reminded me of the confusing pagan history often attributed to December 25th in an attempt to rob us of the true meaning of Christmas. Nevertheless, he was successful in accomplishing his mission. People were riveted to their TV sets and constantly gazed at the night sky as Halloween drew near. Kids were still giddy about the coming candy bonanza and hoards of teens remained oblivious to the real danger but most people were swallowed up in the nauseating apprehension of the menacing peril we faced. Parents wondered how to deal with trick or treating without putting their children at risk.

For me the irresponsible media coverage was just another maddening example of the loss of reality that had turned my world upside down. October was nothing more than a hellish prison to me. My ship was rudderless as I drifted along aimlessly under the moon's surge that month. My total lack of concentration was threatening to put a major dent in the 4.0 GPA I had aspired to for that semester. Even Doctor Mosely's gentle admonishments fell on deaf ears. I couldn't get the sight of Wes' dead body out of my mind and Dr. Greene's shocking revelation ate at me as if I had a giant ulcer in the middle of my gut. I missed my work with Wes. Although I had been reassigned it wasn't the same. I'd never been AWOL from work before in my life but just couldn't answer the bell sometimes. My internship was rightly in jeopardy. In an odd way, I missed being part of the investigative team. While it had exposed me to so much troubling information, it at least afforded me with some closeness and camaraderie that now was sorely lacking. I missed the challenges that kept my restless mind occupied.

Never before had I felt so all alone. I let a distance grow between me and Professor Mosely. There were no lifelines available to me. It was so bad that I considered pulling up stakes and heading home to Portland but I knew that would only hurt Walt and Gretchen and I didn't want to destroy the last bit of peace in my otherwise insane world. What troubled me the most? Was it the pressure of being under suspicion for the murder of Wes Woodson or was it the wall I'd built up between me and Faith? She should have been my anchor in the storm but I couldn't bring myself to open up to her. We still saw each other fairly regularly in spite of the excuses I dreamt up to sometimes avoid her. Although she had cut me plenty of slack in consideration of my grief over Wes, her considerable patience wore thin. "Seth, how long are you going to continue to punish yourself?"

I shot back angrily, "What do you mean by that?"

She paused and looked away to avoid fueling my anger then raised her eyes to mine; deep, soulful, understanding eyes. "Seth, I can see the way you're hurting and it hurts me too. I want to help you but I don't know how. We seem to be drifting apart and it scares me."

I wanted to jump down her throat. I wanted to wag an accusing finger in her face and call her a hypocrite and liar for leading me on when she was the source of my heartache and troubles. However, it wasn't time. I couldn't bring myself to broach the subject I dreaded. Maybe I was a coward or maybe I wanted to prolong putting off the inevitable. No matter what she had done to betray me I couldn't bear the thought of burning the tattered remains of the bridge between me and Faith. So instead, I put on a disguise of my own. "I'm sorry Faith. I don't mean to be angry or distant. It's just that I have so much on my mind."

She leaned closer with those piercing blue eyes, "I know Seth but Wes wouldn't want to see you this way. He'd want you to move on with your life and make him proud. We can't bring him back but we can honor his memory and what he meant to you."

I kept the mask in place, "You're right Faith but there's more to it. There's something I haven't shared with you." A look of concern creased her face and I continued, "Detective Sloan suspects me of having something to do with Wes' murder." She was stunned and remained mute as I filled her in on the details. I had wanted to keep this to myself but dropping the bombshell had the desired effect. She cut me some more slack for my otherwise inexcusable behavior.

Flip Flanagan happened to be on the TV as we sat next to each other in stony silence. Finally I begged, "Please turn that off or change the channel. I can't stand that guy and his bombastic bull crap." Flanagan was in the middle of another discourse on our supposed pagan heritage when Faith hit the remote.

"I know Seth, it burns me too. You'd never know that October 31st is the eve of All Saints Day. It has nothing to do with ghosts, goblins or satanic rituals. It was conceived as an alternative to pagan celebrations and is meant to honor all the Christian saints that have gone before us into heaven by the grace and mercy of God through the all-availing, atoning sacrifice of Jesus Christ. I wonder how many people still remember why Martin Luther nailed his Ninety Five Theses to the church door at Wittenberg on October 31, 1517. He didn't pick that date at random. He knew it was the eve of All Saints Day. His was a message of grace. If anything we should celebrate All Hallows Eve for the restoration of God's word of truth that he accomplished through his servant." In spite of my suspicions and the bitter thoughts I harbored, I still marveled at what I once believed was the essence of Faith's character. Although I knew it was for my own good, I rued the day when Dr. Greene brought me into his confidence.

I seemed to be descending deeper and deeper into the pit of despair as October lurched forward. We were only a week away from Halloween when Sloan called me out of the blue. He asked me to meet with him in Clayton but cut me off without an explanation. When I arrived at Police Headquarters and was ushered into the conference room, I was stunned to see the whole team assembled. Everyone was present except for the Chief who apparently had a conflict and couldn't join us. My mind raced to figure out why we had been asked to reconvene. Had Sloan determined my innocence? Had new evidence been brought to bear? Had a suspect finally been identified? Our curiosities were satisfied soon enough as Sloan revealed a new letter from the killer.

> Detective Sloan,
>
> I am truly sorry for the evil I perpetrated against your comrade but I feel you bear much of the responsibility for this deed. You betrayed me after I came to you seeking benevolence. Instead of earnestly helping me to bring my reign of terror and bloodshed to an end, you foolishly tried to set a trap for me.
>
> Did you really believe I would not see through your lies? You may take me for a fool but I have a functioning brain. The moment it was announced that all the harvest and festival locations would be closed except inexplicably Creve Coeur Lake, I knew you were setting a snare for me. Well, I set a trap of my own. I do regret the abomination I committed against the ranger but you have no one to blame but yourself. You know that I cannot control myself once the transformation occurs. My uncontrollable

rage was unleashed by the moon's power ... and vengeance toward you my unfaithful friend.

In spite of your complicity, it is I who must suffer the remorse ... the agony of a tortured conscience. I can no longer bear this burden. This must come to an end. With that thought in mind, I shall afford you one last chance to prove yourself worthy in aiding me in this cause.

I cannot stand the thought of my ravenous alter ego being loosed on Halloween with the night providing a smorgasbord of dainty, costumed delicacies to satisfy my evil lusts. I can see only one way to avoid disaster while proving it is not me but the moon's curse that wreaks the havoc. I have fashioned iron fetters suitable for the beast and will restrain myself before the moon rises in the Halloween sky. This will be done under one condition. You, Detective Sloan must witness the transformation. And you must come alone. Once you've seen the savagery and pain I suffer during the malignant metamorphosis, I'm hopeful you will be filled with pity rather than a desire to destroy me. Perhaps you will find it in your heart to help me.

If you can agree to these terms, please let me know by flying the flag at half-mast on Halloween morning. That being the case, I will call you with the location before the clock strikes eight.

Lew Carew

Sloan offered this explanation, "Thank you all for taking the time to join me today. I have no intention of re-commissioning the team or putting any of you in harm's way. However, I obviously have a tough decision to make and would appreciate your input. No one has better insight into Lew Carew than you."

Everyone nodded silently and then I took it upon myself to break the ice, "Do you trust this guy?"

"Of course not, but what choice do I have?"

I offered the first suggestion, "What about setting another trap? Doesn't he have to be somewhere near here on Halloween morning to see the flag?"

Sloan sighed with resignation, "I don't see how we could ever pick him out of the crowd. And in any case, it didn't work out so well the first time around."

Tracker Joe offered a novel thought, "I bet one of my hounds could pick him out of the crowd with one scent of him."

Sloan remained pessimistic, "Don't you think he'd be a bit suspicious if we had dogs posted on every corner? We all saw what he is capable of when he feels betrayed. I don't want to find out what he might do if we set him off on Halloween."

Everything we could dream up was fraught with flaws. I was ready to throw in the towel, "It's too bad Michael is not here. He's a great one for thinking outside the box."

Greene spoke up, "He's booked on a speaking engagement out of town."

Sloan too was ready to drop the gavel, "Boys, I appreciate your help but it's clear what I need to do. I'm going to have to play this one by the book. He may be setting me up but I can't take any chances. There's too much at stake."

I floated one last trial balloon, "Are you going to take anyone with you?"

Sloan remained steadfast, "This guy is too sharp. He has an uncanny way of sniffing out funny business."

I objected, "Can't you wear a wire or GPS tracker to lead your back-up to the secret location?"

"Kid, I gotta play this one straight. If something went wrong and this maniac took out his revenge on some cute little tyke in a Curious George costume, I'd never be able to forgive myself. No, I'm going to play this one strictly by the book and let the chips fall where they may. Thanks guys and wish me luck."

When I returned to campus, I was surprised to find Dr. Mosely waiting outside my door. "Hey Doc, what's up?"

"Do you mind if I come in for a chat?" I opened the door, waved him in and offered a seat on the couch. He had something serious on his mind because he elected to sit at the kitchen table on a hard wooden chair rather than relaxing. "Tell me Seth, do you feel better now that you're not a suspect?"

I was puzzled, "I didn't realize I'd been taken off the list. Did you hear something I missed?"

"No, it wasn't anything I heard but I hope you realize that you wouldn't have been in the room if you were a suspect." I waited for an explanation. "Sloan is a cagey bird, my boy. I think the only reason he shared that letter with us was to read our faces and confirm his hunch that none of us are involved. In my opinion, it was no coincidence that he scheduled our meeting when Michael Muraco had a conflict."

The light bulb went off in my head, "Sloan told me he was suspicious of Michael during our last meeting."

Dr. Mosely offered a wry smile, "And why do you suppose he opened up to you like that? I'll tell you. He likes to read faces. I believe he was putting you on the spot to see if you might have any connection to his prime suspect."

It started to make sense to me. Lew Carew had too much inside information not to be tied to the investigation in some fashion.

Doc confirmed my suspicions, "Sloan was convinced it was an inside job from the time he received the first letter from Lew Carew. Everything after that was a clever process of elimination for him. He never trusted Michael Muraco. He couldn't bring himself to believe in the Loup Garou no matter how well the legend fit our circumstances."

I protested, "But Michael is so convincing!"

"Yes, he is, Seth. Perhaps he believes it in his own mind. Just maybe, as Dr. Greene surmised of Lew Carew, Michael suffers from some form of lycanthropy. That I don't know. But rest assured that you are not a suspect. I believe our friend, Detective Sloan is a blood hound tracking another singular scent … he is on the trail of Mingan Muraco."

Dr. Mosely switched from conjecture to a stern warning. "Seth, I shared my opinion with you to give you some peace of mind. I know this has been tearing you up inside. So take this simply in the spirit offered."

"What do you mean, Doc?"

He squinted over a thin smile, "I know how you are Seth. Your first impulse will be to try to help in bringing Michael to justice. I implore you, do not think about it. This belongs in the hands of the police. Whoever is the killer; be it Michael or someone else, he is extremely dangerous. I still do not believe Lew Carew is a raving lunatic or wild, unruly lycanthrope. His evil mind is brilliant and he knows exactly what he's doing. There is something beyond ideology at play here. He is possessed by white, hot anger … a rage so ferocious he is capable of anything. Remember what I've said and whatever you do, stay as far away from Lew Carew as possible." What could I say other than okay?

The Professor wasn't done with me yet. I could almost see him removing an arrow from Cupid's quiver. "Faith also tells me that you haven't been yourself lately. Is there anything else bothering you?"

It felt good to confide in Dr. Mosely and I took some comfort in the fatherly advice he'd offered about Lew Carew. However, I wasn't ready to open up about Faith. I still didn't want to believe she had betrayed me. How could I bring myself to raise such a horrible accusation with Dr. Mosely? Anyway, they were partners in crime in my opinion. He shared some of the blame for the way I'd been misled and then had my heart ripped out. So instead of getting it off my chest, I played another charade, "No, there's nothing else bothering me beyond Wes' death. I'm still having a tough time. But it really helps to know that I'm not implicated in any way. Thanks so much Doc."

It was a Friday and the day before Halloween and I was supposed to hang out with Faith at her parents' house. Normally, I'd be champing at the bit since Deborah and Dan had a night on the town and wouldn't be home until almost midnight. Unfortunately, my state of mind was so pitiful I dreaded what I'd normally consider a golden opportunity. I thought about cancelling but couldn't come up with a credible excuse. Faith did her best to get things back to normal, "Hey Seth, come on in." She tried to plant a wet one on me but I turned my cheek to her. She did her best to ignore my rude behavior and let what amounted to an insult pass. "What would you like to do?"

I responded without enthusiasm, "Wanna go out someplace and grab a bite?"

She looked wounded, "What in the world is the matter with you mister? We have this big house all to ourselves and you want to go out? Come into the kitchen and look at what I've made special, just for you." It was one of my favorites, an oozing, warm cheesy batch of tasty chicken enchiladas in soft, grilled tortillas with just the right amount of jalapeno to make them spicy but not overwhelming. The flour tortillas were toasted just right to a golden brown on the outside to where air pockets formed crispy bumps that I loved to crack like popping some kind of savory bubble wrap. She also had rice, refried beans, home-made guacamole dip and plenty of frosty, cold Budweiser.

I felt like a jerk for being so unappreciative. It was a very nice gesture and my stomach was growling so I was able to enjoy the meal and put on a happy face for a while. I downed three Buds in rapid succession in an attempt to numb my injured feelings but it only served to loosen the strings I'd attached to my bitter tongue. Faith tried to build on what she thought was positive momentum, "Do you want to watch a movie downstairs?"

Normally, the come hither look in her eyes would have had me scrambling down the stairs but I hesitated, "Why don't we watch it upstairs since we're already here."

She wouldn't take no for an answer and grabbed my hand and pulled me, "Don't be silly. The TV downstairs is so much bigger and all the DVDs are down there."

I sat in the middle of the couch while she popped in a DVD and then cozied up next to me. Like a fool, I inched away but she scooted over to close the gap. We kept up this comedy until I was trapped by the arm of the couch then pretended to be engrossed in, of all things, some incredibly boring chick flick while Faith pressed up against me and tried to dock her lips on mine. Finally, she couldn't take it any more ... not just the way I rebuffed her that night but everything that had built up over almost a month. She began to sob in desperation and anger, "Why are you acting this way? I didn't kill Wes! Why are you taking it out on me? Is that what you call fair?"

Maybe it was the Budweiser or the pressure was just too much to bear but I blew up at her accusation. "You wanna talk about fair do you? You've got some nerve going off on me about what's fair!" I couldn't tell if she was more shocked or puzzled but the intensity of my anger stunned her. Her sobbing was replaced by a quivering lower lipped punctuated by occasional gulps for air.

Faith's eyes were incredibly sad. "I've had this bottled up inside me for almost a month waiting for you to come clean!"

"Come clean … come clean … come clean about what?"

"You know exactly what I mean … Zeb Greene, that's what!"

Faith was so dumbfounded she couldn't speak. I couldn't take the silence, "He came to me earlier this month and told me all about you putting the moves on him. I guess when he turned you down you decided to stick with old Seth for a while, eh?" Her mouth formed a perfect circle and I thought her eyes would pop out of her head. She couldn't quite spit out her apoplectic response before she broke down crying uncontrollably with her face pressed into the couch. Even though I was the injured party I felt like a heel. I didn't know what else to do and reflexively patted her and rubbed her back.

She sat upright like she'd been launched out of a jack-in-the-box and screamed, "Don't you touch me!"

Something was very wrong. Why did I feel like apologizing? We both sat there frozen for the longest time until some semblance of composure returned. Faith spoke to me in measured tones, "I didn't say anything to you because I wanted to forget. I felt it would be better to put it behind me rather than dragging you into a huge mess. I'll tell you now though, Seth Lomax, since you've elected to believe a lying scumbag of a man without even giving me a chance to explain. Yes, there was something going on behind your back between me and Dr. Greene. But it wasn't at my choosing. He was the one who tried to renew our relationship and turn it into something it never was. I told him again and again that we could be nothing more than friends but he wouldn't take no for an answer. He badgered me to the point where I had to get downright hostile and burn our bridges completely. I wasn't trying to be mean; I just wanted to be left alone. I went out of my way to keep things from getting ugly. And do you know what I got for my trouble? That animal hurt me! He tried to molest me and when I fought back he hurt me! That's what you saw on my wrist. If you would have lifted my sleeves and removed my top you'd have seen my arms, chest and neck covered in ugly, horrible, purple and green bruises!"

I was mortified. I felt fortunate when she collapsed in my arms because I felt so full of shame that I couldn't look her in the eyes. She cried and cried and I just held on for dear life, at first to try to console her and then to hide my own tears. Painful memories flooded my mind with reminders of all the grief and punishment I had poured out unjustly on her. I muttered over and over, "I'm so sorry, Faith." We sat there intertwined for what seemed like an eternity before we could start rebuilding the bridge between us. "Faith, I'm so sorry. I should have never doubted you. I was such a fool. Please forgive me."

She smiled and her face was still beautiful despite the puffy redness and tracks of her tears, "Seth, I should have told you right away. I'm sorry too, honey. Please forgive me." We embraced again and shared a deep, rejuvenating sigh of relief. She gave me a peck on the cheek which led to many exchanges and then deep, hungry kisses as we rushed to make up for lost time.

I didn't want to kill the mood but I couldn't hide a new and different anger that was welling up inside me. Zeb Greene was not only a rat of the tallest order but a sick pervert to boot. As Dr.

Mosely had opined long ago, Green's altruistic intentions were completely phony from the outset and he was, as Mosely surmised, a sicko looking to score with a student almost ten years younger than him. I fumed at the way he lied and used me to cover his tracks with Faith. We forfeited a month out of our lives thanks to him. As I envisioned Faith struggling under his weight and bearing the brunt of his slimy paws clutching her wrists, arms and neck, I couldn't contain my rage. Faith tensed up again, "Seth, what's the matter now?"

"I'm sorry; I just can't stand the thought of that sick weasel man-handling you. I need to settle the score with Zeb Greene."

She grabbed my shoulders firmly but gently and pierced my eyes with her longing gaze, "Seth, let it go. It's not worth it. It will catch up to him. The only thing that is important now is you and me." I welcomed another warm embrace but didn't take her kind and wise advice. There would be a reckoning with one Zeb Greene.

I wasn't there to see it but knew the flag in front of the government center in Clayton was at half-mast the next morning. Not too many people noticed it since everyone was wrapped up in preparations for Halloween ... while fretting over the threat of Lew Carew. The media drum beat was pounding louder than ever and concerned parents had to offer insincere assurances to children who were old enough to pick up on the incessant, disturbing warnings. Most of the people who noticed the flag assumed some government honcho had passed away. One onlooker knew better. As for me, I was preoccupied with vengeance. I called, went by his office several times and even tracked down his residence but Greene was nowhere to be found. I thought sarcastically that maybe the sicko professor was enjoying the day cruising the local high schools and malls for the next young, unwilling object of his perverted affection.

The day spun away and I resigned myself to perhaps not being able to settle the score with ZPG until another day but I remained determined and persistent. In the meantime, Detective Sloan continued to be resolute as well. He passed the time mulling over the situation and preparing as best as he could until the sun began to drop below the horizon. As nightfall proceeded, the kids ventured out with parents in tow to begin the happy quest to fill their trick or treat pillows, satchels, sacks, bags and plastic pumpkins. Sloan left the office to kill time cruising nearby neighborhoods. He ironically longed for the good old days when the typical threat was some creep burying pins or razor blades in a candy bar. His phone rang much earlier than anticipated, well before the rising of the blood moon. The display simply read private caller, number unknown. The muffled, deep voice was brief and to the point. He was instructed to drive to a wooded stretch of farmland way out west off Interstate 70 near New Melle, Missouri. The detailed directions guided him to a particular, secluded spot down a dark gravel road well off the beaten path far from the nearest home.

He went as far as possible in his car and then proceeded on foot. He almost didn't need a flashlight except for the many branches of the tall oaks that blocked the light reflecting off the moon which was still ascending brightly overhead. Lew Carew had said the path would take a sharp turn about three hundred yards from the gravel road then slope down sharply into a meadow where he would be waiting beneath a broad sycamore. The distinctive tree was unmistakable from one hundred yards away with the moonlight shining across its smooth, expansive, pale bark. Sloan pulled his service revolver and approached cautiously, listening intently for any sign of life. There were no bugs or animals and the few remaining leaves were motionless in the cold, still, dead night air. His eyes darted nervously up and down looking for trip wires, pits or snares.

At thirty yards out, the detective's flashlight caught an unnatural shape at the base of the tree. There was still no sound or movement. He advanced even more cautiously until the image was unmistakable. The Chief was slumped against the tree with his long, matted black hair suspended from his bowed head. One hand was clasped tightly at the wrist in a thick, iron shackle that was chained to the sycamore with a long, heavy steel spike that was sunk deeply into the massive tree trunk. A large hammer rested on the ground nearby. His other arm hung limp at his side with his hand resting near the gun that had brought his miserable life to an abrupt end with one devastating shot fired directly into his left temple. A few wisps of remaining steam still rose from the fresh wound.

Sloan had suspected Mingan Muraco for quite some time. But he didn't anticipate things ending this way. He fully expected the Chief to set some kind of trap to make him his blood moon victim. Apparently, this Loup Garou did have a conscience and it got the best of him. There were some questions Sloan would have to answer to fully satisfy his cop's curiosity. Where was the wolf? Would they be able to find his lair somewhere or did Michael let it go or dispose of it in some way to perpetuate the myth of the Loup Garou? Fittingly, there were silver bullets in the remaining chambers of the pistol the Chief had used. There was no suicide note, no epilogue from Lew Carew so they would have to speculate about his motives. Perhaps there might be a way for the medical examiner to dissect his brain to determine if in fact he suffered from lycanthropy. Sloan must have suspected he was just a loony tune. The only artifact left on the body was a razor sharp buck knife. The detective would ask the forensic team to look for traces of blood from Hanley Wilson's bloody pentagram. They would also try to match the Chief's blood to the DNA found at the other scenes. Sloan was dog tired from the strain of waiting for the Chief's call all day but had to be relieved to know that the kids would be safe that Halloween night and tomorrow would be a new day. A long night lay ahead but soon it would be over and, in the morning, he'd have the pleasure of finally passing along the good news at the press conference.

As luck would have it, I was talking to Faith on my phone when Zeb Green returned my call at 8:30 on Halloween night. I was in the car heading to meet her at her parents' house where she was handing out goodies to their giddy little visitors. When I hung up, I saw the missed call and dialed my voice mailbox to get Greene's curt message that I could meet him at his house. I quickly called Faith back and told her I'd be delayed. She pressed me for a reason until I admitted I was headed to a showdown with Zeb Greene. Faith tried her best to discourage me saying that she didn't trust him … that he was unbalanced. I lied and said I just wanted to talk to him face-to-face to lay the whole thing to rest. I assured her I'd finish with Greene and be there before 9:30.

Greene's house was at the end of the block on the outskirts of the trendy central west end of the city, right on the edge of where affluence blended abruptly into the surrounding decay and crime. It seemed isolated because no one ventured that far for candy and the neighbors kept to themselves with doors bolted tightly at night. They were mostly singles or young couples without children who were out at posh Halloween parties elsewhere. When I knocked on the large, ornate, wood, glass and wrought iron door, I could hear the ominous echo emanating from within the cavernous entry way. Zeb opened the door wearing an odd ensemble of jeans, boots and down vest as though he'd just done a photo shoot for Cabela's.

I thought maybe he was dressed that way to be ready to rumble. He didn't turn on the porch light or ask me to come in. Instead he stepped outside and walked down the steps to the front lawn.

It was fairly dark since the nearest street lamp was halfway down the block. I could still see that he had a smug look on his face that didn't betray a hint of fear. To the contrary, he appeared quite self-confident. "Apparently, you've been hot on my heels all day, Seth. So here I am. What is it that you want?"

It didn't matter that I was on his home turf. I wasn't going to give into any mind games. "I think you know why I'm here." He just nodded as a sly grin slithered over his face. "I want you to tell me why you lied to me about Faith!" I leaned toward him with my fists clenched and body tense but he didn't budge.

He was oddly calm as he retorted, "What was I supposed to do; tell you how I roughed the bitch up when she refused to put out?" He threw his head back and laughed maniacally. I stared in disbelief for a moment then lunged forward to teach him a good lesson. Before I could close the gap between us, he reached inside his vest in one swift motion and pulled a gun on me. Faith was right … the guy was bonkers. I froze thinking all I'd have to do is back down and walk away but was caught completely off guard when he pointed and fired without blinking an eye.

When I awoke, I found myself bound to a chair in a run down, ramshackle cabin in the middle of nowhere. I had no way of knowing that we were way out Interstate 44 past Fenton and Eureka about as far away as possible from Detective Sloan and his fellow officers. There was a sharp pain in my left shoulder where I'd been hit with a tranquilizer dart. My head was still filled with cob webs. Greene approached me with that smug look still affixed to his face and slapped me several times to help bring me around. I thought this couldn't be happening to me! I half expected him to bust out laughing and have Ashton Kutcher rush out to tell me I'd been punked. I knew I was sadly mistaken when a look of rage enveloped Greene's twisted face.

"So what do you think now, Sir Lancelot? Are you glad you came to save the reputation of your fair damsel? You made a big mistake, didn't you, you dumb, ignorant fool!" He paced rapidly as he ranted as if he had to let off the energy building up inside to avoid completely blowing his top. "Make no mistake though. This is not about your bouncy, blond bimbo. Did she tick me off? Sure she did. But not as much as you! I thought you had potential … until you started hanging out with Miss Goody Two Shoes and that demented Australian Neanderthal. You think I betrayed you by trying to get some mileage out of that dumb, bumpkin winch? Who betrayed who, Seth? It's time you admitted that you're the real culprit here!" He was so worked up that he was spraying spit everywhere. I was waiting for him to start foaming at the mouth like a rabid dog.

I'd be lying if I said I wasn't scared out of my gourd. The guy was missing more than a few cards from his deck and seemed just on the verge of becoming completely unhinged. I tried to derail the rampage express, "I don't know what you're talking about. Please calm down, Dr. Greene."

He pounced like a jungle cat and slapped me so hard I saw stars. "Shut your mouth, traitor! Yes, that's right … you're nothing but a lousy, miserable traitor! You've betrayed the cause … you've betrayed the earth … and all for some stupid, little girl with the brain the size of a pea! I thought you had brains but obviously I was wrong. You fell for that charlatan, Mosely, and his insipid line of banal bull crap! You should have known better but no … you've swallowed their creationist propaganda like pabulum. Do you really believe that nonsense or did you sell out just to try to get in that girl's pants? Are you that shallow Mr. Lomax?

The decibel level was rising to the point where I feared for my life. I knew I had to do something to buy some time. Pleading ignorance or appealing for sympathy was obviously the wrong way to go so, out of desperation, I decided to go on the attack. "Who's kidding who, Zeb?" I paused and braced for another slap but he was momentarily stunned. He was not used to being addressed on a first name basis by a student and didn't expect such abject disobedience from someone in as helpless a position as mine. It encouraged me to press the attack further, "Do you expect me to believe this is not about Faith? Don't try to lay all this environmental mumbo jumbo on me. You can't stand the fact that Faith rejected you in favor of me!" His face grew even redder and he seemed to fill with pressurized steam but he remained frozen in place so I piled it on thicker. "Then you have the nerve to tell me you have another girlfriend. Ha, that's a good one! That's your problem. You don't have anyone because no girl would be caught dead with a creep like you."

He was seething but still immobilized so I continued the onslaught. I remembered how Faith said Greene had a strange relationship with his mother … how she manipulated him and seemed to exercise so much influence over him. It was just a shot in the dark but what else did I have? "Maybe it's because for all your worldly wisdom and academic credentials you're still living in mommy's shadow." I knew I had struck a nerve by the look of pain and astonishment that flashed across his face. "You just can't escape her apron strings, can you? Maybe you're problem is that you can't find a girl just like mommy. Yeah, I bet you have sick dreams about dear, old mom, don't you?" That one did it. I pressed the wrong button because he flung the door open so hard it shattered the glass panes and he stormed off into the night. My heart was pounding uncontrollably as I awaited the madman's next move.

Reality surpassed my worst fears. The beast snarled and panted as it fought the chain that slowed its swaggering, strained advance through the doorway. It must have been a freak of nature at what seemed like twice the size of a normal gray wolf. The tongue hung suspended like a slab of raw meat in a butcher shop. Its fangs were impossibly long like a set of ivory steak knives dripping with saliva. The hunched back was so incredibly high it nearly reached up to Greene's chest. I could see the sinews rippling through its legs and under its coat across a broad chest and shoulders as it strained against the heavy chain. Most fearsome though were the menacing eyes that fixed their evil gaze upon me as it snarled wickedly, tried to lunge and snapped its steel trap jaws with a loud clack. I braced for death as Greene released his grip on the chain but the animal heeled obediently as Greene barked a single command. It was incredibly well trained to follow his orders and carry out his demented whims.

There was no way for me to hide my fright and Greene fed off the fear instinctively like a junk yard dog. He spoke calmly now in a manner that disturbed me more than his previous raging diatribe. "I'd like you to meet my friend, Lew Carew. Actually, his name is Caesar. Give him your paw Caesar." The obedient monster raised one massive paw causing Greene to laugh diabolically. "I raised Caesar from a pup and he's quite the obedient student as you can see. You cannot imagine the countless hours and attention I've given to my devoted pupil. Unlike you, he's extremely loyal and will do anything I ask … even kill. He's very good at it and knows how to keep it tidy as you've seen. But we have something different in store for you, Seth. You need to learn a lesson about nature and man's low standing. You need to see that when pitted against one another on equal footing, man is no match for nature. I want to see what happens when you pray to your creator for help. For your sake, I hope your God is listening."

He patted the murderous, giant wolf and caressed its massive head and neck as if it was a common house pet. "For all your flaws, you deserve a sporting chance so I'm going to cut you loose and there will be no more drugs administered. We will rest here peacefully and give you a five minute head start before I unleash Lew Carew. Let me warn you though. Do not attempt to take to the trees to elude him. That would be a big mistake for I will track you down and shoot you with another dart if that is the case. I'll drop you to the ground where you'll be treated to the helpless feeling of his jaws around your throat ... clenching and ripping the life out of you. No, you'll be much better off taking your chances on foot. I hope you're in good shape and up to the challenge because Caesar needs his exercise. It's not often that he gets free rein to hunt on his own. Doesn't this sound fun?" He unleashed another sinister smile, "Oh there's one more thing. As if you didn't have enough incentive already, here's something else to motivate you. When you fall prey to Lew Carew, Faith will be mine. Just so you'll know; I'm going to do unspeakable things to her before I kill her."

Fear coupled with rage made me want to tear out Greene's throat but I had no choice but to go along with his sick game. So when he cut me loose, I readied myself for the race of my life ... a race against terror and a horrific death. As I sprinted out the door, the last words I heard were; "Run well my friend. You have five minutes ... not a second less and not a second more." I was completely disoriented. There was no way of knowing which direction might lead to a highway or road so I just darted straight ahead trying to put as much distance between me and the cabin as possible. The moon was high overhead in the sky and incredibly large. It was one of those nights where you can see the dark spots forming the face of the man in the moon. Its luminescence aided my escape by helping me to avoid trees and branches as I hurried away.

Although I was in good shape I knew it would be foolish to try to maintain a sprint for five minutes so I settled into a brisk, steady pace. My adrenaline was pumping madly but I forced myself to try to think rationally. I looked at my watch to be able to keep track of the precious little time I had. As I dodged trees, rocks and other obstacles I figured the wolf would make up ground quickly to where maybe I'd have two or three minutes more before he'd overtake me. Then what should I do? I had no doubt that Zeb Greene was serious about the tranquilizer dart so I wasn't about to start climbing a tree. The terrain was foreign to me so there wasn't much of a chance I'd find a cave where I could seek refuge from the wolf. The beast's keen sense of smell ruled out any thought of trying to find a hiding place. Would I come across a pond where I could submerge and breathe through a reed? No, that kind of stuff only happens in the movies. I assumed correctly that we were far enough off the beaten path that I wouldn't be able to find help from a neighbor or passerby.

As the first two minutes passed it became abundantly clear that I would have to face the wolf, one-on-one. I needed a weapon to have any chance. Glancing down as I ran, I spied a perfect tree branch that lay nearby and snatched it up. It was nearly six feet long, two inches in diameter and still strong and solid. I had to work harder to maintain my pace while carrying my spear in waiting. It's a good thing that I have a head for numbers because it wasn't easy to calculate a plan in my head but the challenge helped me to avoid succumbing to panic. I figured it would take me a good minute to fashion the branch into a sharp point assuming I came across a good sized, coarse rock. That would give me perhaps four minutes before putting the make shift spear to use. I wondered if it really mattered how much distance I put between myself and the wolf before the inevitable battle ensued. Then I remembered Greene. I needed to get as far away as possible to avoid a two-on-one confrontation.

I picked up the pace a bit but was wary of saving as much strength as possible for my clash with the monster. Then, I caught a glint of the moon and hurried toward a large outcropping where I feverishly began scrapping the end of the branch into a surprisingly sharp point in a brief amount of time. Since I had a bloodthirsty gray wolf on my tail, it did wonders for my productivity. When I passed the five minute mark, I began to listen for signs of the terrible predator. As expected, only a couple of minutes passed before I heard the crunch of the leaves and thumping of its massive paws pounding the ground. When it got close enough that I could hear its panting breath, I knew it was time. I screeched to a halt in a small clearing, clasped the spear in both hands and readied myself for a battle to the death.

The canny wolf stopped a few yards short to size up its prey. It paced sideways in an arc around me and snarled viciously, never unlocking its eyes from mine. Its body was tensed and coiled to strike a deadly blow at any moment. I was almost paralyzed with fear staring into the face of Lew Carew. Its head was lowered, ears pinned back, teeth bared in a fearsome pose of pending doom. It instinctively knew to be wary of the spear and tested my abilities with the lunge and parry of a fencing champion. My reflexes were excellent but I was still amazed at the lightning quickness of the wolf and its ability to change direction so effortlessly. It seemed to toy with me as I thrust the spear time and again. He was the mongoose to my cobra. Time was running out and I had to make a move before Greene could come up in reinforcement. With nothing more to lose and my life on the line I decided to revert to an old, Hollywood stunt. I lunged again then pretended to stumble and fall backwards while lowering the spear to the ground. Lew Carew leaned back on his haunches preparing to leap on top of me and tear my throat apart. This was my one shot. I held steady waiting to raise the spear at the last moment to impale the lunging beast.

Just as I was about to realize my chance for an improbable victory, a voice rang out, "Caesar heel," and the beast immediately sat still. It was too late. Greene approached gun in hand and launched another dart into me before I could react. This time it was different. It didn't knock me out cold but held me in a tingling grip of paralysis and suspended animation. Greene stood over me sneering as I tried fruitlessly to sit up or move my arms and legs. "There, there Seth ... don't you worry now. It will be over soon enough. Look, I've even brought my camera phone to capture your death mask. I'll be sure to share it with Faith before I have my way with her." I was so angry and helpless that I wanted to cry but wouldn't give Greene that pleasure. He backed away and with one small motion released the wolf to do his bidding. I saw first-hand what poor Mike & Carol Sue, dear Wes, Billy, Brantley and the others had experienced. The wolf approached slowly with what appeared to be a devilish grin on its face and bared its drool covered, glistening fangs as it prepared to plunge them into my waiting throat. I closed my eyes and began to pray to God Almighty, "Yea, though I walk through the valley of the shadow of death, I will fear no evil: for thou art with me; thy rod and thy staff they comfort me ..."

I didn't cease praying even when I could feel the wolf's hot breath blanketing my face in putrid waves. Then a miracle occurred. To this day I'm convinced it was God's intervention. A shot rang out and the wolf yelped as it collapsed heavily to the ground in a heap next to me. The next voice I heard was a winded one with an undeniable Aussie accent, "Drop that gun Greene or I'll put one through your wicked heart too." Good old Noah Mosely was, thankfully, by the grace of God, way ahead of me once again. He knew I would not heed his warnings and acted as my guardian angel that day. Mosely had hovered close and followed my every movement including my about face to Zeb Greene's house. Once I recovered and had a chance to chat with Doc I quizzed him as to why he didn't enlist the police. He said he tried to seek help from Sloan after Greene shot me with the tranquilizer dart but he was off on a wild goose chase. He had no choice but to stay on Greene's tail. He laughed heartily in noting that he still had enough left in the tank to keep up with Greene through the woods … just barely … in the nick of time … by the providence of God.

EPILOGUE

WHAT IS THE MORE UNSETTLING proposition, that we are the product of random chance or an omnipotent designer with uncompromising, impossible standards? I had learned so much from Dr. Noah Mosely; certainly enough to know this was not a valid question. God is omnipotent and is most definitely our creator but he does not hold us to uncompromising, impossible standards. No, that only applies to the ungrateful, vile, rebellious fools who reject God and choose to place themselves under the law's strict hand. Our God, the only true God, is a God of infinite love and compassion. He loves us so much that he took our sins upon himself in the person of Jesus Christ to be the end of the law for righteousness, a righteousness we don't deserve. But he lavished it on us anyway at such a great price. God did all this as a free gift to us, even granting the faith to believe in him as a gracious gift rather than a work we must perform. We don't do anything to earn heaven and can't take any credit. We can only incur all of the blame if we reject so great a gift. Thank God that we are not products of random chance that occurred impossibly, mysteriously over eons of time through cruel evolutionary death and struggle.

I owe a lot to my friend Noah Mosely. He taught me how to see things through a different set of glasses, spiritual lenses. Doc taught me that my Christian faith and empirical science are not mutually exclusive but go hand-in-hand. So much of what I was able to grasp would have been impossible to see through the worldly blinders of conventional wisdom and *settled science*. Doc Mosely was never drawn off course by imaginary werewolves whether conjured through myths and legends or evolutionary babble and pseudo-science. He always saw things clearly and was many steps ahead when the rest of us were fumbling our way along, hopelessly lost. He's not superhuman. It's just that his wisdom is grounded solidly in God's word, the precious Bible that I've come to cherish.

It turns out his earliest profile of the killer fit Zeb Greene to a tee. Mosely's focus on motive as the key to the crimes proved prophetic. In something akin to the Hitchcockian confession of Norman Bates, a shattered Zeb Greene spilled his guts to the authorities. He truly was a tortured, twisted, rage-filled soul thanks in large part to his domineering mother. Through his formative years, Zeb suffered the neglect of a single parent home where his mother often vented her wrath over the inconvenience he presented to her. At other times, especially as he grew older, Gloria smothered him under her cloying control as she forcefully indoctrinated him with her radical philosophies. In something close to the Stockholm syndrome, Zeb worked tirelessly to be the devoted son, adopting Gloria's ideology and taking it to another level to garner her favor. It was a manic relationship ranging from cruel barbs where she taunted him as a bastard and accident to lavishing him with doting praise for his strict adherence to her rigid life paradigms.

Deep beneath the surface of his seemingly calm exterior slathered with the veneer of admiration, laid deep seated resentment for the witch who so often tormented him with such vindictive glee. Buried further within his subconscious was also a monstrous rage emanating from an unspeakable secret ... the sexual abuse of his mother which, in his poor, warped mind was translated into the maternal love and comfort he craved but provided a painful reminder of her disaffection for him in any normal sense other than one where she found it useful for her own perverse, selfish desires. He developed a powerful Oedipus complex but, unlike the classic Freudian version, Zeb was unable to entertain a son's twisted desire to kill his father. Thanks to Gloria, Zeb had no psychological outlet ... he never knew his anonymous specter of a father and, thus, suffered intense frustration that turned into the unquenchable rage he directed outward toward other *villains* who committed crimes against mother earth. This is what I unwittingly tapped into when I taunted Greene in the cabin about his mother.

In a way, Greene embodied the legend of the Loup Garou. No, he didn't transform into the mythical beast ... at least not physically. But he possessed the deadly instincts of a predatory beast combined with such keen human intelligence that it made him as extraordinarily dangerous as the Loup Garou. He was not burdened by conscience or weighed down by remorse. Zeb Greene was a true adherent of evolutionary faith and murder was of no moral consequence ... it was nothing more than a random occurrence whereby the old, foolish and weak inhabitants of the animal kingdom meet death by chance when they stumble into the path of the wise, strong and superior. He was doing mankind and the world a favor by ridding it of useless, dangerous dinosaurs like Merle Polk, Ray Slaten, Hanley Wilson, Brantley Earl and evolutionary mutant misfits like Mike, Carol Sue and Billy the Armadillo. He admitted that he felt some regret in having to kill Wes Woodson who was a friend to the environment but confessed that it could not be avoided. He ranted how his just wrath had been poured out to make an example out of Wes only after he had betrayed and tried to trap him.

Dr. Mosely was also on target when he said the killer was cold and calculating rather than an out-of-control lunatic. Greene plotted his murders strategically and carried out his plans like a master tactician. He consciously birthed and fed the werewolf mania to cover his tracks. It gave him added pleasure to concoct the notion of nature taking out its vengeance upon evil mankind. Greene went to great lengths to stage the scenes properly. Imagine carrying such a beast away from the crime scenes to manage the prints in just the right way to create the illusion of a wolf transforming into a man. The peaceful repose of the dead victims' bodies had nothing to do with regret or repentance. He wanted to create an image of death that went beyond what a normal wolf might dispense. That's why he carefully controlled Lew Carew to limit his bloodlust to the victims' throats. He was able to achieve this through considerable research and hard work in using aconite, a by-product of wolf's bane. It had been replaced long ago by modern, much safer anesthetics but served his purpose perfectly in immobilizing the victims while leaving them conscious to satisfy his sadistic desires.

He displayed extraordinary talent and patience in training the wolf to serve him so well ... and remarkable premeditation. Greene picked the unusually large pup from a litter at the wolf sanctuary he served in Colorado and raised him like a pet or better yet a child. They shared a bizarre bond built on iron clad trust and loyalty. Greene confessed with perverse glee how he was able to bring Caesar along to Missouri without raising an eyebrow due to his work with the zoo and the local wolf sanctuary. He leased the remote cabin for the express purpose of keeping Caesar hidden, out of harm's way from nosy authorities. The only time anyone but the victims saw Caesar was a rare conjugal visit to the wolf sanctuary to pass his genes along to a new generation … a scary thought. Greene revealed the depth of his depravity when he explained to the authorities how he had trained Caesar to kill. Without a kernel of remorse, he proudly detailed how he selected stray dogs at first then homeless men who would never be missed. After Caesar practiced his craft under Greene's guidance, Greene carefully disposed of the bodies. He knew how to cover up his evil deeds until it was time to unleash his terror upon the public.

When it came time to put things in motion, everything was incredibly well thought out. He managed the crime scenes meticulously to feed the werewolf mania. He swept tracks clean and carefully dotted the area around the Armadillo's body with only Lew's hind prints. Imagine the deadly beast remaining so compliant to his master. It would have been almost comical to watch if not so tragic. Greene guided Lew through the traps set around the deer. When he picked up the wolf to leave a dead trail, it was his scent that Joe's hounds followed. Thereafter Greene took pains to avoid being near the dogs. He mixed the Chief's blood with wolf DNA. His hand stirred the concoction used to stamp the wolf's paw print. He deposited hair in just the right places. He kept the lantern from bursting into flames when he struck Brantley Earl. He manipulated our thoughts through the letters and dropped subtle hints in our team meetings to eventually point everything toward implicating the Chief.

Other than Doc Mosely, no one was better than Greene at thinking ahead. Before he recommended Mingan Muraco to Sloan, he knew he would make him the fall guy. If it were not for his weakness for Faith and uncontrollable urge for retribution against me, he might have pulled it off. The Chief was a victim in more ways than one. He was robbed of his DNA and the knife that Greene used to carve Wilson's chest. Ultimately, he forfeited his life at the hand of Greene who staged his suicide. How Michael must have suffered emotionally in those last moments knowing that he had been betrayed by the person he considered his spiritual brother in arms. Perhaps Sloan would have eventually caught on when blood toxicology revealed aconite in Michael's body too. It would be hard to explain how someone could be immobilized yet raise a gun to their head. In any case, we were all very thankful that Greene had been apprehended and his bloody reign of terror brought to an end. Sloan was especially thankful that he didn't hold the press conference until after the Chief was cleared and the real culprit was revealed.

As for me, Walt and Gretchen's first impulse when they heard the sordid saga about my incredibly close brush with death was to pull me out of Wash U and bring me back home immediately. I convinced them otherwise. Although I had come to St. Louis with a lot of reservations about living among the Midwestern hayseeds, I'd changed my mind. In spite of turning part of my life into the most bizarre nightmare imaginable for that year, it had provided great blessings beyond my wildest dreams. I was able to pursue a fantastic undergraduate education and gained experiences that other people wouldn't enjoy in a lifetime. I lost a friend and mentor but gained another who was also part father and part brother. Then of course there was Faith, a priceless treasure like no other. Most importantly, somehow in the midst of all the madness, God used all these trials, tribulations and testing to draw me nearer to him and strengthen me in the one, true, Christian faith.

No, I stayed in St. Louis and finished my degree at Wash U. I'll never forget when Noah Mosely presented me with a unique graduation gift. "Here you go my boy. Congratulations on reaching such a meaningful milestone. I hope this little reminder will help you going forward ... to see things through spiritual lenses."

I was thankful but puzzled, "Doc, why a pen instead of maybe some glasses or a magnifying glass?"

"Oh I agree that a pair of replica glasses would have been clever and quite symbolic but I think you'll find this to be even more powerful in shaping your outlook on things. This is not just any pen. Well perhaps the pen is rather ordinary but it's the ink that stands apart. You see, it's filled with Jurassic ink that is 155 million years old." Doc chuckled at my astonishment and handed me a sedimentary stone with a perfectly preserved squid fossil with the ink sac intact. This fossil was removed from the Jurassic rock layer in Wiltshire, England in 2009. There were thousands of other squid that died in the same place ... almost as if deposited together by some cataclysmic event eh? You can actually write with the ink if you like. It's still good. Now, I wonder how the sac and its organic contents were so freshly preserved for 155 million years ... hmmmmm." The graduation card that accompanied this special gift included a reference to Ephesians 1:18 ... "The eyes of your understanding being enlightened; that ye may know what is the hope of his calling, and what the riches of the glory of his inheritance in the saints."

I'll stick around a bit longer, at least until the next year after Faith graduates. I've signed up for graduate studies to get to work on a MBA ... just in case. I'm not going back to my internship at the Parks. I want to leave my memories of Wes well enough alone.

Instead, I've signed up to work as a graduate assistant to a nutty, old professor with a quirky Aussie accent. I don't plan on wearing an outback vest like him with all the pockets but I will keep his pen and fossil squid close at hand. It will serve as a good reminder. But I won't use it to write anything. I'm guessing the ink will stay good for a while longer.

Faith and I finally got around to making the trek out to Portland to meet Walt and Gretchen personally. After seeing her in the flesh, Walt gave me a big, goofy grin and thumbs up behind her back. When they realized that what was on the inside was even better, they both encouraged me to go back to St. Louis for a while and not let her get away. Before packing up to head home, I had a heart-to-heart with Walt. He understood right away … and floated me a *loan* to buy a ring. I was so giddy, I could have howled at the moon.

ACKNOWLEDGMENTS

I want to acknowledge the writings and teachings of people who have helped me gain a better understanding of God's creation and our true origin. There are many. In particular, I'd like to credit John Mackay, Ken Ham, Brian Young, Dr. David Menton, Pastor Keith Ellerbrock and the late Pastor William Bischoff.

As a work of fiction, Murder by Chance just scratched the surface regarding the wonders of God's creation. I heartily encourage you to dig deeper into the foundational truth of God's creation by enlisting the following resources as a start:

- John Mackay, Creation Research
  (www.creationresearch.net)
- Ken Ham, Answers In Genesis
  (www.answersingenesis.org)
  - Dr. David Menton, AIG Contributor
- Brian Young, Creation Instruction Association
  (www.creationinstruction.org)
- Harry Rimmer, The Harmony of Science and Scripture,
  The Berne Witness Company, 1939

Most importantly, I want to point you to the Holy Bible which is the one source of absolute truth that guides these men along with all faithful pastors, teachers, disciples and believers everywhere.

Giving thanks unto the Father, which hath made us meet to be partakers of the inheritance of the saints in light: Who hath delivered us from the power of darkness, and hath translated us into the kingdom of his dear Son: In whom we have redemption through his blood, even the forgiveness of sins: Who is the image of the invisible God, the firstborn of every creature: For by him were all things created, that are in heaven, and that are in earth, visible and invisible, whether they be thrones, or dominions, or principalities, or powers: all things were created by him, and for him: And he is before all things, and by him all things consist. (Colossians 1:12-17)

About The Author

Steve Stranghoener's formal training in education and history was supplemented by the rich and varied experiences gained during a distinguished career with a multi-national business concern. In his spare time, he spent the past thirty years pursuing an unusual passion as an avid student of theology and church doctrine. This created an odd amalgam for a story teller ... someone able to straddle the great divide between secular and Christian world views. The author enjoys fiction of all types from the classics to contemporaries but has a penchant for mysteries and thrillers that explore man's dark side while instilling hope and extolling faith. In his own writings, he is consumed with our dual natures and the struggle between good and evil that rages within. His favorite book is the Bible which provides the answers to the greatest mysteries of all, in this life and the next. Steve Stranghoener lives in St. Louis, Missouri with his wife where they enjoy spending time with their growing family of children and grandchildren.

Other books by Steve Stranghoener ...

- Asunder: The Tale of the Renaissance Killer
- The Last Prophet: Imminent End
- Tracts in Time

These books are available at www.amazon.com.

CPSIA information can be obtained at www.ICGtesting.com
Printed in the USA
LVOW081027250312

274547LV00004B/2/P